THE ASTRAL

BOOKS BY V. J. BANIS

FOR BORGO PRESS / WILDSIDE PRESS:

THE ASTRAL: TILL·THE DAY I DIE
AVALON
CHARMS, SPELLS, AND CURSES FOR THE MILLIONS
COLOR HIM GAY: THE MAN FROM C.A.M.P.
DARKWATER
THE DEVIL'S DANCE
DRAG THING; OR, THE STRANGE TALE OF JACKLE AND
    HYDE
THE EARTH AND ALL IT HOLDS
THE GAY DOGS: THE MAN FROM C.A.M.P.
THE GAY HAUNT
THE GLASS HOUSE
THE GLASS PAINTING
GOODBYE, MY LOVER
THE GREEK BOY
KENNY'S BACK
LIFE & OTHER PASSING MOMENTS: A COLLECTION OF
    SHORT WRITINGS
THE LION'S GATE
MOON GARDEN
THE POT THICKENS: RECIPES FROM THE KITCHENS OF
    WRITERS AND READERS (editor)
SAN ANTONE
THE SECOND TIJUANA BIBLE READER (editor)
SPINE INTACT, SOME CREASES: REMEMBRANCES OF A
    PAPERBACK WRITER
STRANGER AT THE DOOR
THIS SPLENDID EARTH
THE TIJUANA BIBLE READER (editor)
A WESTWARD LOVE
THE WOLVES OF CRAYWOOD
THE WHY NOT

THE ASTRAL

TILL THE DAY I DIE

by

V. J. Banis

The Borgo Press
An Imprint of Wildside Press

MMVII

CONTENTS

PROLOGUE

It was everything just as she had always heard it described: the tunnel, the light, blinding white light, and there was everyone waiting to greet her. Gosh, that was her father, wasn't it? And there was Aunt Fanny, and....

"Catherine." She heard her name distinctly, from somewhere behind. She looked back, and saw Jack in the distance. Jack? That wasn't possible, surely, not after all these years?

"Catherine," he called again, "Come back. You can't go yet."

Ahead, her loved ones waited for her, willing her to come to them. When she tried to look at them, however, actually to see them, there were no images. It was more as if she felt them. She simply knew they were there, and she wanted to join them, truly she did. She couldn't go back. She wouldn't.

And yet...she glanced back once more at Jack and all the years fell away, and in an instant, she remembered the feel of his arms about her, his lean, hard body against hers. How could she remember anything so physical, here, now?

Someone—*some thing*—separated itself from the light, something of light itself, but so bright, so intense, that she could not bear to look directly at it, and shielded her eyes.

"You must go back." It was like a voice inside her head; she could hear it and yet she knew that no sound had been made. "He is there. You must find him. There is something that you must do, that only you can do."

"I can't go back. Please, spare me. The pain—I know what happens. It's more than I could bear."

"He is there."

"Who?"

But it was too late, already she could feel herself returning, the voices were fading, the light retreating, further and further until....

Until she was back, in a bed, and the pain was crashing through her, seeming to crush her in its horrible embrace, and somewhere a triumphant voice was saying, "We've got her. She's alive."

CHAPTER ONE

"Can you hear me?"

Catherine forced her eyes open. A white-jacketed man leaned over her. She was in bed. A hospital bed. She tried to move her hand, to wipe away the fog that misted her vision, but the hand wouldn't move. Neither would her head. It felt as if it were in a vise. Her legs…it dawned on her that she was strapped to the bed like a victim in one of those corny horror movies, only this horror wasn't make believe.

"What…?" Her voice was weak, rasping.

"Don't try to talk, not yet," the doctor said. "You're going to be all right. You've had a narrow escape."

"We need to talk to her," someone said. "We have to ask her some questions."

"Not now," the doctor said, his voice firm.

There were two strangers behind the doctor, a dark suited man and a woman with frizzy orange hair. Beyond them, Walter, her husband, watched her with anxious, red-rimmed eyes. Seeing him, she remembered all of a sudden: the parking lot, her daughter, the yellow bearded man. Somehow she was sure she knew, knew already what she was going to hear, but she had to have it confirmed. Despite the doctor's order not to talk, she managed to croak one word at Walter: "Becky?"

Walter bit his lip. He began to cry, tears spilling from his eyes and streaming down his cheeks. He shook his head and sobbed aloud, "She's dead, Cathy. Becky's dead."

I should have died instead, she thought, *it would have hurt far less.*

* * * * * * *

The scene kept playing over and over, like a tape loop, on the screen of her mind. She saw herself come out of the market. It was a warm Friday, late spring in Los Angeles. She had been shopping for a special dinner to celebrate Becky's last day of school, and she saw, puzzled, the empty Buick where Walter and Becky should have been waiting, the wide open door setting off alarm bells inside her head.

Her eyes raked the crowded parking lot and as if by magic her gaze went directly to them, to Becky and the two men trying to force her into a rusty black pick up. She saw Becky fighting and kicking, heard her cry: "Mommy, Mommy, help me!"

"Becky! Stop, let her go," Catherine shouted. She dropped the bags of groceries and ran toward the truck. Startled people turned to look but she had eyes for nothing but the little girl struggling in the arms of two men.

One of them clambered into the truck, dragging Becky with him. The other, tall, skinny, shoved her toward the middle of the seat and tried to get in after her.

Catherine caught the door as he started to swing it shut. "No," she screamed, "I won't let you."

The skinny man, green-eyed, with an artificially bright yellow beard, swore at her and tried to kick her away with one foot that caught her in the belly. She gagged with the pain, but her hands still held on to the door.

"Get away, bitch." He bared his teeth in an angry snarl and yanked the glove box open, pulled out a gun and waved it wildly. "Let go of the damned door."

"Mommy," Becky sobbed loudly. The truck's engine roared to life.

Somewhere behind her, Catherine heard Walter cry, "Catherine! Becky!" but she couldn't, wouldn't take her eyes from the man with the yellow beard. His face was so close she could smell his beer-laced breath and the scent of his sweat.

"Give me back my daughter!" This couldn't be happening, not to her, not to Becky, it must be a nightmare. She sobbed with terror. The truck began to move, but still she would not let go of the door. "Give her back."

He aimed the gun in her direction, held it practically in her face, and fired. It felt as if she had been struck alongside the head by a rock. She seemed to be falling upward. Her fingers slipped from the flailing truck door. Gears ground, tires squealed. Her head hit the pavement and blackness fell over her like a thick, dark blanket.

* * * * * * *

"It's my fault, totally," Walter said, his voice breaking. He waited for her to say something, waited for expiation. When none came, he went on: "It was only a couple of minutes, I swear it. We walked over to look in the window, at the toy store, you know, and then we came back, and I had just put Becky in the car when this man came up and said I had dropped my wallet. I felt my pocket and, sure enough, it was gone.

"'Back there,' he said, 'back by the toy store,' so I walked back to look for it, but I couldn't find it, I was just looking around when I heard you scream, and I saw...." He choked back a sob.

Still Catherine said nothing. She would have to forgive him. Someday. She understood what guilt he was suffering. It would kill him to remain unpardoned. She couldn't do that to him.

For now, though, her grief was all but killing her, it was all she could manage. She couldn't even look at him, let alone give him the forgiveness he needed.

"They found her at the beach. They had...."

She found her voice then, an icy, a toneless voice. "I don't want to hear it. Don't mention that to me, ever."

He shrank down in his chair and sobbed helplessly.

* * * * * * *

She had hardly any more to say to the investigators who came the next day to see her: L.A.P.D. Sergeant Jess Conners, and the woman with the frizzy orange hair, who introduced herself as Agent Chang with the Federal Bureau of Investigation. "Child Abduction and Serial Killers Unit," she added. "CASKU."

"Agent Chang," Catherine acknowledged.

"Most of the guys just call me Chang." She hesitated briefly. "We're sorry to trouble you now. I know how difficult this is for you, but in these cases the sooner we can gather information the better our chances are of resolving them."

"Cases?" Catherine felt as if her tragedy ought to be, must be, unique. Hers was a pain she did not choose to share. She didn't want to be a "case."

Agent Chang seemed to understand. "We think these men have done this before," she said, gravely sympathetic.

Catherine wanted to help, truly. She gave them what she could, though it seemed little enough.

"It was an old truck, black, rusty. A GMC, I think."

"And you didn't see the license plate? No, of course not," she answered herself. "Can you describe the men for me? There were two of them?"

"Yes, two men, one burly, I barely got a glimpse of his face; he was big, that's all I know, like a bear. Short hair. Dirty. The other one, the one who…the one nearest me, his hair was longer, almost to his shoulders. He was tall. Six foot, at least, and skinny. A hard face, savage, high cheek boned, a mole on his chin. Large nose, crooked."

"Like it had been broken?"

"Yes, it might have been. It bent to the right, here." She indicated with her finger. "Green eyes. Yellow beard, unkempt, scraggly. No, not blond, yellow. Like it had been dyed."

"Voice?" the man asked; a policeman, she remembered, though not his name.

She had to think. "A drawl. Southern, maybe."

Later, she worked with the police artist, over and over as he worked at a laptop, plastic transparencies appearing one atop the other, going through the process repeatedly, refining the image he was creating of the man with the yellow beard.

"Yes," she said to the face he finally offered her, "that looks like him." As nearly as she could remember. Remembering was painful, doubly so—the pain in her head and the pain in her heart. She had mostly been trying not to remember.

She was less helpful with the sketch of the other man. Despite more than an hour of work with the artist, she couldn't really say if the result looked much like him or not.

"I barely looked at him," she said with a weary sigh. "Not more than a second or two. I might recognize him if I saw him again, but…." She shrugged.

"Anyway, we've got one of them." Chang said emphatically, "Don't worry, Mrs. Desmond, we'll find them. We'll get these monsters, I promise you."

"You've got to go now," the little Filipina nurse, Millie, told the federal agent. "She has to rest."

Catherine was grateful for Millie, as grateful as she could be now for anything. Millie understood, she asked no questions, offered no well-meaning condolences. She simply did everything she could to ease Catherine's discomfort.

Agent Chang got up obediently to go. Catherine looked at her, into her eyes. She was well intentioned. Catherine knew she was. She meant her words to be comforting. What comfort could they give her, though? Becky was gone.

* * * * * * *

"That's got to be the worst thing that can happen to a mother, losing a child," Conners said outside the hospital room. "Has to be a special kind of hell, doesn't it?"

"It is," Chang said.

"My mom always says she hopes she goes before I do."

"Every mom says that," Chang said.

He started to say something more, but when he glanced sideways at her, her grim expression discouraged him from pursuing what was obviously an unwelcome topic. "At least this time we can eliminate the parents," he said instead. Incidents like this made headlines but it was rare for a child to be snatched off the street. Most cases involved family or close friends.

"It was ballsy," Chang said. "Grabbing her in broad daylight, and in such a public place."

"Super ballsy. Weird ballsy, actually," Conners agreed. "But maybe it means we have a better chance of catching them. Easy to trip up when you're that bold."

"Let's hope so." She wanted that. Wanted it very much. "Those bastards."

Though at five foot four inches she had barely qualified for the Bureau, her success rate in nabbing the perpetrators of child kidnappings and abuse was the best in the agency. Not, she insisted often, that she had any special skills or was any smarter than anybody else. Simply, she wouldn't quit. She pursued her quarry with relentless determination until, most times, she finally tracked them down.

To her way of thinking, the men she pursued were the worst of the worst. It was trendy today to regard even these criminals as victims themselves: of their own childhood, or abuse, or some other circumstances beyond their control. She had no such compassion for them. She thought the earth would be a better place if they were removed from it, and she had made it her job to accomplish that as often as possible.

Her doggedness was legend among her fellow agents. It had earned her, as well as a modicum of envy, a respect that few of the Bureau's women agents enjoyed. They called her "The Bulldog," and thought she didn't know.

Conners was silent, not wanting to intrude on her thoughts. Crime in Los Angeles was the province of the Los Angeles Police Department, but a child kidnapping was one of those special circumstances that brought the F.B.I. into the picture. Some L.A.P.D. officers resented working with the Bureau. In particular, he had been razzed for having to work with a female agent. He didn't mind, though. He had worked with Chang before, knew her nickname. Everyone agreed she was the best. "The Bulldog always nails them."

There had been some snickering suggestions, too, that she was a dike. He doubted that. He had yet to catch any particular sexual signals from her, though his instincts told him that if anyone were ever able to melt that glacier of ice that she wore so blatantly, they would probably discover a volcano waiting underneath. Truth was, he thought she was cute. Small breasted, hard bodied; even the kinky red hair turned him on.

He had been careful not to act on that feeling, however, though he had been plenty tempted. There was also a story told that she had torn the balls right off of some guy who had tried to jump her. He was ninety-nine percent sure it was another piece of malicious dirt, but he was careful, both literally and figuratively, to keep his dick out of their relations. Much as he would truly like to be the one who melted that iceberg, he also truly wanted to hang on to the family jewels.

On the other hand, you couldn't always keep those naughty pictures from slipping into your mind.

As for Chang, if she could have her druthers, she would work all her cases alone, but it didn't happen that way. Protocol demanded that she liaise with the L.A.P.D. That being the case, she much preferred Conners to the other officers she had worked with in the past. He was the only one who hadn't treated her with sometimes barely concealed resentment, even disdain.

He was also the only one who had not hit on her at the first opportunity. She was mostly grateful for that fact. She had no—absolute zero—interest in getting involved with anyone, had neither the time nor the energy nor the inclination. Her job was her life.

She had enough womanly vanity, though, to be a tad disappointed at his total lack of interest. He was good-looking: nothing flashy, but nice. Only a few inches taller than her, short for a cop. That, combined with a boyish and astonishingly innocent face—he must get carded every time he walked into a bar—made him look more like a college kid than the experienced police officer she knew he was. He was stocky, with firm muscles and enormous hands that suggested real strength, and the way he held himself, the way he moved and walked, told her that he was most likely dynamite in the sack—and damned well knew it.

She'd had a thing with a guy just like him in college, the last real thing she'd had with any guy. She had broken if off cold after two breathless weeks. He was just too good. She couldn't afford the distraction. Not then, not now.

As if he had read her thoughts, he glanced at her and flashed a grin. *Nice teeth*, she thought, and then, *Jeez, Roby, like you're buying a horse. Why don't you check out his rump while you're at it?*

Which she did when he walked ahead of her to unlock the car. Of their own volition, her eyes dropped to his buns, nicely rounded, looking like they were carved out of granite.

She snapped her eyes away from them. Buns were not a part of her business plan. She had bad guys to catch. Totally disgusted with herself, she slid into the car seat beside him.

"Crapola," she said aloud. She hated shit like this.

* * * * * * *

Mommy, Mommy, help me!
Becky....
Catherine fought against the restraints that held her to the bed, the tubes that connected her to monitoring equipment.

Even when the nurses came running, even when the sedative had relaxed her body and her struggles had ceased, the cries still rang in her mind:
Mommy, Mommy....

CHAPTER TWO

"This will seem a little strange to you," the woman doctor said. She was one Catherine hadn't seen before, a pale blonde woman. The light from the window formed a golden halo about her head. After three weeks they had finally removed the last of Catherine's bandages. With the wrappings gone her scalp felt oddly naked.

The doctor raised a small penlight in front of Catherine's face and flicked it on. Intense light filled Catherine's vision. "Don't blink."

It reminded her of that other light, blinding, pure. She had told no one about that, had resolutely refused even to think about it, but the light shining into her eyes, blinding her, brought it back. It began to seem to her that she could see something in *this* light—almost see something, if she just looked a little harder.

She was only vaguely aware of what the doctor was saying: "You must travel. You must learn it. Try, now. Just a little way. I will help."

Suddenly, she was in the corridor outside. There was her nurse, Millie, coming along the hallway toward her, a clipboard in her hand. Millie looked up and saw her. She blinked, disbelieving, her eyes wide.

As suddenly as she had left it, Catherine was back in her bed, pain threatening to make her head explode. She moaned aloud. She had forgotten the doctor tending her until she said, "Hurts, doesn't it?"

Catherine opened her eyes. That brought fresh lightning bolts of pain crashing into her skull. "Who?" she started to ask, when the door flew open. Over the doctor's shoulder, Catherine saw Millie dash into the room and come to an abrupt stop. The doctor did not turn, did not even seem to notice the sudden entrance.

"You're here," Millie said. "I thought...."

The doctor smiled and waved a hand to indicate the tubes connecting Catherine to the various life support systems. "How could she go anywhere?" she asked.

For a moment more, Millie gaped. With a mystified expression, she shook her head. "Of course. How silly of me, how could you go anywhere?" She backed out of the room, her puzzled eyes studying Catherine's face.

Catherine looked at the doctor. "Why did you say that?" she asked.

"Say what?"

"That, what you said, about traveling?"

The woman chuckled and slipped her penlight into the pocket of her tunic. "My dear, I'm afraid it will be a while before you do any real traveling. You rest now." She got up and strolled toward the door.

"Wait," Catherine said, "I—I'm confused."

At the door, the doctor paused for just a second to look back and smile. Up until this moment she had been utterly professional and sweetly bland, a face you could almost but not quite remember, the sort of someone you might know only slightly from church or perhaps one of your child's teachers. There was nothing bland or sweet about the smile she flashed across the room at Catherine, however. It was fierce, almost demonic. And challenging.

"Of course you are. It will get better, I promise. You'll be fine. It just takes time."

* * * * * *

It felt strange to be back in Los Angeles. Jack McKenzie took the freeway ramp for Hollywood Boulevard, swerving out of the way of a brainless driver determined to get around him to exit first. That, at least, hadn't changed: the Los Angeles traffic and the nutty drivers. No, that wasn't true. The volume of traffic had doubled, at least, in the dozen or so years since he had been here.

One thing that blessedly hadn't changed was Musso and Frank's. The restaurant sat where it had sat for ages, defending its faded elegance against the growing seediness of Hollywood Boulevard. He left his car in the parking lot in the rear, slipping the attendant a ten to insure that he kept an eye on it, and entered by the back door and the little corridor that went past the kitchen. To the right was the newer dining room with its lunch counter and brighter lights.

He went to the left, however, to the older of the two rooms, with its monumental mahogany bar, the faded and vaguely pastoral murals, the high-backed wooden booths where generations of stars, politicians, moguls had sipped their cocktails and eaten the unchanged list of daily specials. The waiters might have been the same ones who had served him in the past. None of them were young and all of them were pros. To a man, and here and there a woman, they eschewed the trendy we-are-all-buddies-together style of service. If you wanted a waiter-as-friend, you could get that all over this town. Here, what you got was the business of good food and good drinks, properly, efficiently served.

Peter Weitman was already in one of the booths, and already sipping a martini. A second one waited in its little bowl of ice for Jack. In the years since they had last met, Weitman had added some extra pounds to his never-trim build and traded much of his hair for them, but the eyes in the round face looked up at Jack with undiminished shrewdness.

"I hope your tastes haven't changed," he said, indicating the waiting martini as Jack slipped into the booth across from him.

"Not that much." They shook hands quickly. By that time, a waiter had appeared to pour Jack's drink into the chilled stemmed glass. Jack nodded his thanks and took a sip. "Ah. Nobody does it better, I swear."

Peter lifted his glass. "Welcome back to La-La Land." He had a sip of his own drink. "How does it feel?"

"A little funny. You forget the essence of the place. They never seem to capture that in movies or books. For all its tackiness, it does have a charm of its own."

"Admittedly a wacky charm," Peter agreed. "You have to live here to get that." He hesitated and looked down at his martini. "Did you hear about Catherine?" he asked without looking up.

Jack skipped the pretense of asking which Catherine. They both knew there was only one Peter would mention.

"I heard that she married Walter. That was years ago. I don't suppose you're going to tell me they're divorced." He said it lightly, but he couldn't help the little surge of hope that rose up inside him.

"Her daughter was killed. Kidnapped."

"Jesus!" Jack slammed his drink down so hard that the stem on the glass broke. In an instant, a waiter was there. "It's okay," Jack said, snatching a handkerchief from his jacket pocket and using it to stem the little rivulet of blood.

"I'll bring a new glass," the waiter murmured, whisking up the broken one and deftly wiping the table. One quick, practiced glance had told him the problem was not one of overindulgence. Else, no further drinking would happen on his stint at this table. Musso's wasn't that kind of establishment and there wasn't a name, or a tip, big enough to bend that rule.

They sat in silence until the waiter brought a new glass, already filled with a fresh drink. He set it down and gave Peter and the menus a meaningful glance. Peter shook his head and the waiter disappeared again.

"God, she must be crazy with grief," Jack said finally.

"She was nearly killed herself." He told him the whole story, so far as he knew it. Jack listened without interruption, sometimes looking down into the crystalline purity of his martini, sometimes up at the dingy murals over the booths, almost never directly at Peter.

He was thinking, what a horrible thing it must have been for her. If only he could have been there to comfort her. He couldn't, of course. She didn't love him. He could have borne that, if she had only let him love her; but she was married to another man, had married him within weeks of the day he had left Los Angeles, so whatever love she felt for Walter must have been there all along—all the time that she was with him.

Since he had arrived back in the city, he had been to nearly all the places they used to haunt. Yesterday he had lunch at The Apple Pan: a hickory burger with cheese, and apple pie alamode. The day before, he had been to the pier at Santa Monica, where he had resisted the urge to ride the merry-go-round. A couple in love could do that and get nothing more than amused glances from passers-by. A single man could only engender suspicion.

He had been to Disneyland and Knott's Berry Farm, Angel's Flight and The Bradbury Building, the Farmers' Market, The Witch's House that the tourists never discovered, and The Original Pantry in the seedy part of downtown, where he'd eaten a French Dip in honor of its invention there. A one man tourist trail, and all of it empty of pleasure, all of it spoiled for him by the absence of the one with whom he had shared it in the past, with whom he could never share it again.

Sitting across from him, as he talked, Peter watched all these emotions flit across his friend's face. *Should I have said anything*, he wondered? *Or kept my trap shut?* He would have learned of it sooner or later anyway, wouldn't he? For such a big city, Los Angeles could be a small town in that regard.

He finished his story and waited for Jack to respond. The silence grew uncomfortably long. He was about to speak up himself when at last Jack looked directly at him for the first time in many minutes.

"Let's talk about that job you mentioned," he said.

* * * * * * *

It was nearly a month before she could go home. Brain damage, they explained, in terms too technical for her to grasp: stroke danger, seizures, black outs. A whole litany of dire consequences, none of which mattered to her in the least. If she couldn't die, couldn't trade places with her daughter, what did it matter how she lived?

She never saw the woman doctor again, the one who had spoken to her of traveling. No one seemed to know who she was. Even Nurse Millie was unhelpful.

"There are so many doctors here," she said when Catherine questioned her. "It's hard to keep track of them all." Millie was different now. She still took pains with her ministrations, but the easy intimacy that had existed between them before had vanished. She was wary with Catherine. Sometimes it seemed as if she were uncomfortable in Catherine's presence.

"Who could blame her?" Catherine asked herself. "*I* am uncomfortable in my presence."

* * * * * * *

Walter brought her home, his air one of gentle solicitude. She had managed to give him at least some of the forgiveness she knew he sorely needed.

"It wasn't your fault," she assured him, this on the day before she left the hospital. "You are not to blame for their evil. How could you have known—how could any sane person expect that?"

He was grateful, of course, but it seemed to her as if her forgiveness embarrassed him in some way. They both knew it was not over, that perhaps the guilt would never go away. Perhaps she could never altogether stop blaming him, but it was a start, at least.

They had to try, if they were to save their marriage. If they were to save themselves. To linger in that hell of self-torture could only lead to insanity. She had felt since the moment she regained consciousness in that hospital bed that she was teetering at all times on the edge of that abyss. Sometimes she thought it might be easier to plunge into it.

Her mother was at the house when they got there. "I won't be in the way," Sandra Dodd promised, wary, because up till now, when she had visited at the hospital, her daughter had been distant and uncommunicative. "I'll just finish getting dinner ready and then I'll go home. Unless," she added, and could not keep a hopeful note from her voice, "you want me to stay."

"It's okay, Mom," Catherine assured her, making the effort to smile gratefully. "I can manage."

"Maybe she should stay for a night or two," Walter said. "I'll have to go to work. I've been away from the restaurant so much, and you know what happens when the cat's away. People are getting sloppy."

"I'll be all right," Catherine said, and, more emphatically when they both looked uncertain, "Really."

She glanced around at the living room that should have been familiar, and looked utterly foreign to her. She focused on a vase filled with yellow roses that sat atop the piano. "Thank you for the flowers, Mom," she said, to soften the stubbornness that she knew left mother and husband uneasy.

"Oh, they're not...." Sandra hesitated. Part of her wanted to let the mistake stand, but she found that she couldn't. "They aren't from me." Catherine raised a questioning eyebrow. "They're from Jack. Jack McKenzie." She didn't add that they had been coming every week for nearly a month.

"McKenzie?" Walter said. "I didn't even know he was back in town, did you?" The look he gave Catherine was accusing.

"I've rather been out of circulation." She took the note from the roses and read it.

"What the hell does he want?"

She handed him the note. It was simple to the point of austerity: "My sincere sympathy. Jack McKenzie."

Jack McKenzie. As if he needed to add his last name. As if she might have forgotten who he was. She suddenly remembered hearing his voice in that dying moment. That was why she had kept the memory of that incident so resolutely locked away inside her mind, why she had mentioned it to no one. To remember that eerie moment was to remember Jack, and she didn't want to think of Jack; *wouldn't* think of him. That, surely, was the feather that would tip her over the edge into the bottomless pit if anything would.

Walter took the card, read it for a long moment as though the message it contained was a lengthy one. "Have you seen him?" he asked finally.

She sighed. "I haven't spoken to Jack since he left thirteen years ago."

He was on the verge of saying something further, and thought better of it. Instead, he crumpled up the card and threw it violently into the wastebasket by the desk.

"Did I hear a baaing sound?" Sandra asked. "I do believe there's a lamb stew calling for my attention."

She left the room to give them tactful space for anything that needed saying. There was, she thought, quite a bit of that, none of which she needed to hear.

Whatever that might have been, however, remained unsaid in a silence that eddied around husband and wife. Catherine went to the bay window and stared out at the back garden. The flowers were wilted, the grass brown from lack of water, the leaves of the maple tree hung down dispiritedly. She supposed it was a measure of her healing that she could even notice such things, though she hadn't yet reached the point of caring much.

"I'd better get to the restaurant," Walter said to her back. "If you have any…if you need anything, call me on my cell."

"I'll be all right," she said again. Relenting, if only slightly, she came to give him a perfunctory kiss.

When he had gone, when she heard the car door slam, heard the Buick pull out of the driveway and move off down the street; when she was sure he wasn't coming back but was truly on his way to the restaurant he owned in Santa Monica, she went to the wastebasket and retrieved the card, smoothing it out. She too studied it for a long while, as if seeking some coded message invisible to the undiscerning eye.

They had been rivals, Walter and Jack, if unequal ones. It had always been Jack who had ruled in her heart, though she liked Walter well enough, and felt kindly toward him for his unrequited love.

"You're sweet. I do like you, honestly," was the best she could give him then, and that, of course, was not enough for a man in love. Even as she said it, she was aware of its inadequacy.

What can I do, she asked herself? She couldn't help being in love with Jack anymore than Walter could help being in love with her. Not just love, either: her feeling for Jack had been a burning, an overwhelming passion that never left her for a moment.

Maybe, she sometimes thought even then, more passion than love. Waking or sleeping, he was always there. She had only to close her eyes and see him drawn in flames upon her lids: the dense dark curls of his hair, his blue gray eyes that seemed to see into her heart, his lips, too full, perhaps, for a man, but sensually thrilling to her. Especially when he kissed her, when he kissed her lips, when he kissed her *there*, the delirious prelude to that moment when he lowered his lean, hard body onto hers and she gave herself up to him so utterly.

I mustn't think of this, she told herself severely. I mustn't remember. From the kitchen she heard the rattle of cups and silverware as her mother set the table. She started to throw the card away again, but her hand refused to do her bidding. Instead, she dropped it into the pocket of her denim skirt.

She ran her fingers through the shapeless fringe of reddish blonde hair just beginning to grow back in over her scars. He wouldn't find her so desirable if he saw her now, she thought grimly. And, probably, that was just as well.

She followed the aroma of lamb stew into the kitchen.

CHAPTER THREE

Summer became autumn. The house stifled her. Everywhere she looked she found memories of Becky. She tried to watch television, and instead of Oprah, she found herself watching Becky's one time favorite show, Daffy Danny's Alley. It was a passion that Becky had shared with a great many pre-teens and one that (thankfully so far as Catherine was concerned) she had quickly outgrown. Catherine had come into the den one day to discover Becky watching cartoons instead.

"No Daffy Danny?" she had asked.

Becky's answer was brief and to the point: "He's smarmy."

An opinion Catherine shared. Danny was Danny O'Dell, host and hand-puppeteer, an altogether too fey young man—or, probably not really so young, but who worked hard at that illusion—who wore too-short trousers and a too-tight checked jacket and a tam with a red pom-pom and who mugged a little too outrageously for the benefit of the squealing girls in the studio audience.

In the past she had gritted her teeth while Becky sat enrapt, from "Kids, what time is it? It's Daffy Danny time," through every "daffy laffy," to the last "daffy bye-bye," delivered with a big kiss thrown at the television screen.

Now, of course, she would have kissed Danny O'Dell herself if it could have brought her daughter back to her.

She clicked off the television with an angry gesture.

* * * * * * *

She went back to work finally at Dean and Summers, Publishers, half days to start, both glad to have her time occupied, and sorry to have to face the well-meant expressions of sympathy, the worried glances that she pretended not to see when she went past people. As if the jungle drums had alerted them, everyone seemed to know when she was coming, were waiting for her appearance in the drama of their lives.

Alden Summers had passed away years back, but the firm still carried his name on the masthead. She went first thing to Fermin Dean's office. Fermin's secretary waved her in with a friendly but guarded smile.

"Catherine," Fermin greeted her with evident delight. He was tall and gaunt, silver haired, one of those people who seem to be in motion even when sitting still. He bounded up from his chair and came round his desk to clasp her hands. "It's good to have you back. Though when you see the load on your desk, you'll know just how much I've missed you."

"I'll be glad for the work. I can use the occupation," she said.

"Don't overdo it. And, I mean this, Catherine, make your own hours, please, come and go as you want."

Even with his warning, she was not quite prepared for the workload waiting for her despite everyone's obvious efforts to keep things moving along. As chief editor for their art books divisions, one of Dean and Summer's major divisions, her input was nearly indispensable. Books that ought to have been in production by now had been held up for months and newer projects waited for her green light. A mountain of correspondence, most of it submissions for book proposals, filled up one half of her desk and overflowed onto a chair.

She threw herself into her work. It was the best antidote she had found yet for the pain. Not, of course, that the pain ever quite went away, it merely curled itself up into a little knot in a far corner of her mind, where it ever waited to come back out into the light.

She saw that her coworkers eyed her cautiously, and knew that many of them wanted to talk. She understood that they were saddened for her, and horrified by what had happened; but there was a certain thrill there, too. Murder, ghastly murder, tainted everyone with its evil glamour, even those at a distance, those whose involvement was only vicarious, the more so the more gruesome it was.

She had no desire to satisfy their grisly curiosity and avoided the hesitant glances. Fortunately, most of them kept their distance. Her assistant, Bill—black and gay—worked closely with her each day, but she had learned early on that he was a very model of discretion, a fact for which she could be grateful now.

Only Mrs. Pendergrast from their young adult division ventured beyond her door with personal condolences. "Catherine, you poor,

poor thing," she cooed and leaned over Catherine's desk so far that Catherine felt she meant to embrace her, and cringed inwardly. "I just can't tell you how awful I feel for you. If there is anything I can do, anything at all."

"As a matter of fact." Catherine held up a pile of sketches, needing to divert all that dripping sympathy, "These need to go back to art, if you wouldn't mind dropping them on your way."

"It would be a pleasure." Mrs. Pendergrast's voice was a shade less cordial. One did want one's sympathy to be appreciated.

Later, in the ladies room, Mrs. Pendergrast shared her insights with Mrs. White from accounting. "Such a tragedy," she said, repairing her lipstick. "Of course, let it be said, I would never, ever leave my Samantha unattended. You just can't be too careful these days."

Mrs. White patted her hair and frowned. "But, that isn't quite the way it happened, is it?"

Mrs. Pendergrast ignored the question. "I keep her practically glued to my side every minute when we're out. People may call me over-cautious if they like, but no one will steal my little girl."

After two years of marriage, Mrs. White was still childless, and afraid to question her doctor because she was sure he would share her husband's opinion that the fault was hers. She could not help thinking, however, that if God ever granted her the little baby girl she prayed for, she would be ever so vigilant as well.

Of course, she did understand that it had been the husband looking after the Desmond girl, but, really, you just couldn't leave something like that up to a man. Certainly not a man as easily distracted as her Robert.

* * * * * * *

At first, Catherine went every day after work to Forest Lawn Memorial Park, to bring flowers to Becky's grave. Becky had so loved flowers. *"Red and orange and yellow and white and blue...."*

"I don't think there are any blue flowers, darling."

"Purple?"

"Yes, definitely purple. And pink. You forgot pink."

"And pink. And purple and blue...."

She said nothing to Walter about her visits. She had no desire to share this pilgrimage with him, with anybody.

She and Becky had used to come here in the past, not as morbid a destination as one might have supposed. There were fountains and gardens, and an uncanny look-alike of Michelangelo's David.

The winter rains came. They did not in any way deter her, though by now she went only once or twice a week. The gravesite was on a knoll from which bright green lawns, salt and peppered with gravesites, spilled down to the Golden State Freeway with its endless rush of cars, their sound a murmur at this distance. She stood without umbrella and let the cool droplets fall upon her, in hope that they would wash away her grief, or at least the numbness.

Both remained. Her soul was condemned to hold on to every memory, until surely it must break from overloading. She knew that she must one day come back to herself. She had to return to the world of the living. She could not continue as she was. If you were condemned to be alive, you ought at least to live.

At home, she and Walter shared the house, they moved about in the same finite space and yet they remained light years apart. Sometimes she could hear him in his office, crying. Most of the time he watched her warily with red-rimmed eyes and sniffled until she thought she must scream, but how could she, eyes tearless, rail at him for his grief? She wished that she had solace to offer him, but of that her heart was empty.

He spent more and more time at the restaurant, pleading increasing numbers of diners. She had no doubt that he found it more comfortable away from her, just as she was relieved to see him go. It was not that she hated him, nor that she even consciously blamed him for what had happened. They could hardly share their home day by day, however, without reminding one another of what was missing from it. And you could only say, "it's all right," so many times before *that* began to sound silly.

He had lost ten pounds and gained ten years. He looked faded, like a shirt too often washed. It wasn't only Becky those two men had killed, she thought grimly. They were killing Catherine and Walter Desmond day by day, inexorably and she felt helpless to prevent it.

A casual question one day—"Will your mother be coming for Christmas?"—made her aware of the time she hadn't noticed passing.

The question caught her by surprise. "Is it December?"

"The second." The gravity of his tone made it sound the most important thing in the world.

Which meant, she realized, that Thanksgiving had come and gone without her noticing. They had always made such a big deal of it in the past. Becky had been quite set in her preferences. The turkey's wings were hers, both of them, and woe betide the foolish mortal who thought to claim one. The pie must be pumpkin.

"Punkin pie, punkin pie, punkin pie." She used to chant it while her mother cleared the table, brought in the pie, took the ice cream—pumpkin ice cream it must be—from the freezer. "Punkin pie."

"I hadn't thought that far ahead," she told Walter. She got up and began to clear the table, but she did manage to rest a hand, briefly, on his shoulder. She really did wish she could comfort him.

He sniffled and said nothing.

When he had gone, she went into the garage and got down a box of Christmas ornaments and carried it into the living room. The first one she unwrapped turned out to be Becky's favorite, the little Christmas angel they had bought the year she was born. She set that aside and found another one: the papier-mâché camel with one leg missing. Becky had insisted they hang it anyway each year, legs or no legs.

"Jesus will love him anyway, won't he, Mommy?"

There were, it seemed, memories attached to every ornament. She put them back in the box and taped it closed again, and carried it out to its shelf in the garage.

A car, a fire engine red Bronco, pulled into the driveway just as she came back into the kitchen. It was unfamiliar to her and at first she didn't recognize the woman who got out and walked briskly to the door. Not until she had rung the bell and Catherine had studied her long and hard through the glass in the front door, stared at the red hair that clearly refused to obey any bidding of brush or comb, did she realize that it was the FBI agent who had interviewed her in the hospital. What was her name, she wondered as she opened the door?

"Mrs. Desmond." The visitor stepped inside.

She remembered then. "Officer Chang."

"Agent Chang." She smiled to show that no offense had been taken. "Just Chang. Or you can call me Roby, if you like, there's no need to be formal." When Catherine still looked blankly at her, she added, "Roby. As in Roberta." She saw the familiar puzzlement and waited for the customary question. Catherine Desmond's glance took in her decidedly Asian face, heart shaped, sloe eyed, and went up to the frizzy hair. At least she put the question a bit differently from most.

"You must get told a lot, that doesn't sound Chinese."

"Not as much as I hear, 'funny, you don't look Jewish'."

Catherine laughed briefly. She must have done that often, before, Roby Chang thought, and felt her throat tighten with anger at what had been done to this woman. Watching her, she was surprised to discover how beautiful Catherine Desmond was. When she had seen her earlier, in the hospital, her face had been purpled with bruises, her head swathed in bandages. The gold hair, glinting with its own copper highlights, had mostly grown back out, the bruises had faded from a face that just missed classically beautiful and was the better for it. She was taller, too, than Chang had realized. Five nine, she guessed, maybe five ten, and full-figured. She was no fashion model, but rather what the boys described as "a babe."

"Daddy's the Chinese part," she said aloud, "Momma was a Jewish princess. Still is, to tell the truth, but she would have a fit if she heard me say it. That explains this, too." She put a hand up to her spiky orange hair. "I'm afraid I'm the classic American mongrel."

Who looked not at all like an F.B.I. agent, Catherine thought. It wasn't just that she was little, nor that her heart shaped face and the frizzy red hair gave her a comic-cute look entirely at odds with any kind of police work. Her costume, too, was something less than authoritative: jeans, a gore-tex jacket, some kind of boots that Catherine couldn't put a name to.

"Maybe hybrid is the better word," she said aloud. Really, she chided herself, how was she to know what an F.B.I. agent should look like? "Come in, please. Can I get you something? Coffee? A drink?"

"Nothing, thanks, I won't stay long." She looked around, avoiding Catherine's eyes.

"Have you come with news? Have you found them?" Catherine asked, hope flaring for a moment.

Chang looked directly at her then and Catherine knew the answer before the agent shook her head. "Nothing, unfortunately. Actually, I was hoping you might have something for me. I thought maybe you had remembered something after all this time, some detail that you forgot earlier." Her look was so earnest, so pleading, that Catherine hated having to disappoint her.

"Nothing that I didn't tell you before."

Chang hesitated a moment. "There's been another one. Several, actually, over the last few months, but a couple of them look awfully similar to your...your case. Yesterday a girl got snatched from a shopping mall. The mother got just a glimpse, but the description she gave us sounded like the same two men."

"That poor woman. I wish...I wish I could do something to help her." Catherine swallowed a lump that rose in her throat and looked away. "There's something that I've...I've struggled for hours at a time to understand: how anyone could do what these men do. Can you help me to understand that, Agent Chang?"

Roby Chang sighed deeply. She had struggled with that same question many times and every answer she came up with ultimately seemed inadequate.

"I think it's the innocence of their victims," she said. "These animals—I won't call them men, they aren't that—they see that innocence, what we perceive of as something beautiful and precious, and to them it appears as a stain, as a flaw in their scheme of things, and they feel compelled to remove that stain." Like all the others, this answer too sounded inadequate when she tried to put it into words.

"So this comes down to a philosophical question?"

Chang shrugged helplessly. "It's difficult for people like us to understand these creatures. There's more to it than that, of course. Money."

"But, they never asked for ransom. They didn't even...there wasn't time for that."

Crapola, Chang thought silently. She took a deep breath. She wished she didn't have to say this, but she knew that it had to be said. "Often, they take pictures, films. There is a big market for that sick sort of thing. Kiddie porn, it's called."

Catherine turned away from her and leaned against the window frame, head bent. After a moment, she asked in a breaking voice, "Are you telling me that somewhere there are pictures, movies, floating around that show—that show my Becky being violated?"

"There may well be. What I don't get is, why did they...?" For a moment she had gone into agent-mode, thinking aloud. She caught herself and gave Catherine an apologetic look. "I'm sorry."

"No. Go on, please. What is it that you don't get?"

"Well, I...are you all right with this?"

"No, but go on anyway. I want to hear."

"Well, like I said, there's movies and pictures, they're worth a lot of money. And then, after that, usually, they, you know, they pass them on."

"For sex, you mean?"

"Yes." Chang was clearly embarrassed with the information she was imparting to Catherine's back. Should she go on? Or try to soft pedal it? Yet her instinct was that this woman truly wanted— *needed*—to know. "The point is, these children are worth far more to them alive than dead."

"Then why...?"

"If I knew that...." Chang shrugged again.

Catherine was quiet for so long that Chang wondered if perhaps she should simply leave. When Catherine finally did speak, it was to say, her voice cracking, "I tried to protect her. I tried to shield her from the evil of the world."

"Yes, of course you did. Who could dream that such evil would come down upon you?" She had seen this same bewildered grief in other parents who had lost a child to murder. You wanted to protect, and when you failed, when something of this magnitude happened, you felt as if it were you who was at fault. She had seen marriages, families torn apart by such guilt. Even when justice was served, even when memory faded, no one ever really recovered, no parent of a murdered child ever afterward swam blissfully in the river of forgetfulness.

She pulled her shoulders back and thrust her chin forward. "Mrs. Desmond, I want you to know, I mean to get these monsters. And I will, I promise you. However long it takes, I'm going to see them burn in the chair before I'm finished."

Catherine suddenly turned toward her, fists clenched, and said, with a fervor long missing from her voice, "I want to see it. I want to be there to watch them burn, to see them writhe in agony. Promise me that, Roby Chang. Promise me I will be there when they die."

Chang blinked, surprised by her vehemence, and heartened too. When she had interviewed her before, in the hospital, Catherine Desmond had been like a zombie, all her feelings locked away somewhere inside. Anger was good, in Chang's opinion. It was often a first step in recovery.

"It's a date. I promise you, you'll see them die," she said with a grim smile. She took a card from her wallet and handed it to Catherine. "Meantime, if you think of anything...sometimes memory does funny things, you know, you're reading a book or walking down a street, and the most trivial thing will trigger something in

31

your mind. If you think of anything, anything at all, call me. Day or night."

* * * * * * *

Catherine had planned to go into the office for the afternoon, but now she changed her mind. Roby Chang's visit had unnerved her. She called in and made her apologies, was embarrassed by how quickly, how understandingly they were received.

The free time left her restless, however. She sat at the piano, picked listlessly at a Chopin prelude. Jack McKenzie's yellow roses, a new bouquet of them, sat in their usual place atop the piano. Walter never failed to glower at them when he saw them, but he kept his objections to himself.

Her out-of-practice fingers hit a wrong note. She slammed her hand down on the keyboard, creating a discordant cacophony, and got up, banging the lid down on the piano and making the roses tremble nervously.

She went to the window and glanced out, and saw again the sorry state of the back yard. Despite the cold and a gentle rain, she donned a parka, pulled the hood over her head, and went out to do some gardening.

A blue jay scolded her as she pulled up dead pansies and primroses with violent yanks. She imagined herself ripping out the hearts of the men who had murdered Becky.

Later, muddy and exhausted, she took a shower and thought about Walter. She had been cold, unyielding with him, though he too had grief to bear and, worse yet, a burden of guilt as well.

She had ignored her mother, too. The sorry truth was, she had been so wrapped up in her own suffering she had given not a thought to the suffering of others. She lashed herself with the recognition of her self-absorption.

Since her return from the hospital, she had been sleeping in Becky's room. That night she returned to her own bed, to Walter.

He welcomed her into his arms, and after several long moments of silent embrace, he tried dutifully to make love to her. It was a failure on both their parts. After what seemed an eternity of writhing and rubbing, he heaved a deep sigh and rolled off of her.

"I'm sorry," he said.

For a reply, she took his hand and gave it a forgiving squeeze. Later, when he began to snore gently in his sleep, she went back to Becky's room.

Lying there in the darkness, the futility of their attempt at sex stayed with her. Yet now that she was in another bed, another room, now that she considered it at a safe distance, she realized that nothing sexual had happened between them for a long while, even before. She had not minded, had welcomed the absence, she supposed, and so had been willing to overlook it, had scarcely even been conscious of it. If she had been able to see the future, she might well have considered another child...but who could possibly have foreseen what happened.

She did not find it flattering to face the truth of what she had done: it hadn't been only out of consideration for Walter, for their marriage, that she had returned to his bed. Far back in a corner of her mind, she had thought of replacing what had been lost. In a way, she was glad the attempt had been unsuccessful. That wasn't the right motivation to bring a child into the world. Becky had been precious to her, and another child might well be too, without being a "replacement." Anyway, if she were going to be truly honest with herself, Walter was no longer the man she would have chosen for a father.

She got up and went into the bathroom—not the master bath, which was too close to where he slept, but the one across the hall from Becky's room. The door closed, all the lights on, she shed her robe and took a long, hard look at herself in the mirror.

She had never been beautiful, not even as a young woman, but she had known without conceit (and with a probably too immodest pleasure) that she was attractive to the opposite sex. That, however, had been years ago. Was she still? She honestly didn't know. Walter didn't count. She had not for many years thought of him in terms of sex, opposite or otherwise. And, it seemed, the same with him.

She had a good complexion, what they used to call "peaches and cream," and eyes the color of old cognac, with gold flecks that glinted when she was angry or excited. She was thirty-two. Well preserved, she thought with all due modesty. Until this last year, she had been careful of diet and exercise, and though no doubt some softening had set in during that time, she could not yet detect any evidence of it.

Or not much evidence. When she got on the scales, she saw that she had gained a full five pounds. Too much time abed, not enough exercise.

Even so, she didn't exactly look chubby. Would a man still find her attractive? Would—*the time for pretense in your life is past, my girl, she told herself*—would Jack McKenzie still find her attractive?

Memories crowded in upon her, sweet, stinging. She had been seventeen when they had met. Eighteen when they first made love—the night of her eighteen birthday, to be exact. His scruples, not hers. Certainly not hers. Despite her most ardent efforts to convince him otherwise, he had stubbornly insisted that he wanted her to be an adult when it happened. "I'm not robbing any cradles, my love," he insisted. He was eight years older than she. Eight years wiser, she could see now, though at the time she had seen it only as sheer pigheadedness.

Pigheadedness that somehow allowed her to convince herself that he didn't love her when he said they would have to wait to get married.

"Why do you have to go away, to the Middle East?" she demanded. "You could make a writing career here, couldn't you?"

"Because I plan to be a war correspondent." He had been so calm, so reasonable, that it only enraged her all the more. "Iraq is where the war is going to be, Iraq, Kuwait, Saudi Arabia. That's where I have to be."

"Then I'll go with you."

The tolerant smile he gave her infuriated her. "There's no way I would take you there. The danger, the hardship—no, my darling, you will wait here until I come back. Assuming I do come back. There's always that chance."

"And if I won't wait?"

"Kat, don't be silly. If it will make you feel better, we'll get married the first day I step on U. S. soil again, I promise."

"Why don't we get married now, and you go do your Mid-East thing, and I'll wait here for you. We have a week for a honeymoon, surely, before you have to leave."

There was that damned smile again. "Suppose I didn't come back. Suppose I left you pregnant. What family do you have? Your mother, who is caring for a bed-ridden husband at the present? And I have a cousin in Oregon, who probably barely remembers me. Do you imagine I want the woman I love left with that sort of burden to bear alone? You'd be middle aged by the time you worked through it all. No, you're young, you're single, I want you to enjoy your life, have fun. You're still a kid. Go out with other guys if you feel like it. There'll be plenty of time to work on marriage when I get back."

He went, and she sent his ring to him without even a note, and before six months had passed, she married Walter.

She thought again of her husband and that futile effort at making love. Yes, now that she remembered, she could see that part of their marriage had begun to fade long ago. How many years could it have taken him to realize how much spite there had been in the hasty "yes" she gave him when, the field rid of his rival, he had once again pressed his suit?

What a fool she had been. Now Jack McKenzie was back in the city. Somehow, knowing he was here, close by, made it all the worse.

The shooting had left an ugly scar at her left temple. She tugged her hair down over it, pulling and fluffing until she had managed to hide it from sight. After a moment, she made a grimace of regret at herself and gathering her robe from the floor, tossed it about her shoulders. Before she turned the light out, she gave the image in the mirror one last glance.

She could not help wondering: how would Jack McKenzie see her now?

In the master bedroom, Walter heard the bathroom door open. He tensed, his hand paused in its ministrations. The door to Becky's bedroom closed a moment later, and he let out the breath he had been holding. His hand began to move again. He closed his eyes and resumed the fantasies playing across the screen of his mind.

His hand moved faster.

* * * * * * *

It seemed to Catherine that she had barely closed her eyes when a voice said, "Wake up."

She opened her eyes but the white light that filled the room blinded her and she could see nothing.

"You must come," the voice said, "Come see."

The light faded, and she was standing in an unfamiliar room, a seedy room with faded wallpaper hanging loose from the ceiling and dust motes dancing in the pale light from a single overhead bulb. There were two men on a bed—and a little girl with them. They were...God in Heaven, what were they doing?

On cue, the girl cried out with a sob, "Don't, don't, please."

A giant bear of a man, his back to Catherine, chuckled. The other one—long, skinny—said, "Shut up, or I'll tape your mouth again."

Catherine tried to scream, to call out to them to leave the girl alone, but no sound came. She took a step toward the bed. She must make them stop. This was too horrible to bear.

Despite her silence, perhaps because he sensed her presence, the skinny man raised his head and looked in her direction, looked directly at her. Her heart thudded. It was him: the man with the yellow beard. The beard was gone now, shaved off, making his face look different, but she would never forget those eyes; nothing could disguise that face from her.

"What the hell?" he said. He jumped up from the bed and took a step in her direction. The other man looked too, she had a quick glimpse of his face as he said, "Trash can?"

The next instant, she was back in bed in Becky's room, lightning shards of pain crashing through her head.

CHAPTER FOUR

She leaped up and staggered to the bathroom, barely reaching the toilet bowl in time to vomit wildly into it. Even when her stomach was emptied the dry heaves continued for long minutes.

Finally, weakly, she sat on the edge of the bathtub. As her head began to clear, she thought of Agent Chang. She ran to the den where she had left the F.B.I. agent's card and was actually dialing the number before she thought to wonder what she was going to tell her. That she had seen her daughter's kidnappers in a dream? With another little girl, perhaps the very one who had disappeared yesterday?

She returned the receiver to its cradle. Chang would think she was insane. Maybe I am, she thought. How could she explain what had just happened? Who would believe her? I don't believe it myself, she thought despairingly. Yet it had been so real.

Had it been only a dream? Though it sickened her to imagine it, she summoned the scene she had witnessed back into mind. Even now, when she was awake, it was startlingly vivid. She saw Yellow Beard jump up from the bed, heard him exclaim. Heard the other man on the bed say, "trash can." Which made no sense.

Dreams didn't, though, did they?

* * * * * *

She woke with the memory of that horrible nightmare still fresh in her mind. The Times had the story of the kidnapped child on the front page. Catherine looked long and intently at the grainy photo of a grinning twelve-year old schoolgirl. Was it the girl she had seen in her dream? She couldn't say with any certainty. She'd had only the briefest glimpse of the child's tortured face before Yellow Beard had seen her and jumped from the bed.

She wished she could share her experience with someone, and at once dismissed her husband. He would shrug it off as hysteria,

hysteria and grief, which had brought on a terrible nightmare. Even she had to logically suppose that was the truth. If only it hadn't seemed so vivid, so like she had actually been there.

Her mother? As if that thought had communicated itself through space, the phone rang and it was her mother. "I have to do some shopping," Sandra Dodd said, her tone making a question of it, a hopeful question, "And I thought you might join me? We could have lunch together."

Shopping and lunch had been a monthly ritual in the past, one of the many that had fallen by the wayside. "Dominique's in the mall?" Catherine suggested. That had been their favorite spot.

"At twelve?" Sandra was obviously delighted.

After she had hung up the phone, however, Catherine was less sure. The thought of the mall crowds, the early Christmas crowds especially, intimidated her. She used to enjoy going out, had savored the noise and bustle, had particularly enjoyed the Christmas season. Now, though, she felt the urge to stay in her safe retreat, with a husband as little interested as she was in interaction, where no one could assault her.

Only, they had, hadn't they, had assaulted her, if only in her dreams? Staying in was no safer than going out, if her mind wasn't free. Hadn't she been haunted all these months by memories? By the time she was dressed to go out, her mood was decidedly cheerless.

Walter at least seemed pleased. "It'll do you good," he said when she told him her plans. "Tell you what, I'll try to make it home for dinner tonight and you can tell me all about your shopping. We'll make a regular evening of it." He gave her cheek a peck as he went out.

Ready to leave, she paused to look at herself in the hall mirror. What a grim looking creature, she thought, and laughed bitterly at her own reflection. You simply could not play the role of tragic martyr, no matter how justifiably, without looking just a trifle ridiculous.

* * * * * * *

The mall parking lot was crowded and she had to drive around for several minutes before she finally found a space. Even so, she was early. She sat for a brief while, listening to the sound of rain on the car roof and trying to screw up the courage to go inside.

Don't be an ass, she scolded herself. She shoved the door open, and walked with determined steps through the rain, forgetting to put up her umbrella.

Dominique, the restaurant's petite and pretty proprietress, was happy to see her. "Mrs. Desmond, how delightful," she greeted her, "We've missed you."

Which meant, Catherine imagined, that she did not know the reason for the absence. Just as well, she thought, as she followed Dominique to their favorite table in a sheltered corner. That was one person, at least, who would not regard her with pity, liberally laced with curiosity. She ordered a glass of Chablis and told the waitress she would wait for her mother to join her.

When the wine came, she took a sip without tasting it and turned the glass round and round in her fingers while she looked about at the other diners. They were a decidedly mixed lot: more women than men, lots of children, and a few teenagers, eschewing the fast food outlets favored by their contemporaries and looking their most sophisticated. In the background, Bing Crosby dreamed faintly of a white Christmas.

At the table next to hers, a young boy, eight or perhaps nine, got up from the table and told his mother he was going to the restroom.

"Give me a minute," she sighed. She emptied her coffee cop and started to collect her packages.

"No, I want to go alone," he said firmly.

It was a youngster's predictable push for adolescent independence and after a moment's consideration, the mother nodded. "Straight there and straight back," she said, and motioned to the waitress for more coffee. She could use another cup, she was thinking, and besides, her feet hurt. When had Christmas shopping ceased to be fun and become work anyway?

Catherine watched the boy stride away, shoulders proud and straight, and felt a sudden wave of fear, of horrible expectation. He looked so very young, so vulnerable with his thin wrists showing out the cuffs of a shirt he had nearly outgrown, probably all too quickly. She thought of everything that might happen in those few unsupervised minutes, thought of the brief time, no more than seconds, surely, in which Becky had been taken. What if someone were there, in the restroom, waiting…?

Without thinking of what she was doing or how she might appear, she leaped up so suddenly that she startled the approaching waitress.

"Please." She stepped the few feet to the woman's table, "Please, you mustn't let him go alone. It isn't safe."

The woman looked up at her in surprise and suspicion. She glanced at the waitress as if to say, who let this fruitcake in? Aloud, to Catherine, she asked, "What's not safe? The mall? For Pete's sake, there's a million people here today, it's not like I'm sending him into a den of lions."

"You can't imagine," Catherine started to say, but the woman interrupted her in an icy voice: "I think you should mind your own business."

"Ma'am." The waitress tried to intervene, holding her coffee pot in front of her like a shield.

"I'm sorry, I...." Catherine realized suddenly how she must look. Probably they thought she was mad. She backed away in confusion and knocked over a chair. Other diners were looking, some of them concerned, some amused.

She snatched up her purse, the umbrella forgotten altogether, and dashed out of the restaurant. "Tell my mother something has come up," she told a startled Dominique. "Tell her...she'll understand."

She ran through the corridors of the mall, ignoring the puzzled looks of the shoppers she jostled and sidestepped, ran through the glass doors to the parking lot—and ran into Jack McKenzie.

Ran into him literally. Head down, she plunged through the glass doors, already fumbling in her purse for the car keys—and collided with someone, nearly fell down from the impact.

Hands caught her arms to steady her and an astonished voice said, "Catherine? My God, it's you."

She stepped back, looked up—and felt her heart stop inside her. "Jack?" She made a question of it only because she could not believe this could possibly be happening.

"Have I gone downhill that badly?" he asked, making a joke to hide his own confusion. She looked wild-eyed, frantic. God, what more could have happened to her? He wanted to take her in his arms at once, kiss and comfort her, and held himself in check by a sheer effort of will.

"No." She shook her head emphatically. "You look...." She was going to say "wonderful," but amended it to "...good. I just...I wasn't expecting to see you."

"Well, no, of course you wouldn't be. Me neither." He glanced around and up and seemed to realize for the first time that they were standing in the rain. "Look, maybe we should step inside."

She looked up at the sky too. "Oh." She sounded as surprised as he was by the raindrops.

He held tightly to her arm, as if she might try to break away from him, and pulled the door open with his other hand to lead her inside. They paused by the skating rink. On the ice below, a pert young woman in pink and white spun elegantly, showing off for a trio of male admirers.

It seemed as if neither of them could think of anything to say. He realized belatedly that he was still holding on to her and let his hand drop. "How are you?" was the best he could manage. He tried to say the rest with his eyes.

Eyes that, she thought, looked altogether too shocked at seeing her. What did he see, anyway: a woman he had once loved, a woman now thirteen years older? Not gray and doddering, that was silly, but faded nevertheless? The thirteen years stuck in her throat.

"I'm all right," she said hoarsely. "Thank you for the roses."

He shook his head. "Catherine, I felt so awful for you. I wanted...I wanted to come to you, but I didn't think...."

She managed a lopsided smile. "No, it's best that you didn't. Walter...." She left it at that. She lifted a hand unconsciously to tug a damp curl over the scar at her temple, and as she did, the sparkle of her wedding ring caught his eye.

"Yes," he said, the shards of light seeming to pierce his heart. He took the gesture for deliberate. "Walter."

The silence now was awkward. And painful. He took a step back from her. "Well," he said again.

"Are you...?" She wanted to ask, *are you married, are you in love, is there someone to whom I should direct all my hate and enmity?* Instead, she asked, "Back to stay?"

"For a while, at least. Peter gave me a job at the station. Peter Weitman, you remember him?"

"Yes."

"Channel Three at four. I reveal my ignorance on the state of the world." Another try at a joke, as unsuccessful as the previous one.

She looked long and hard at him. He had changed, of course he had. The truth was, she thought the changes were for the better. The hair was close cut now, and there was a dusting of gray at the temples, which gave him an air of distinction. The gray-blue eyes that studied her with an intensity that took her breath away were still as piercing as ever and his mouth...she had a sudden memory of his mouth upon her, not simply a mental memory, but a bodily memory, she could practically feel him down there, the way he had…She felt her cheeks redden as if he could read her thoughts.

"Catherine," he blurted out of a sudden, too painfully aware of her expression of embarrassment (was it that awkward for her, just seeing him?). "I'm sorry about everything in the past. But that's what it is, the past. Surely now we could be friends."

Which, she thought, settled that nicely, didn't it? Put her squarely in her place, in case she might entertain any ideas of something more, of his kiss….

"I don't see why we shouldn't." She made her voice businesslike. "I've got to go. It was good seeing you. Welcome back."

Just like that, she was gone. He stood and stared after her, watched her dash across the parking lot, saw her climb into her car, waited until it had disappeared into the rain.

So much, he thought, for the fantasies that had kept him burning in his bed night after night. She had looked right through him, had looked downright unhappy to see him—could not, in short, have made her disinterest any plainer.

And what had he expected, anyway? That after all these years she would throw herself into his arms, would tell him that she did after all love him, that nothing mattered any more but them, together at last?

Just by passing by she has stolen my heart. Surely, all those thousands of years ago, Ramses had meant those words to be joyous, but remembering them now, they filled him with anguish.

He cursed himself for a fool and looked around in a daze. He had forgotten entirely what he had even come here for. Disgusted with himself, in despair, he followed her path out into the rain of the parking lot.

* * * * * * *

At home, Catherine stripped off her sodden clothes and slipped into a robe. The telephone rang but she ignored it. A fire was already laid in the living room fireplace, and she lit it and poured herself a glass of cognac.

She didn't often drink these days, was afraid that she would find that too convenient a relief. Now, though, the burn of the alcohol in her throat was welcome.

She was still unnerved by the meeting with Jack. Seeing him…my God, how that had shaken her. The thought of resuming sexual relations with Walter had sickened her. She'd had to force herself to make the effort, futile as it had turned out to be. A day ago, an hour ago, she would not have imagined that she could feel—would ever again feel—desire of that sort.

Yet she had only to lay eyes on Jack McKenzie and she had been panting like a bitch in heat. *No use dressing it up in fancy words, my girl.*

It wasn't only sexual heat, though, now that she'd had time to consider. It was another kind of heat as well that had permeated her. Seeing him, however briefly, however disappointingly, was like stepping from an icy cold outside into a warm, fire lit room. She could almost feel the frigidity within her begin to thaw, like the heat from the fireplace leaching the chill from her body. She turned her glass in her hand, watching the gleam of firelight caught in the amber like some prehistoric insect.

The clock struck, giving her a start. Walter had said he would be home for dinner. She couldn't bear the thought of struggling through an evening with him. Though she and Jack had done nothing more than chat in a desultory fashion, she felt oddly guilty. Surely Walter would see her desire written on her face.

She dialed the restaurant, meaning to plead an excuse. She would say she was going to a movie with her mother, or perhaps that she had a headache and wanted to be alone.

None of which turned out to be necessary. A girlish young voice she didn't recognize informed her, "Mr. Desmond isn't in today, it's his day off. Can I help you?"

She hung up without reply, relieved and puzzled at the same time. He had said he was going to the restaurant, hadn't he? Oh well, she thought, he surely isn't finding my company any more enjoyable than I do his.

For a moment, she considered trying his cell phone, and decided against it. Out of the blue, it occurred to her that he might be having an affair. And what if he was, she wondered? She could hardly blame him. Could hardly care, truth be told. Anyway, after the desire—*oh, hell, call a spade a spade,* she thought—after the lust Jack had inspired in her, she wasn't in a position to cast stones, was she?

Maybe, she thought wryly, in Gilbert and Sullivan style, they had become the very model of a modern messed-up marriage.

The phone rang again. She almost answered it, thinking it might be Walter, and then changed her mind, letting it ring for several long minutes before it finally stopped.

* * * * * *

Walter was not home for dinner after all. She was already in bed when she heard him come in. She listened, and concluded from his stumbling around and muttered remarks that he was drunk.

She got up to see if he needed help, but when she came near to the bedroom door, she heard him crying. She crept back to her own room, Becky's room, where she lay in the darkness and imagined, though it would have been impossible, that she could still hear his muted sobs.

Or perhaps they were Becky's sobs that she heard. With that thought, there seemed to come to her a chorus of weeping. Children, a vast multitude of them, crying.

CHAPTER FIVE

At first, when she woke in the morning, she could not quite think what was different—something about the light? She turned on her side and saw the glow of sunlight beaming into the bedroom. Going to the window, she pulled the curtains aside. The rain that had fallen for days had ended and the sky was blue and high above.

What was really odd, she thought, as she slipped out of the oversized tee shirt she used for a nightgown, was the fact that she had slept the night through, like the proverbial log. For months her sleep had been fitful, periodic, punctuated with awakenings when she would find herself bathed in sweat and the bedclothes tied in knots.

She was in the shower when she realized with a sense of discovery that something had happened to her, something was different inside, in the very core of her being.

She tried to analyze it, and came back to her meeting yesterday with Jack. It was as if that electrical shock of seeing him, of sexual remembering, had jump-started her feelings, all the emotions she had so carefully locked away.

Out of nowhere, she began to cry—the first tears she had shed since that horrible moment in the parking lot, clinging to the door of a truck, fighting for her daughter.

She sat on the edge of the tub and let them come. The sobs wracked her body, the tears rolled down her cheeks unstopped. It was painful, but at the same time, she felt alive in a way that she hadn't been before. It was like being born again. Was this what the church people meant when they said that?

Walter gave her a concerned look when she came into the kitchen. Probably, she thought, he had heard her sobbing in the bathroom. "Are you all right?" he asked.

"I'm going to be," she said, and gave him a hug and a kiss on the cheek. He seemed pleased, if a bit mystified. She was grateful that he didn't question her further. She didn't have the answers yet herself.

She did, however, have some plans made. When Walter left, she went to the garage and took down the boxes of Christmas ornaments and without opening them set them on the front step, and called Goodwill to pick them up. She told Goodwill the boxes were Christmas ornaments, but in her mind it was a big chunk of self-pity she was disposing of.

Then she went to see her mother. She drove up Beverly Glen, seeing for the first time how green the hills were from all the rain, and took Mulholland Drive, following its twisted route across the ridge of hills that separate the valley from West L.A.

In the summer the valley would be thick with smog and visibility limited to no more than a few miles, but now, the air washed clean by rain, it spread out before her in all its immensity, seeming to go on and on forever before it collided with the purple-gray mountains in the distance.

She turned off Mulholland to weave her way down Laurel Canyon into the valley itself. It was Saturday, nearing Christmas, and traffic was busy. People were intent on going here and there, some of them chatting with companions in their cars, some of them appearing to talk to themselves. They looked happy, sad, frenzied, spaced out, the whole gamut of human expression. The sidewalks were mostly empty. People didn't walk much here, though there were groups of children playing, and a mailman plodded wearily along his route, a terrier yapping at him from behind a wire fence.

Perhaps after all it wasn't so bad to be alive. She still had her grief. Probably she would have that within her for the rest of her life, but maybe there could be room as well for the rest of it, the common threads of humanity that held life together.

Her mother was still in her bathrobe, not one of those pink and frilly woman's things, but a man's white terry cloth robe, several sizes too big for her. Somehow Catherine found it endearing.

Sandra was surprised to see her, and faintly alarmed, not sure what to expect. She had been worried since she arrived at Dominique's yesterday and found Catherine gone. Several times she tried to phone, but there had been no answer. Now, suddenly, here Catherine was, stopped just inside the front door.

"It's funny," Catherine said in the way of greeting, "I was thinking that no matter where you have lived or for how long, coming to your mother's house is always 'coming home'."

Sandra gave a timorous smile. "Strange you should say that. I said almost the same words to your grandmother many years ago."

"Oh, Mom," Catherine said, and then they were in one another's arms, both of them crying and talking at the same time, and even laughing, and it was minutes before Sandra could steer them into the kitchen.

They sat at the little table there and had coffee and bagels and cried and laughed some more and after a while, to the great good pleasure of both, their chatter settled into the kind of frank, woman-to-woman conversation they had enjoyed so often together in the past.

They spoke of Becky, the first time Catherine had been able to speak of her to anyone: of how precious she had been to both of them, and they shared the horror they had suffered over what had happened, and the anger that had been too long suppressed.

"I've been so selfish," Catherine said, "I was so wrapped up in the pain of losing a daughter, I forgot that you had lost a grand-daughter."

"I felt as if I had lost a granddaughter and a daughter." She made of it less a rebuke than a statement of fact that produced another round of tears and hugs and a spilled cup of coffee.

"It's all right, really, I do understand," Sandra said as she mopped up the coffee. "When your father died—it's nearly ten years now—but I thought for a long time that my life was over. I simply couldn't imagine how I could go on without him."

"It's so strange, you seemed at the time to be handling it so well."

"I wasn't any better at sharing my pain than you have been. We're two of a kind, I suppose. The point is, time is the answer. It's such a cliché, but time is what does it. It's early days yet. Wait, be patient, the wounds will heal. She'll never leave you, and that's all right too. It just won't hurt so much when you think of her. When I think of your father now, it's mostly with pleasure."

They both thought of that for a moment while Sandra got up to pour some more coffee.

"Do you ever," Catherine asked and hesitated slightly, "Do you ever miss the, you know, the physical part?"

"Sometimes." Her mother smiled shyly. "Until he got sick, your father was a very passionate man."

Which Catherine found awkward to contemplate. One never wanted to think of one's parents that way, though she was sensible enough to realize how altogether silly that was.

"But you're still young." Her mother was fifty-four and could surely pass for ten years younger. "Haven't you ever thought about finding someone else?"

"Yes. I actually did, well, 'see' someone a few times. You remember Mr. Adams, the widower?"

"Johnny Depp?" Catherine said with an incredulous laugh—that was their nickname for the neighbor across the street, who did indeed look uncannily like the actor. "Are you telling me you slept with Johnny Depp?"

"He's a very handsome man." Her mother gave her a stern look, which quickly deteriorated into a giggle. "And slept is not quite the right word. He always went home afterward."

"Well?" Catherine raised an eyebrow. Inwardly she was scoring her mother some serious points. Mr. Adams, "Johnny Depp," couldn't have been more than thirty-something. A teacher, he had been married only a few years when he lost his wife in an auto accident. Despite the obvious efforts of numerous women in and out of the neighborhood to provide solace, there had never been any suggestion that he was seeing anyone—until now.

Sandra shrugged. "Well, nothing, really. Oh, not that he wasn't very willing, and so far as I can say, he seemed to have all the moves right. It's just that for a woman, for some women anyway, at least for me, it doesn't really work on a purely physical level, it needs that special something. Not love, necessarily, but something more than just bodies banging together. I think for me, if he's someone special, a private glance across a room is very thrilling, and if he is not, it doesn't make much difference what he brings to you in looks or technique or, if you want to know, size."

Catherine gazed pensively into the distance. "I think you're probably right. I think it's the same with me."

"You're thinking of Walter?"

Catherine looked directly at her mother. "I was thinking of Jack McKenzie," she said frankly.

"Oh." Sandra sounded not particularly surprised.

"I seem to have loved him forever. And to have been unhappy about it nearly as long."

"Oh, my dear, love has nothing to do with happiness. You can be quite happy with someone and not love him. And you can love him and despise him at the same time. It's something spontaneous and, it seems to me, quite unmanageable. And endless, too, I don't think once you love someone you can ever really stop loving, although you can certainly end the relationship."

"I'd have to agree. I know I tried hard enough to get Jack out of my heart, but try though I will, he's still there."

"I don't think I shall presume to advise you on that score. You remember your Dante, don't you? When he first starts his journey it is Socrates, the intellect, who guides him, but when they reach a certain point, he turns the job over to Dante's beloved Beatrice. Which was Dante's way of saying, as I see it, there comes a time when reason be damned, you have to let your heart lead the way."

What a dope I have been, Catherine was thinking, to have deprived myself of this wonderful woman.

* * * * * * *

She stopped at the mall again on her way home. At the entrance to Macy's Christmas department, she had to pause to steel herself. All the bustle, the noise, Christmas music piped over speakers, the babble of voices and the jangle of cash registers. In the far corner a line of children waited to see a thoroughly unconvincing Santa. Or perhaps the children were happy to allow themselves to be deceived—children were often wiser, she thought, than parents gave them credit for being.

She made herself go in. She picked up two strings of lights, and got a third one for good measure. Four boxes of ornaments, that ought to be enough, wouldn't it? Tinsel, some garlands. She even got an angel for the treetop, and immediately named it Becky.

Those purchases made, and they were the hardest, she went to men's and found a cashmere sweater for Walter, and to women's, where she picked out a Pashmina stole for her mother. She chose black first, and then, thinking that too funereal, traded it for a fire engine red; but she could hear her mother saying, "What on earth would I wear that with?" She settled finally for one in pale lilac.

"It's going on sale tomorrow," the silver-haired saleswoman whispered in a conspiratorial voice. "I'll ring it up for you at the sale price."

"That's very kind of you," Catherine thanked her. That was something she must work at remembering: there were kind people in the world too, good people. One mustn't think that everyone was evil. To do that was to let the villains win.

She took her packages to gift wrapping and had them wrapped. That, she decided, she still wasn't up to. Anyway, she had never been very good at it.

Satisfied that she had taken several good steps in the direction of recovery, she left the store. On her way home, she stopped at her regular flower shop, Rose's Roses. They had ordered their Christmas trees from Rose Leiberman for years, always—Rose's little joke—calling it a Hanukah bush.

The tinkle of the bell over the door and the familiar blend of flower shop scents, the sweet of fresh and the rotten of aging flowers, welcomed her.

The pale, blonde woman by the window was new to her however. In the past Rose had always managed the shop alone. "I was looking for Rose," Catherine replied to her greeting.

"I'm here to help you," the woman said.

A new employee, then. Catherine was disappointed. She would have liked to see Rose herself, but Rose was getting up in years and the shop was probably too much for her to handle alone at this hectic time of year.

"I'd like to order a tree," Catherine said.

"You must keep trying," the woman said.

"Oh. You mean you don't have any trees this year?"

"Traveling is like a muscle, the more you use it, the stronger it gets," was the puzzling response.

Catherine tried to digest that, but could make no sense of it. "I'm sorry, I don't think I understand." Did she know this woman? She looked vaguely familiar, but standing just in front of the window as she was, with the bright sunlight streaming in around her, it was difficult to make out her face. If one were fanciful one might almost imagine that the light made a halo about her head.

"I'm sorry about the pain, but it will get better too with practice. It does sort of go with the territory, unfortunately. You were shot in the head, after all."

Catherine gasped. "How could you possibly know...?" she started to ask, taking a step towards this strange woman.

"Mrs. Desmond! Catherine!" Rose Leiberman came through the curtained doorway from the back room. "What a wonderful surprise."

Catherine turned to greet her and was swallowed up in a determined embrace, crushed against Rose's enormous bosom. "I was so sorry, so very, very sorry," Rose said. "You poor darling."

Catherine felt a cold draft across the back of her neck. It was a moment before she realized the shop door had opened and closed behind her. She jumped back and looked around. The woman had gone.

"Oh, wait," she cried. She ran outside and looked up and down the street. A huffing Springer Spaniel impatiently tugged along a thin man on the end of a leash. Two boys tossed a football back and forth, and a young woman in purple Spandex that ought to have been too skimpy for the chilly day teetered perilously on a pair of inline skates. The woman was nowhere to be seen.

Rose looked at her curiously when she came back in, the bell over the door jingling. "Is something wrong?" she asked.

"That woman. She just disappeared. I wanted to talk to her. Did you know her?"

Rose looked around the shop, confused. "Woman?"

"She was just there, by the window, she was talking to me when you came through the doorway."

Rose looked in the direction of the window. "Oh, I suppose she was just a looky-loo, we get lots of them this time of year." She dismissed the subject with a shrug and turned her friendly smile back to Catherine. "Let me guess, you've come for a Hanukah bush?"

CHAPTER SIX

At home, Catherine poured herself a glass of wine and, kicking off her shoes, curled up on the sofa in the den.

She could no longer ignore the fact that something peculiar, something downright weird, was happening to her. But what, exactly? What had that woman at the flower shop meant, about traveling? Hadn't someone said the very same thing to her previously?

She tried to think back over all of it. The nightmare. On the face of it, there was nothing peculiar about that. Why wouldn't she have a nightmare about the men who had kidnapped her daughter?

It had been so real, though: the shaved off beard, the face. Had the mole been removed? She wanted so desperately to tell Agent Chang about those changes in his appearance, because she wanted so desperately to see those men caught—but how could she tell Chang what she had seen in a dream without sounding like a madwoman?

What if it was *all* just a nightmare? What if she had in fact died when she was shot, and all the rest, everything that she had experienced since, was just some epic, drawn out dream?

She tried to place things in some logical sequence. There had been that moment in the hospital when she had imagined herself in the hallway outside her room, and that had seemed real also. And it must have seemed real to Millie, too, because remembering now that moment when the nurse burst into the room, recalling her expression, she realized that Millie had fully expected to see an empty bed. So Millie must have seen her in the corridor as well. Surely two people couldn't share the same delusion.

She thought about the woman doctor. Like the woman today at Rose's shop—they could have been the same person, she realized suddenly—the doctor too had mentioned travel. Had she been only a dream, too, or had she been real? Yes, of course, she was real. She and Millie had exchanged words.

Or had they? The doctor had spoken, and Millie had spoken, but had they actually spoken to one another? She couldn't remember their exact words, but now she didn't think that they had. For that matter, had Millie even seen the doctor? And if not, did it mean she wasn't real?

Even that hadn't been the beginning, though. There was that eerie experience when she had been, if not dead, certainly dying. It had gotten blurry in her memory, like a faded photograph and she had deliberately pushed that memory away. There had been light, she remembered that much, blinding light, and someone had spoken to her about a job to do. Something only she could do.

So many questions, to which she could think of no answers. What had the woman in the shop said today: "You must practice. You mustn't let the pain hold you back from traveling."

Okay, then, say that she had been "traveling," in some sense. Was she having, what-did-they-call-them, out of body experiences?

Dean and Summers had published a book on paranormal experiences a few years back. She went to the bookshelves lining the wall, and found it, *An Almanac of the Paranormal*, and looked through the table of contents until she found a heading for "astral projection." Yes, she thought, skimming through that chapter, it sounded like what had been happening to her.

There was a lengthy discussion of what the author described as a spiritual double, what the ancient Egyptians had called the Ka, which could sometimes leave the body during sleep or during a trance and return to it, so that individuals might seem to be in two places at once. According to the author, this "travel" often began as a spontaneous thing. Which, if you thought about it, was certainly what had happened with her.

She put the book aside for a moment. It sounded to her like a lot of mumbo-jumbo. Yet she couldn't deny that something had happened to her, that unless she had simply had the most bizarre dreams, she had traveled in some spirit fashion to other locations.

She had a chilling thought: if that nightmare of her daughter's murderers was not a nightmare, then she had actually, spontaneously, traveled to where they were. Was that what she was meant to do, why she had been given this bizarre "gift?" Because, if so, God in Heaven, she didn't want it. She did not want ever again to have an experience like that.

Except, she hadn't been given any choice, had she? It *had* been spontaneous. But surely, she was not simply at the mercy of some extraterrestrial force. There must be some way to prevent that from happening again. She went back to the book. Yes, astral travelers generally learned with practice to control their projections, to choose where and when they will travel.

Well, then, there was the answer. She must practice, learn how to control what had been happening to her. Only, how was she supposed to practice something that occurred on its own? She didn't have any idea what she done on any of those occasions, didn't in fact think that she had done anything to bring those weird experiences about.

"All right," she said aloud, "let's suppose I can travel, to borrow a word, and I just need to practice it. Let's pop in on Mom, why don't we?"

That was certainly something non-threatening, and if she startled her mother, it would be a good intro to telling her all about it. It was assuredly difficult to think of any better way of broaching the subject.

She made herself comfortable on the sofa, closed her eyes and concentrated hard, screwing up her face. Were there some magic words she was supposed to use? The book hadn't said. Abracadabra maybe? Open Sesame? Knock, knock?

After a while, feeling foolish, she opened her eyes. If she were supposed to practice this, they would have to give her some sort of hint as to how. Whoever, she amended, *they* were. And it would help if they explained why she was supposed to practice it. Other than avoiding the hassle of commuting in Los Angeles, she didn't quite see the point. Much as she wanted to see them caught and put away, she did not want, ever, to pay any more visits to those two men, and if that was their idea, they could simply think again. If, that was, that had not been a dream. And there she was, back full circle where she had started, and none the wiser.

The hall clock announced four. She remembered all at once what Jack had said: channel three at four. Putting the book aside, she found the remote and flipped on the television to channel three, and there he was, talking about some problem with the Koreas. She watched him, paying no attention to his words, free now to study him without awkwardness.

He still had that odd mix of vulnerability and independence—the result, no doubt, of being orphaned young, of having to make his own way—that had always been so attractive and, in a way, frightening. Even as a young girl, she had wondered what lay within the still depths of those gray-blue eyes, keen eyes that seemed to look out from the screen straight into hers. The movement of his lips once again sent sensual shivers coursing through her.

She was surprised when a woman with stiff black hair appeared on the screen beside him. "Oh, go away," Catherine ordered the brunette, "I want Jack."

The brunette asked Jack a question and again the camera zoomed in on him. And again, he seemed to look straight into Catherine's eyes, she could almost feel herself falling into gray-blue pools. The light around him appeared golden, like a gilding fog....

Just like that, she was standing in an unfamiliar office, beside a desk.

* * * * * *

"See if you can get me a ticket for the symphony for tonight," Jack told his secretary as he passed her desk, barely slowing his brisk pace.

"The Chopin? Lang Lang? I've heard it's sold out."

"The peanut gallery will do. There's usually something up top."

"One?" she asked after his rapidly vanishing back. Always in such a hurry, she thought regretfully. She had hoped, when she got the job, that he might pay a bit more attention to her. She might as well have been a doorstopper for all he noticed the pains she had taken with her clothes and her makeup, and hadn't she just spent one hundred dollars on a new hair stylist?

"One will be plenty." He pushed open the door to his office, stepped through—and saw Catherine standing in front of his desk.

He caught his breath and blinked, and she was gone. Hadn't really been there at all, of course, or if she had, it had only been a ghost, because he had seen the desk right through her, logic told him that even as his heart insisted she *had* been there.

Great, he thought, I'm going bats.

* * * * * *

Back in her den, Catherine looked for the daily newspaper and checked the concert listings. Yes, there it was, The Chopin "First Piano Concerto", Lang Lang with the Los Angeles Philharmonic Orchestra, tonight, at Disney Hall. That part, certainly, had not been a dream.

She smiled broadly. The Chopin first was the most romantic piece of music she knew. It was also, for her, intensely erotic. Jack had played it for her the night he first made love to her.

What did it say about him, that he was going tonight to listen to that very music? And what an uncanny coincidence it was that she had traveled to him at the very moment he told his secretary to find him a ticket.

Uncanny, indeed. Maybe there was an upside to this travel business. She lifted her eyes heavenward and whispered "Thanks," half expecting to hear an answering, "You're welcome."

Smiling, she dialed her mother's telephone number. "Mom," she said, "Do you still have your symphony subscription?"

"Yes, although I hardly ever go. As a matter of fact, now that you mention it, I have tickets for tonight."

"The Chopin? Two tickets?"

"Yes. And I can't make it. It's bridge night. Did you want them?"

Catherine's smile grew wider. "I'd love to have them. I'll stop on my way. Oh, and Mom, if Walter should ask, we went together."

* * * * * * *

She promised herself that she wouldn't actually speak to him, wouldn't even meet up with him. He needn't know she was there. She only wanted to see him, at a distance, to know that she was under the same roof with him, sharing the same musical experience.

Nonetheless, here she was, standing in the lobby near the main entrance, waiting to see him arrive. As usual, he was late. The lobby began to empty as people ascended the stairs on their way to the auditorium. She shifted her weight from one foot to another and gingerly sipped a glass of wine.

What if he didn't come? He might have changed his mind. Or his secretary might have been unable to find a ticket. Or he could have come up the escalator from the parking garage. She had made a guess that, only recently returned to the city, he would park at the Chandler, across the street, where he had always parked in the past. That would bring him in this way. It was only a guess, though.

He had never liked "flashy" women and she had dressed carefully: an eggshell silk skirt and blouse, the skirt falling to mid-calf—fashion trends notwithstanding, she had always worn her skirts that length, for the most vain of reasons: it was a hemline flattering to her legs. She had tried on her only good jewelry, a single strand of pearls—real oyster, as her mother liked to say—and had swapped them at the last moment for a simple jade pendant that set off her complexion and lent her eyes an arresting topaz glint. A white cashmere trench coat was flung casually over her shoulders. She wore little makeup and didn't need it—some lipstick, peach blush, a little eye shadow—and she had left her hair down, the way he liked it, though it was shorter than it had been when they were younger. One carefully arranged curl hid the scar at her temple.

He wasn't coming, she thought with a sudden burst of impatience. How utterly silly of her to be here like this, waiting for certain disappointment. It was like lifting your glass to drink and finding it empty. She set her wine aside on the bar being carefully wiped clean by an impatient bartender, who snatched it up at once.

She started toward the escalator—and stopped dead as Jack dashed in, at the last minute, just as always in the past—she ought to have remembered that. Windblown and coatless, a man who couldn't deign to notice the weather, he hurried into the lobby.

Her promises to herself went out the door as he came in. At the sight of him, her heart jumped into her throat. She took a deep breath and put her head down and moved in a path that would intercept his, walking quickly because in another few feet his hurried steps would carry him to the escalators. Already the smartly uniformed usher was holding out her hand to scan his ticket.

"Jack." She looked up and directly at him at the last minute. "This is a surprise."

"Catherine." He stopped in his tracks and gave her a measuring look, as if he were not altogether as surprised as she professed to be.

She ignored the look and the pounding of her heart and managed a warm smile. "The Chopin," was all she could think to say.

"Yes. It's one of my favorites."

"I remember."

He looked down at his watch. "We'd better get inside."

The usher scanned their tickets, and realized belatedly that there were three tickets and only two people, but Catherine was past her and already moving up the escalator before she could say anything. She shrugged, and turned instead to another late arrival.

The escalator seemed to move at a snail's pace. Catherine waited until they had almost reached the next level before she asked, "Where are you sitting?" She tried to make the question innocent. If only he didn't look too carefully at her….

He grimaced and nodded his head upward. "The top. Nosebleed country."

"But, no, I have an extra seat right beside me, mother was supposed to come and changed her mind at the last minute. Orchestra. Why don't you join me?"

They had reached the orchestra level. He looked toward the escalator that continued upward, and hesitated. "That's very kind of you, but...."

"Please," she interrupted him. "You did say we were going to be friends, didn't you? And I really hate going in by myself. That's why I waited till the last minute, so all those people wouldn't have time to think, 'that poor wretch, she couldn't get a date'."

He laughed at the ridiculousness of that, and looked at his watch again. By now they were very nearly alone. "Well," he said, knowing perfectly well that he shouldn't, and knowing just as well that he was doomed to lose the argument with himself.

"I insist." She put a hand on his arm and steered them toward the door to the auditorium. The usher waiting there, watching them approach, tightened her lips and looked at their tickets. Inside, the lights were starting to dim already. She had planned to be comfortably ensconced in that empty seat in the back row before the music, one of her favorite pieces, began. As it was, she would just have time to get them to their seats. Some people had no sense of propriety. Worse, probably the music meant nothing at all to these two. She could see as plain as the nose on her face that they were far more interested in one another.

* * * * * * *

He could barely concentrate on the music, so aware was he of Catherine next to him. Their arms brushed and he jerked his away as if it had been burned.

Probably she had forgotten the last time they heard this together, but that evening was branded on his soul. He cursed himself as a fool for giving in to the romantic notion of hearing this piece tonight.

What could he have expected? Even if he hadn't run into her like this, it would have been hell for him. Especially after that eerie moment in his office when he thought he had seen her. She had not been out of his mind for a second since then, and now here she was sitting beside him, as if his very thoughts had conjured her up. If he chose, he could turn toward her and take her in his arms. The heroic music, as brilliant and icy as stars splashed across a night sky, urged him to smother her with kisses as he had done so often in his dreams, tear her clothes away....

He grinned ruefully to himself. And wouldn't that give the symphony audience something to contemplate with their Chopin?

It was over at last. They drifted out of the auditorium with the crowd. There was another selection, Liszt, to follow the intermission, but as if it had already been discussed, they took the escalator down to the lobby, went past the little gift shop and out the exit. Neither had any interest in staying now that what they had come to hear was over.

They stopped on the verandah. Los Angeles could be cold in early December, as tourists often discovered to their dismay, but tonight was balmy, a gentle breeze chasing the clouds. She looked up at a starlit sky, at the swooping stainless steel wings of the concert hall, that seemed to embrace them, searching for something to break a silence that had become too weighted with suggestion.

"Your first visit to the Disney?" she asked finally.

He glanced over her shoulder at the voluptuous curves of the Gehry-designed building. "It's interesting," he said. "Reminds me of a synagogue, I think. It's not ugly, at least, which makes it better than that rock and roll monstrosity he saddled Seattle with." She laughed her agreement. They had always thought so much alike. Except, she thought sadly, when it came to one another.

"It makes me think of a ship," she said, looking back at it too. "I always feel like I should be swaying, and holding on to a rail."

He laughed and nodded, and the conversation faltered. "Where are you parked?" Jack asked.

"Downstairs. You parked at the Chandler?"

"Yes. I'll see you to your car."

Neither of them made a move to go, however. After another long silence, she asked, "Where are you living now?"

"I found a little place in Santa Monica. Tiny, but if you lean far enough out the bathroom window you can get a glimpse of the ocean before you fall."

She smiled, and then surprised even herself by saying, "Can we go there?"

He sighed and she knew before he said it what the answer would be. "I don't think that would be a good idea." Did she really think that, in the privacy of his own apartment, alone with her, he would be able to keep his hands off her? Or was she just mocking him?

Her heart sank. "No, you're probably right." She managed to shape her lips into a semblance of a smile at the same time she was mentally kicking herself. Why did she insist on making this fool of herself over him? Hadn't he already made it clear that the past was over and buried. "Well, goodnight, then."

"I'll see you to your car," he said again.

"No, that's all right, thanks anyway." She started to leave and then turned back to where he stood unmoving. "Would it be all right if I called you sometime? I...it really would be nice to think we could still be friends. I think I need friends just now."

"Absolutely. I'd like that." He found a business card in his wallet and scribbled hastily on the back of it, and handed it to her.

She tucked it into her pocket without looking at it and with a final quick nod, left him. He watched her get into the elevator without a glance in his direction, waited until the doors had glided shut and she disappeared from sight.

* * * * * * *

The garage was nearly deserted. She was almost to her car when she heard footsteps and the muted sound of voices. Garages were notoriously dangerous places. The bad guys had lots of opportunities: unwatched cars to be broken into, unwary parkers to be robbed or assaulted. They could hear someone coming well in advance, and had no end of places to hide.

She unlocked her door hurriedly and looked cautiously around as a couple came down the next aisle over. Nothing there to worry about, it appeared. Nevertheless, she slid quickly into the Jaguar, locked the door behind her and started up the engine.

The couple reached their own car as she drove past. She heard the young woman say, "But I just don't know what to do."

"Never you mind about any of it," her companion said, unlocking her door and swinging it wide for her, "I'll take care of everything. Leave it all to me."

Heading out of the garage, Catherine had a momentary sense of envy. How convenient that would be, wouldn't it, to have someone else shoulder the responsibility for every problem? To be one of those old-time women who let the man do everything for her.

Convenient, she thought, edging out onto Second Street, *and utterly not for me.* She stomped her self-sufficient foot down hard on the gas and merged into the traffic.

Driving home midst the river of cars on the freeway, the lighted towers of the city gliding past, her thoughts turned inevitably, despairingly, to her latest meeting with Jack. She had a sudden thought, not a happy one: what if he were involved with someone else? He had been alone tonight, but that didn't necessarily negate the possibility. She, whoever she was, might have had another commitment.

She frowned into the glow of the dashboard. Part of her knew that, sensibly, it might well be best for him, for both of them, if he were involved with someone.

Another part of her, however, did not like that idea at all. She smiled grimly to herself. What if he were? She could certainly deal with that, if that were the case. Let him try to make love to another woman with her standing at the foot of the bed. This "traveling" might not be such a bad thing after all, once she had gotten the mechanics of it down pat.

She was immediately ashamed of that line of thought. It was petty and childish and whatever the reason she had been given the gift of travel, it certainly hadn't been for anything so puerile.

But the idea didn't altogether go away, either.

At home, she left the Jaguar in the driveway and, before she got out, took his card from her pocket and glanced at it. He had written not only his phone number, but his address as well.

A Freudian slip? Or a deliberate invitation? Her spirits, sunk in a pit a moment before, soared toward the heavens. She put the card carefully into her purse and slid smiling out of the car and turned a little pirouette on the flagstone walk. She felt drunk, and not on the glass of wine she'd had earlier, but on something far headier.

It was ridiculous, it was altogether scary, it was almost certainly immoral and illegal and probably fattening in some way she couldn't yet fathom. Most of all, it was wonderful. For better or for worse, she was—still—head over heels in love with Jack McKenzie. And just at the moment, she couldn't begin to imagine how she was going to deal with that truth. It was enough for now to have faced it, head on, without any pretense.

She started up the walk, but halfway to the front door, she stopped abruptly, the hair on the nape of her neck rising. She had a sense of someone near, someone or something evil.

She turned around in a circle, looking. The halogen lights made the front lawn as bright as day. There was no one to be seen, and yet the sense of a threatening presence remained.

A stonewall and a row of citrus trees—a lemon, an orange, a grapefruit, neatly spaced—shielded the lawn from the street. There were shadows there among the trees, but no sign of any prowler lurking in them.

Frightened, not knowing quite why, she hurried to the front door.

* * * * * *

In a seedy cottage a few miles away, Lester Paterson—Trash Can Paterson to those who knew him, though few of them were friends—woke abruptly, his eyes flying open.

It was her, that woman again. He stared upward into the darkness. On the nearby sofa, J. D. Colley snored loudly.

He knew her, he was certain he did. But who was she, and why was she popping into his mind this way, like a ghost? Not even into his mind, exactly, more like she was actually here, close by. He had a feeling that if he sat up and looked, he would see her across the room, the way he had that other time.

Of one thing, he was certain: whoever she was, she was a threat to him. One that he had to eliminate.

He needed to find her. Fast.

CHAPTER SEVEN

Sunday morning dawned warm and sunny. Outside, the birds argued noisily over matters of territory and precedence. Catherine woke with a feeling of resolve. She had decided before she fell asleep last night that there were things that she must do, and first among those was one she had made up her mind she would not put off, the one she would do right away—before she got cold feet.

She had determined to shed that wearisome past that had weighted her down for far too long now. Like the spoiled child who will eat nothing because he cannot have the apple pie he demands, she had cursed life because it was not what it had been before. Well, it wasn't ever going to be. She had no idea what future lay hidden in the golden light from the window, but of one thing she was sure: she must make it for herself.

The scent of fresh brewed coffee led her to the kitchen. As if she had never smelled it before, she marveled at the welcoming aroma. It was astonishing to contemplate how much of the pleasure of life was made up of those tiny sense impressions, too often not even consciously noted: the fleeting smell of coffee and a faintly lingering one of toast; a glimpse of some purple dyed bird outside the window, the faint insinuation of a car passing on the street outside. They made her feel alive again.

Walter was in the kitchen, sipping coffee and nibbling at an English muffin while he read the morning paper. He nodded at her and went back to his reading. She waited until she had poured herself a cup of coffee before she interrupted him.

"I'm going to leave," she said without preamble. "Today."

His hand paused with the muffin halfway to his mouth, and he sniffed and looked up at her for a long measuring moment. "You mean permanently?" She thought that was unusually perceptive of him. Yet, her announcement could hardly be unexpected, might even be welcomed.

"Yes. I mean a divorce. I'm sorry. I don't blame you any longer for what happened, and I know you have your own pain to bear. But it's never going to be right again between us, Walter. Maybe it never was."

She had fretted much of the night over how he would take this news, and she held her breath while he regarded her solemnly. He was surely no happier in their current situation than she was, but sometimes pique ruled the day. It occurred to her, not for the first time, that though she had lived with him for more than a decade, she really did not know Walter at all.

Finally, he sighed. "I won't make any problems. However you want to arrange it. I'll divorce you if you prefer. Take whatever you want. But you don't have to leave, you know, I can move out and you can keep the house. Without you, without…it's nothing to me." He finally took that delayed bite of muffin.

She shook her head and made an expansive gesture that took in the kitchen and beyond, the entire house. "No, I want to go. I don't want to remain here. This place is too loaded with baggage. If I had been wise, I wouldn't have come back here at all."

He chewed and looked around as if seeing for the first time the house they had lived in nearly all the years of their marriage. "Then we'll sell it and split whatever we get. When will you…." he hesitated and swallowed. "Today, did you say?"

"I don't see any point in putting it off."

"No, you're probably right. Have you found a place then?"

"I'll get a hotel room for now, just take a few personal items with me. The rest can go into storage till I have an apartment."

"Leave it here. I'll stay till we get it sold, and when you're ready, I'll get your things moved. You can tell me what you want to keep and what to get rid of. Like I said, I won't make any trouble. You don't have to worry about that."

To her surprise, he returned his attention to his newspaper. She felt an odd sense of disappointment. Of course, she had hoped that he would take her announcement well. It was only that she hadn't expected such studied disinterest.

She turned to refill her coffee cup and glanced into the mirror over the sink. For a brief second, Walter had lowered the paper and his face was contorted with emotion: grief, certainly, despair—and something that she couldn't read.

It was so fierce it staggered her, literally. She took a step backward and turned to look at him, but whatever that expression had been, it was gone. The brief look he gave her was bland. He lifted the newspaper and she could no longer see his face.

Had she imagined it? No, surely not. What then did it mean? Was he still too consumed with grief and guilt really to be rational? Which was to say, should she perhaps give him more time, stay and try to help him regain his equilibrium?

Which was foolish, she knew that. She was only beginning to recover herself, and until she had fully accomplished that task, what good could she be at helping anyone else? Cliché though it might be, the blind really weren't very helpful at leading the blind.

Maybe she *had* imagined that fleeting look she had seen. Not imagined it altogether, but perhaps her own conflicting emotions had made more of it than had really been there.

You are being a goose, she told herself; *you ought to be thankful for his making things so easy.* She managed a grateful smile. "I appreciate your being so reasonable, Walter, really I do. You've been kind. You've been a good husband in so many ways. I just...." She shrugged. "I just want to free myself of the past."

He looked up at her briefly, seemed on the verge of saying something and then, changing his mind, smiled wanly. It occurred to her that perhaps he knew of her love for Jack McKenzie, knew that Jack was a part of why she wanted a divorce. Maybe that explained that glimpse she had caught of some inner torment that he did not choose to share with her.

She could do nothing to ease that pain for him, however. She had no idea if Jack still wanted her, would ever want her again the way he had before, but of one thing she was certain: he would never have her so long as she remained attached to someone else. Quite possibly not even then, but she had to try. She had thought that through clearly last night, lying in bed.

Walter nodded again. "I understand," he said.

* * * * * * *

She went that same morning to The Sportsman's Lodge on Ventura Boulevard. A long-standing institution by Los Angeles standards, The Lodge had been her Aunt Fanny's favorite stopping over place. "Kate Smith always stays here when she's in town," she had said every visit, though so far as Catherine knew Aunt Fanny had never met the singer on their common stopping ground. Becky had liked it too, delighted especially by the swans that swam in the all too kitschy pond that one passed on the way in.

She got a room overlooking the swans and by early afternoon had unpacked her single bag, had arranged a small pile of books by the nightstand and her laptop on the little table, and placed the single framed picture of Becky atop the dresser. She looked around at the cookie-cutter room and thought, wryly, "Home sweet home."

Only until she found an apartment. She had taken the room for a week, sure that in that time span she could find something that suited her. She wasn't too particular, she needed nothing more than the basics: a reasonably functional kitchen—she wasn't much of a cook—a bath, a bedroom and some place to sit down and prop up her feet.

She had a late lunch in the Lodge's dining room, glanced through rental listings in the *Sunday Times*, highlighting one or two, and went back to her room. She had brought *An Almanac of the Paranormal* with her and, kicking off her shoes, she turned again to the section on astral projection.

That was another of last night's resolutions: since it seemed she had somehow acquired this dubious gift, and since she was being prodded to use it, it behooved her to learn a little more about it and see if she could get any clearer on what it was she was supposed to do.

The book, unfortunately, was big on generalities and short on specifics. Most of those who "projected" themselves did so in visible form, though others learned to do so invisibly. Few of them had any corporeal presence. Not physical themselves, they could not move objects nor did the people they visited feel their physical touch. Some, though, did find a way to "touch" people mentally, to make their presence felt.

All very interesting, and clearly those were aspects of her "gift" she would need to work on. Unfortunately, the writer offered no instructions on how to do any of these things. She sighed and closed the book, putting it aside on the nightstand. She would have to find her own way, it seemed.

She thought back over her previous experiences. Simply willing herself to go somewhere hadn't worked. What had she done when she popped into Jack's office? She had been just thinking about him, hadn't she? Had seen him on the television screen, looked into his eyes, *gone* into his eyes in some sense.

Visiting Jack was all well and good, of course, but that was too easy. There had always been a bond between them, a spiritual connection if you wanted to put it that way, but she had a notion that wasn't why this ability had been presented to her.

On the other hand, she didn't exactly relish a visit to her two nemeses, though a part of her had begun to understand that this might well be the point of it all—but not, please, until she had gotten a better idea how to handle these "trips." No more horrible scenes to witness unprepared. Especially, she did not want them to see her. She did not want, really, *ever* want to see that man's eyes on her again.

She thought of Walter. Yes, that would be safe, harmless. She could try making herself invisible and if he should see her, he would almost certainly think it a product of his imagination. Except that Walter was short on imagination.

She closed her eyes, relaxing, and conjured up an image of their house, saw Walter's face, familiar and yet in some ways utterly a stranger's face—and as easily as that, found herself standing just inside the door of his home office.

For a moment, she thought that he wasn't there, that she had somehow alighted in the wrong spot. Then she saw him, kneeling on the floor beyond his desk. She looked past him and saw to her surprise an opening in the floor of the closet that she had not known was there, a cubbyhole. He was just putting something into it and, as she watched, he replaced the flooring and pulled the turned-back carpet into place over that.

She remembered what she had just read: there, but not seen. All right, then, that was certainly what was needed for this situation. Only how did you...and discovered that it was far easier than she would have imagined. It was like dialing down the volume on the radio. She could feel herself fade, even as the room before her seemed to mist over. She still saw everything, but it was like seeing it through a veil of gauze.

Make yourself felt? She had no clue how one did that either. She stared hard at the back of Walter's head and mentally called his name.

Suddenly he froze, cocking his head as if he had heard something. Or felt her standing behind him.

"Catherine?" he called aloud and turned in her direction—and looked right through her. There was no indication in his expression that he had seen her at all. His puzzled gaze swept the room, came back to where she was standing, and went about the room once again.

Jackpot, she thought triumphantly, and the next instant was back in her room at The Sportsman's Lodge, her head throbbing. He hadn't seen her, and of that she was glad. She hadn't intended to spy on him. He had a right to his privacy, after all, and especially so now that she had abandoned the pretense of wifeliness.

She couldn't help wondering about that cubbyhole though, and what he had been hiding in it. Again she realized how little she knew the man with whom she had lived until today. Pornography? Drugs? Perhaps a cache of money and the makings of another identity? She had read of men who maintained marriages to two or sometimes more different women, different families and careers.

She smiled to herself. No, she couldn't imagine Walter with another wife. He had barely had the energy or the interest for one.

Or, she thought, perhaps she simply hadn't been the right one. A blow to the ego, that idea, but her disinterest in him, in much of their relationship, might have been the very mirror of his feelings.

People married what they needed. She had married Walter out of spite, and out of a now outdated convention that said women were supposed to marry. Mistakes, both.

But why had he married her? She had always supposed that it was because of his ardent love for her, and wasn't that flattering to her? It hadn't been ardent, however, not for a very long time. Not even, if she were to be completely honest, not even at the beginning. There had always been something perfunctory about their physical relations.

Which brought her back to the same question: why on earth had he married her? Or, more accurately, what was it that he had needed of her? Because, surely, she hadn't provided it all these years. She couldn't pretend that to herself.

She thought again of that hidey-hole in his office that he had kept secret from her for Heaven knew how long. She could poke into it, of course. Not in her astral form: as a spirit she couldn't move the box or lift the floorboards.

She would have to visit the house at some time, though, to pack up her things. It was tempting to imagine taking a peek into this obviously most private part of his life, to learn what secret he thought it necessary to conceal from her.

She reminded herself of what curiosity had done to the fabled cat. No, the bottom line was, it was none of her business. Even though they were not yet divorced, had not even begun proceedings, she had settled in her mind as of the night before that they were no longer man and wife.

Leave it at that, she told herself. She changed into her sweats. Another of her resolutions had been to get herself back into shape, starting with a daily run. After that, she would check out a few apartments.

And she toyed seriously with the question of what dinner plans Jack might or might not have.

* * * * * * *

In the end, though, she thought after all that it might be too soon to call him. He might be gun-shy, and she might not get more than one spin of the wheel.

She called her mother instead, who was delighted to join her for dinner. "I've been craving pastrami," Catherine said. "Let's make it Nate's."

They had barely settled into one of the deli's leather banquettes before she made her announcement.

"I've moved out," she said. "I've told Walter I want a divorce."

"I hope you're not asking my advice," Sandra said. "I rarely offer it, for two very good reasons. One, people don't want to hear it, and two, people *really* don't want to hear it."

"Put me down for number two. No, I'm sure. I should have done it long ago, I suspect. Maybe if I had...." She left that unfinished.

"And Jack McKenzie?"

The waitress saved her from answering, handing them both enormous menus. "I could eat a horse," Catherine said, glad for the reprieve. She wasn't sure that she was ready to discuss the subject of Jack McKenzie with anyone. Wasn't sure, in fact, what she wanted to say to herself on that score. Her eyes moved down the familiar list of offerings.

"Something to drink?" the waitress asked, pencil hovering.

"A Dos Equis," Catherine said. "And a pastrami on rye, potato salad on the side." She closed the menu and slapped it down on the tabletop with a hearty thump.

Sandra said, her eyes studiously regarding her menu, "A green salad, hold the dressing. And an Evian."

Catherine glowered across the table. "What kind of meal is that?"

Sandra smiled sweetly back at her. "I've picked up a couple of unwanted pounds," she said.

"And I suppose you're hinting that I might have as well," Catherine said on a defensive note. She remembered those five pounds her scales had so rudely displayed, which she had since put down to the age of the scales, which surely needed replacing.

"I really hadn't noticed." Another affectionate smile. Which meant that she had indeed noticed.

"Two green salads, hold the dressing," Catherine snapped.

"You still want the Dos Equis?" the waitress asked, biting back a smile.

"Make it two Evians."

"And Jack McKenzie," Sandra said.

Catherine wolfed down her salad and sat watching her mother make her way slowly through her own. Sandra was right, of course, she could stand to take off a pound or two, but a salad just couldn't satisfy the soul the way a good pastrami could, in her opinion.

Nevertheless, she managed to wave away the waitress's suggestion of dessert. "I never have dessert," she said airily, pretending she hadn't been admiring the piece of lemon-topped cheesecake that had just appeared on a neighboring table.

To take her mind off food, she asked, "Do you think Walter has secrets?"

Sandra looked appropriately surprised. "I think everyone has secrets. What makes you ask?"

"A secret life, I suppose is what I mean. You know, a mistress stashed somewhere—though I guess now that's no longer any of my business."

"Mr. Adams explained to me one day about drug use in school," Sandra said, in what Catherine thought was rather an odd tangent.

"Isn't that a bit of a *non sequitur*?" She thought for a moment while her mother smiled obliquely at her. "Are you suggesting Walter does drugs?"

"Mr. Adams said, you could tell the cocaine users because their noses get red and runny, and they sniffle a lot."

Catherine sipped the last of her Evian and gave that some consideration. Walter's nose had been reddish lately, and he certainly had been sniffling. "I just imagined it was a grief thing, you know."

"And it may well be. It's just something that occurred to me. Are there any large amounts of money missing, from your bank account, for instance? That would be another indication. Drugs do cost money. Apparently quite a lot of it."

"No. Well, actually, I don't know. We both have our own bank accounts, so I wouldn't know what kind of shape his is in. And there's a joint account, but he's always handled that. The house payments, cars, all the big stuff, he pays them out of that account. I know, I sound like one of those silly helpless women who can't look after themselves, but really, I just wasn't interested and certainly I've always trusted Walter. I haven't even looked at that checkbook in ages."

They regarded one another across the table for a few seconds. "No," Catherine said determinedly. "I'm not going there. If he has issues with drugs, that's his concern now. When I get settled, we'll divide things up, and after that, he can do whatever he likes with his life. Or his money—for which he works hard, I have to give him that."

Of their own accord, however, her thoughts circled back to that little hidey-hole in Walter's office. She pushed those thoughts determinedly aside.

Mind your own business, she told herself....

CHAPTER EIGHT

By Tuesday she had found an apartment, in what she would have regarded as the least likely of all places.

It started when Bill, her young assistant, paused in her doorway to say, "I understand you're looking for a place to live?"

"Word gets around quickly, doesn't it?" She looked up from the mountain of work covering her desk.

"Oh—I wasn't gossiping, if that's what you mean, I just...." He fumbled for words.

She took pity on his embarrassment. "It's all right, it's one of those things where you sort of hope word does get around, isn't it? Someone may know of a place, I mean." She raised an eyebrow.

"Exactly," he said, relieved. "Which is what I stopped to tell you. There's this apartment in my building. I took the liberty of checking it out. I wouldn't have wanted to recommend some dump to you."

"And?"

He grinned. "It's really cute, actually. I'd snatch it up myself, except it's out of my range." His grin faded a little. "Of course, you can't always tell what someone else will like. It may not suit you at all. But, if you want, I'll call Jan, that's my landlord. He's pretty particular about who he takes in, so he hasn't actually advertised the place yet. He prefers word of mouth."

Catherine cast a dubious eye at the pile of galleys scattered across her desk. On the other hand, she did need to find an apartment, and the sooner the better. And Bill's remark had been rather in the nature of a compliment, hadn't it?

"Do, please," she said. "This afternoon if it's convenient."

* * * * * * *

She had not thought to ask, until after Bill had made the appointment with his landlord, just where this little gem was. And

72

should have asked, she thought when she looked at the address he had written down for her. Smack dab in the middle of West Hollywood.

West Hollywood was best known as L.A.'s gay neighborhood. She was reminded of that as she parked her car a bit later and watched a mating dance going on between two attractive young men eyeing one another from opposite corners. Not just in West Hollywood, either, this apartment, but right on Santa Monica Boulevard, the main thoroughfare, the Champs Elysée, the Fifth Avenue of what the locals called "Boys' Town".

She might have known, she reminded herself. Aside from the obvious, that he was black and quite handsome, almost the only personal thing she did know about Bill was that he was gay, and that only because he had never made any secret of the fact.

It wasn't a neighborhood she would even have considered, and she would have skipped it altogether and gone her way without bothering to check out the apartment, were it not for embarrassing a truly capable assistant whose private life she had always considered none of her business. She sighed and got out of her car, locking it and giving one of the mating dance participants a sideways glance. He noticed her not at all. It was a neighborhood that could be hell on a woman's ego, she thought grimly.

She almost changed her mind and got back into the car, but, she reminded herself, Bill had taken the trouble to make an appointment with his apparently quite particular landlord.

Who turned out to be a tall, spare man of fifty something, wearing a billowing silver caftan and one dangly brass earring. He was olive skinned and had a large nose—a classical nose, Fermin would call it. Arabic, she thought, or perhaps Greek. Jan. Janos?

"It's the top floor, and no elevator," Jan said in a whisky baritone, leading the way up steep, narrow stairs that creaked in faint concert with the swish of his caftan. "My legs resent it, but my butt is grateful."

He opened the door for her and stepped aside to let her enter first. She came directly into a small living room whose high, beamed ceiling made it seem larger than it was. Huge windows welcomed in every ray of the pale winter sunlight. There was a well-used fireplace in the wall facing her, and a one-person balcony in front, overlooking Santa Monica Boulevard—one and a half persons if they were on very friendly terms.

It was love at first sight. She strolled into the smallish bedroom, the even smaller but efficient looking kitchen, and the surprisingly enormous bathroom. "Part of the master bedroom at one time," Jan explained when she commented on the odd disparity in room size. "They made these old places over sometimes in imaginative ways."

It was not a lot of space overall, but that just meant she would have less furniture to buy. Back in the living room, she indicated an expensive looking leather sofa that sat alone against one wall. "Bill didn't mention furnishings."

"The previous tenant's. She needed money for airfare, so I gave her cash for it, in the hopes that the next person might want it. If not, I'll have it hauled away."

"Why did she leave?"

"Oh, you know, the usual story. You come to Hollywood to conquer the movies. You knock on all the right doors, but nobody answers them. The nights are longer and colder than you expected and you end up sleeping alone, or with the wrong guy just to keep the night away. The money runs out, the dreams fade, and Mr. Touchdown back in Eaton, Ohio begins to look a lot more attractive to you." He sighed. "Two hundred for the sofa. I'll throw in the dreams."

"Sold." She wrote a check, he gave her a set of keys, and they shook hands.

"I hope you'll be happy here," he said with a grin that flashed a sea of white teeth, and left her standing in the middle of her new home. She turned around slowly, wondering for a second or two if she had been too quick, and deciding that she was entirely happy with her decision.

The little balcony overlooked Santa Monica Boulevard itself, where those two young men were now having a conversation, but on the top of three floors it was high enough to escape much of the noise and the smell of auto fumes, and the bedroom was to the back, which meant it should be quiet enough for sleeping.

And those stairs would be good for her butt, too, she thought with grim satisfaction.

She checked out of the Lodge and went shopping. She bought a lamp and a mini stereo for the living room, and ordered a bed and dresser delivered, and a small television for the bedroom. She imagined herself lying abed watching Jack on the TV, though why she should be lying abed at four in the afternoon she hadn't yet worked out.

She called Rose to have the Hanukah bush delivered to her new address instead of the house, and thought about ordering a second one for Walter, but decided he probably wouldn't care. Probably wouldn't even notice, truth to tell.

Some linen, a coffee maker and some fresh ground coffee—her idea of roughing it was a morning without coffee. Some juice and some cereal and some milk.

Wheeling her cart through Gelson's, she had a last minute inspiration and added some Beefeaters, a bottle of Noilly Prat and some olives to her cart. By five o'clock that evening she was standing on her little balcony sipping a martini and watching a drooping sun trying to cast its evening colors on an uncooperatively gray sky and managing only a pallid mauve for its troubles.

A light rain had begun, really nothing more than a mist, which she chose to ignore. The wet wind blew a wisp of cloud overhead, its underbelly touched with a faint glow. A river of rain-glittered cars and trucks filled the damp street below, reflected the red and green and orange light from traffic signals; though if it was a river, it was a crowded and sluggishly moving one.

A parade of young men—and fewer young women, though more of them than she might have expected—crowded the sidewalks. Voices drifted up to her, snatches of conversation: "If you do, I will never...what do you buy a boyfriend's ex-wife...so over Christmas...." All punctuated by the occasional toot of a horn, the squeal of tires braked too suddenly, a siren wailing in the distance and a cacophony of music that spilled from the bars.

She liked the bustle, the sound and light and color. Her drink finished, she went down and walked till she found a stylish little eatery. She looked longingly at a mountain of French-fries, crisp and greasy, that a waiter carried by practically under her nose, and ordered the steamed fish with vegetables.

Strolling home—and already it did feel like home, she was pleased to realize—she saw that her preconceptions about the neighborhood hadn't been altogether right, or even fair.

Yes, there were a great many slim hipped colorfully dressed young men out for the evening, in the latest fashion, and hip hop, and cowboy regalia and leather and almost every other look one might imagine.

They were only part of the picture, however. A pair of elderly Jewish ladies came out of a small market just ahead of her, arguing vehemently over some private subject. There were punk types with tattoos and multiple piercings and hair the color and style of which suggested an alien species. Here and there a clearly straight couple strolled hand in hand, the men a bit too indifferent, their women not.

What surely must be suburban housewives took advantage of the area's clever stores for some Christmas shopping, and from time to time, the obvious tourist strolled and rubbernecked.

A kaleidoscope of types and cultures and ethnicities, running together to create a varied and lively street scene which she found delightfully exhilarating. She let the tide of pedestrians carry her along and blushed a little when a pretty young woman in a mannish jacket smiled rather too welcomingly at her.

A stray dog gave her a hopeful look, then trudged on by, his tail in a dispirited slump. If she'd had anything she would gladly have shared it with him. She felt utterly expansive, but she was empty handed. A pair of rose-gray pigeons fought over a tag end of a bagel someone had tossed aside and glowered and fluttered at the interruption of her passage.

A roar of music and male voices spilled from the open door of a bar. She was tempted to go in, not so much for a drink as for the camaraderie. They did seem to be having such fun. She realized with a shock how long it had been, far too long, since she'd had fun. Really had fun.

Only, she was sure she would stand out in this bar like a sore thumb. She went on by, humming along with Janis Joplin: "Me and Bobby McGee...." Goodness, she hadn't imagined anyone but her even remembered that song.

Jan was just coming out the apartment building's door, wearing what looked suspiciously like pajamas and a patent leather coat thrown about his shoulders, the dangly brass earring swapped for a dangly silver one—dressier, she wondered? She could see that she had much to learn. They nodded and exchanged quick smiles, like long time neighbors.

Upstairs, she kicked off her shoes and made a bed of sorts on the leather sofa. She toyed with Jack's business card for a moment before putting it back in her purse. The light off, she took a final breath of air on her balcony, and thought of his description of his apartment: if you leaned out far enough, you had a glimpse of the ocean before you fell.

Santa Monica was to the west. She looked in that direction as though, if she leaned out far enough and looked hard enough, she might get a glimpse of him. There was nothing more pathetic than those foolish souls who lived altogether in the past, wasting their todays in pursuit of their yesterdays. It was a very human folly, to wish that something is, that is not, and sadly, there were those who lived their entire lives in pursuit of what would never be.

Yet she truly felt as if fortune had handed her a second go-round, with Jack. He had walked mysteriously, miraculously back into her life at the very time when she was most prepared to realize the emptiness of her marriage to Walter.

She could not blame Walter. He had probably been a better husband than she had been a wife, and he had given her Becky. For that she owed him her gratitude. However painful it had been to lose her, the years that Becky had graced her life had been an incomparable gift.

It was not until she lost Becky, though, that she had finally seen her marriage to Walter in the light of honesty. They had lived together all those years without ever making that essential connection that made a real marriage of what was otherwise just a legal contract. Becky had been the one bright spot, the one thing that allowed her to keep her loneliness at bay. Without her, marriage to Walter had become unthinkable, unbearable.

Walter was gone, though. There was room now for Jack, a space she very much wanted him to fill in her life. Besides, there had been that moment when she was dying and he had called her name. What could that be, if not a sign, an omen?

She went in, carefully locking the balcony door, and settled herself on the sofa for her first night in her new home.

CHAPTER NINE

Late night Hollywood Boulevard was an open-air loony bin, in Chang's oft-expressed opinion: dealers, users and losers, pimps and prosties, gangbangers, preachers, and curb trawlers.

"Every kind of crazy in the world," she told Conners. He looked even more the innocent surrounded by all this nuttiness. She felt like a baby sitter giving her charge a lesson in nightlife reality.

Though technically, Hollywood was its own community, it was to her just another neighborhood in the admittedly wacky city of Los Angeles. Oddly, she loved L.A., the way a seasoned tar loves the sea, rolling with its waves, ever mindful of the sharks and reefs and sudden storms that await the unwary sailor, and yet cheerfully embracing all to her bosom.

"Who're we looking for anyway?" she asked.

"There's a couple of informers I've used from time to time; I thought we'd do a little digging." A transvestite hooker in garish makeup looked him over with interest from a doorway, glanced at Chang, and lost her interest.

"What made you become a cop?" Chang asked out of the blue.

If he was surprised he didn't show it. "The bucks, what else? Plus I heard women fall all over you."

"Well," Chang said and glanced back at the hooker. "There you are."

"She did think I was cute, didn't she?"

"She thought you had the money for a blow job."

"What?" He gave her a look of mock surprise. "You don't think I'm cute?"

She did, but she wasn't about to tell him that. "I think I don't like guys who fish for compliments." He laughed, flashing those perfect teeth. You couldn't dent this guy.

The owner of a food stand, Mediterranean Cuisine, according to the faded paint of its sign, recognized Conners and called to offer

78

him a falafel sandwich, which Conners declined with a smile and a wave.

"Actually, a falafel sandwich sounds good," Chang said.

"Not his sandwich. Trust me."

"You think his establishment isn't up to the most exacting hygienic standards?"

"That place isn't up to dumpster standards. I had a snack there once, spent the weekend married to my toilet."

"Listen, I was thinking, the Desmond thing," she said, "At the time, you said it was weird ballsy, the way it was done. What did you mean, exactly?"

"Just that. The other snatchings, they took the kids from inside crowded malls, you can be clear away before the alarm is given. That one was so out in the open, where they could be seen. If Desmond had been a man...."

"You mean, if her husband had been the one to go after the little girl?"

He shrugged. "Might not have made any difference. The guy had a gun. You can shoot a man as easy as a woman."

"So, what do you make of it? Why the difference in M.O. on that one?"

"Might have been just opportunity. Maybe they had a special order to fill. You know, some scumbag customer specifically asks for a girl that age, blonde hair, so on. They see the kid, go for it. They had the father distracted, didn't expect the mother back so quick. Ah, here's my boy now."

"My boy" turned out to be a twenty-something speed freak with bad teeth and long, unwashed hair. He saw them bearing down on him, looked around as if seeking an escape route and, finding none, waited for them resignedly.

"Weasel, my man," Conners greeted him with a clap on the shoulder that produced a wince and a pallid smile. "How's it hanging, fella?"

"Officer Conners. What brings you to our star-studded street this time of night?" Weasel asked with regret in his voice. There was a trace of the south in it, too. Probably he had run away from West Virginia years ago, Chang thought, headed for the bright lights of the big city, and had decayed like most of them did. The town ate up kids like him and spit the shells back out to litter the streets.

"We're looking for some information. I told my friend here nobody knows the town better than old Weasel."

Weasel twitched and tried for another smile that refused to come off. He was in constant motion, eyes rolling, hands and feet doing a meth-jitterbug. "Always glad to help, Officer Conners," he said, swallowing rapidly a couple of times.

"Kiddie porn," Conners said.

Weasel jumped as if he had gotten a jolt of electricity and his eyes spun convulsively. "I don't do that shit," he said in a voice several octaves higher. "I don't go near that stuff."

"Wease. Wease," Conners said, putting his hand on the bony shoulder again, "Like I told my friend here, there isn't anything comes down on the Boulevard the Weasel doesn't know about it."

"Drugs, sure, whores, shit like that. The kid stuff—no way, man, you can't pin that on me." He looked around again, appeared ready to bolt.

"We aren't trying to pin anything on you," Chang said in her most soothing voice.

"But we could, Wease, we could," Conners added. "If we wanted to be hard-assed. Course, we don't, you understand. We just want some help."

Chang reached into her shoulder bag and found her wallet. She peeled off a twenty, saw the gleam of interest in The Weasel's eyes, added a second one to it. "All's we want is information," she said. "Like, who on the street is peddling it? Movies, pics, whatever. Somebody is. We just need to know where to look."

Weasel stared at the money, his eyes for a change almost still, and licked his lips. He looked around again, to see who might be watching them, and looked back at the twenties. Chang added a third one.

"There's a newsstand down by Wallace. I heard he's got some shit like that, under the counter. Just for regular customers, people he knows really well, you know what I mean. Like, I haven't seen it myself, I wouldn't even *look* at that shit. That's just what someone told me."

He shuffled a step closer to her, one trembling hand lifted slightly toward the money. She held it toward him and he snatched it in a quick, frantic gesture and before they could say anything else, he darted past them and was hurrying down the street, shoving the money into the pocket of his filthy jeans.

"Nervous type," Conners said.

They found the newsstand, a dingy and dimly lit cave. A few newspapers and an array of girlie magazines, most of them undisguised porn, lined one wall, and a cash register and a counter occupied the other, a dirty glass top covering an assortment of stale candies and gum. A customer leafing through the magazines saw them enter, stuffed the magazine back on the shelf, and slid past them out of the store, his gaze carefully downward. A swarthy bearded man with large, nearly black eyes stood behind the register and looked them over warily, his expression suggesting that he too would like to disappear.

"You the proprietor?" Chang asked.

"Who wants to know?" His tone was surly, but he began to breath rapidly as his blood pressure mounted.

Chang flipped her badge open for him. "We want the kiddie porn," she said.

He looked from one to the other of them, and past them to the girlie magazines on the wall behind. "It's all legal stuff," he said, nodding in that direction. "Go ahead, take a look for yourself. No kiddies there."

"The under the counter stuff," Chang said. "For the special customers. We're special, see."

"I don't know what you're talking about. I never seen anything like that. This is a legit business."

Chang sighed, assumed a sad expression. "Well, sir, I thought we could handle this discreetly, just between the three of us," she said in an aggrieved voice. "See, we've got an informant says you've got some goodies under the counter. What we could do, now, is I can call in for a warrant, and my partner and I will wait here till it comes, just to make certain you don't dispose of anything, and then when we find it, we'll take you in. These days the D.A. gets real livid about kiddie porn. But, see, this is the thing for you to understand: we're not interested in you, not really. What we want is your distributor. So, here's what I suggest. You give us your stash, all of it, and you write down your distributor's name for us, and we go away. And as long as you don't get anything more in stock—and, understand, we will come back from time to time to check on you—but, as long as you don't, well, we won't make you any trouble. Now, what do you say, could anything be fairer?"

His eyes went back and forth again. His breathing was really fast now, and his face had broken out in sweat. He looked inches away from a real cardio-problem. After a moment, he reached under the counter, opened a drawer, and took out a large manila envelope.

"It's all I got," he said. "I swear to Christ."

Chang picked up the ballpoint pen next to the register and handed it to him. "Don't forget the name," she said. "And phone number."

* * * * * * *

"You've rented an apartment in Boy's Town?" Sandra sounded genuinely surprised.

"It's a very diverse community, mother." Catherine switched the phone to her other hand as she inked a contract.

"Oh, I know, I love it, I just somehow never imagined you there. You've always been a bit…." She hesitated.

"Prissy?" Catherine suggested. Fermin had once, over a lunch with one too many cocktails, described her that way and it was a word she had sometimes since applied to herself in more critical moments.

"Sheltered, I think, is the word I would use. Self possessed. You've always stood at the castle window looking down at life, dear. I should think that would be a bit more difficult in such a vibrant neighborhood."

"What an extraordinary thing to say." Catherine stared at the phone in annoyance.

"But true. Things have happened in your life, some good, some terrible, but they have always happened *to* you, never by you, darling. When it comes to the business of living, you've just never gotten down and dirty. Yes, now that I think of it, West Hollywood might be just the place for you."

"I'm glad you approve." If her mother noticed her sarcasm, she gave no sign of it.

"And there is one upside to consider, as a woman now living alone: if a strange man bursts into your apartment he's more likely to be interested in your dresses than your body."

"Not funny, mother."

Her mother was unrepentant.

* * * * * * *

She bought Bill a bottle of Dom Perignon as a thank you. Even if he weren't into wine, that was a safe bet. You could surely always use a bottle of bubbly over the holidays, couldn't you?

Oughtn't she to know that, however? In fact, she knew almost nothing about him apart from the fact that he was gay, not even if he had a partner—and was that the right word these days? Significant other? Friend? For a woman whose business was words, she felt incredibly ignorant.

"I'm presently single," he said when she asked, and added with a grin, "But shopping, in case you meet any prospects."

"I'm not likely—well, maybe I am now." She smiled back. "Anyway, I do owe you one."

"You must have made a hit with our Jan. She can be hard to impress."

"I rather liked him—her?"

"He's a dear," Bill said, switching sexual gears again. Which made Catherine think that maybe her mother was right: maybe she had been a bit too sheltered over the years.

She pondered that in the ladies' room. The last really decisive action she had taken in her life had been marrying Walter. From the day she had taken that plunge, she had been treading water.

No, she corrected herself. That was no longer true. The *last* decisive action had been leaving Walter—and maybe that meant she was truly on the mend, not just from Becky's loss, but from the stagnation of her life.

She turned to look at herself in the mirror and as she did, the lights brightened, as if someone had turned a rheostat up. For a startled moment, she thought she saw someone in the glass behind her, but when she looked over her shoulder there was no one there.

You must go to them. The voice seemed to be inside her head.

"Them?" Catherine said aloud. It took her a moment to understand. "Those men? No, no, I can't, I won't."

There's another little girl. Debbie will suffer a living hell. You must stop them.

"But how can I? I can't. There's nothing I can do."

Mommy, Mommy.... It was Becky's voice, calling to her.

"Oh, God, no," Catherine cried, but it was too late. Her image in the glass faded into the golden glow, the light seemed to explode, blinding, scorching....

"Excuse me, Ma'am."

She was in a department store, Nieman's, she thought. The man in front of her said, "I wonder if you could help me with something?"

She started to reply, and realized he was not looking at her at all. He was looking through her. Literally. She suddenly realized who he was. She'd had only glimpses of him before, and then he was always unkempt. Now his hair was neatly trimmed and he was clean-shaven. He wore chinos, and an expensive looking leather jacket over a burgundy turtleneck. He might have been any one of the hundreds of unaccompanied males in the store for Christmas shopping.

For all the pains he had taken to clean himself up, however, he was unquestionably Yellow Beard's companion, the one she thought of as The Bear. And he was speaking to someone behind her.

Heart racing, she looked over her shoulder at a matron dressed all in blue: a navy coat, a sky blue dress, turquoise shoes, and purse. Even her pewter hair had highlights of blue in it. She pawed through a rack of blouses while at her side a young girl of maybe ten or eleven fidgeted impatiently.

"Mommy, can't we go?" the girl asked.

"In a moment, Debbie." The mother looked in The Bear's direction. "Yes?" she answered him a bit coolly.

Catherine stepped back to watch. The Bear held up a sweater in one hand and a scarf in the other and gave Lady Blue a sheepish grin. "I'm no good at this kind of thing," he said. Catherine was surprised to see how good an actor he was. His expression oozed an oafish sincerity. "I'm looking for presents for my wife, but I don't know, do these colors look right together?"

"Oh." Lady Blue's smile was warmer now. She had a high opinion of her own taste, and was always glad to share it with someone less gifted. She stepped toward him and looked doubtfully at the avocado green sweater and the nearly chartreuse scarf. "Is she fond of green?" she asked. She herself was not. Green made her look sallow. Of course, there were *some* who could wear it.

"Well, now you mention it...." He screwed up his face for a moment, seemed to notice her costume for the first time, and grinned, a warm and thoroughly convincing grin. "I think she wears blue a lot more than green."

She nodded. Blue was ever so much better. "Ah. Let's look at what they have in blue, why don't we?" She turned toward the display of sweaters and he turned with her—and managed, Catherine saw, to place himself between her and her daughter.

Mother and stranger began to discuss sweaters, holding them up for one another's inspection. This one she liked, but got a shake of his head.

"Don't look like her." He offered an alternative and she pursed her lips before deciding against it and offering another.

As Catherine watched, Debbie began to drift away. She paused to look at a mannequin in a pink taffeta gown and looked back at where her mother was still earnestly engaged in conversation with the stranger. She wandered a few feet further.

Debbie will suffer a living hell....

No, Catherine thought with sudden determination. She hadn't wanted this, did not want to be here, but here she was, and clearly she was meant to stop what was obviously a kidnapping in progress.

But how, she wondered? And where was Yellow Beard? Surely he could not be far away. Her eyes scanned the crowds. He was here, she was certain of it. Where?

A man stepped from behind a column. At first, her anxious gaze went over him and right on past. Something clicked, and she looked again. It was him, Yellow Beard—only, the beard had been shaved off, just as in her dream.

That was not the only change, either. His hair, long and yellow and straggly before, was a medium brown now, short and as nicely cut as his partner's.

It was his face that had changed the most, however. The mole was definitely gone. In its place she could see only a faint mark where it had been. What she hadn't fully noticed in that previous, brief vision of him, however, was his nose. That, too, was different, straight where before it had been decidedly bent. It was a face etched permanently in her mind, but if she had only that police picture to go by, she wouldn't have recognized him. She might have walked right by him in a busy department store and never even have seen him.

Any doubts she might have had faded entirely when she looked into his eyes. Even knowing he could not see her, she felt a chill of fear. The evil in those eyes was unchanged. Eyes trained on little Debbie like a hawk's, watching her edge ever closer to him. And closer to the door that led into the mall, where a man and a small girl could be lost in minutes in the teeming crowd of shoppers.

Catherine looked back at the child's mother, still oblivious to her daughter's straying. She stared hard at the back of the mother's head, willing the woman to feel her presence, her energy. It had worked with Walter, once, in the quiet of his office—but would it work in a crowded department store, with a stranger who was engaged in earnest conversation?

For long, agonizing seconds, it seemed as if nothing were happening. Lady Blue remained fully caught up in her shopping advice. Catherine worried over the child, wondering if she had drifted any closer to Yellow Beard, but she dared not look, dared not risk a break in her concentration. In frustration, she decided that she must, after all, let herself be seen. She moved into the woman's line of sight.

Suddenly, the mother frowned and glanced around. "Debbie?" she called, and then more loudly, "Debbie, where are you?"

"I'm right here, mother," Debbie called back.

"Don't you be wandering off, you get right back here, haven't I told you never to go off like that? You gave me a fright."

"I was just looking around." Debbie returned obediently to her mother, who stooped down to tug an errant scarf into place around her daughter's neck and brush a sandy curl back from her forehead.

"You just stay right here beside mommy, that's a good girl. We'll go in a minute. Now, as I was saying...." But when she straightened and turned back toward her shopping student, he was gone. She looked around, puzzled, but he had vanished.

"Well, I guess he changed his mind," she said in a disappointed voice. She dropped the sweater she had been holding on the counter. It really was a lovely shade, she thought, robin's egg, too bad it wasn't right for her. From the way the man had described his wife, though, she was sure it would have been perfect.

Some people, she thought, tossing her head. She took Debbie's hand. "Let's go look at the toys, shall we?"

Catherine looked around. Yellow Beard, too, had vanished.

* * * * * * *

Trash Can Paterson moved quickly, carefully, through the holiday crowds, showing no outward sign of the anger that raged within him. Ahead of him Cooley walked hurriedly toward the exit and the van waiting in the parking lot. Neither of them took any notice of the other.

Paterson swore over and over to himself. A woman, arms filled with packages, stopped just in front of him. He resisted the urge to shove her aside and stepped around her instead. *Don't call attention.* It was his mantra on these shopping expeditions. Attention could be fatal.

They had nearly been successful. They came so close. Everything had gone smoothly, like clockwork. The little girl had practically walked into his arms—and then something had happened, something to alert the mother.

She had been there, he was certain of it, even though he hadn't actually seen her. He had felt her as sure as if she had been standing alongside him. It was her who had interfered in some way that he couldn't quite figure out.

Who was she? He had to find her.

* * * * * * *

"Are you all right?"

Catherine took a breath and looked at herself, pale and shaky, in the mirror. Over her shoulder, she saw Mrs. White regarding her anxiously.

"Yes, thanks." Catherine relinquished her hold on the counter's marble edge. Despite the lingering pain in her head, she was able to smile reassuringly. She left a nervous Mrs. White looking after her.

Score one for our side, she thought. They were right: it was something she could do. She had foiled what surely would have been another kidnapping, perhaps another death. She had to restrain herself from a fist pump and settled instead for startling Mrs. Pendergrast with a triumphant smile.

Back at her desk, however, she admitted more soberly that, wonderful as it had been, it wasn't enough. Fending them off one time didn't stop them. Those two must be caught, put behind bars and out of action altogether. That, apparently, was why she had been sent back, why she had been given the gift of astral projection, what she was intended to do. Exactly how she was to do that, she had no idea as yet, but she knew now clearly that she could never stop until she had achieved that goal.

Still, she had made a start today, a significant start. Take that, you bastards, she thought with a grim smile.

Her sense of triumphant exultation was short-lived. It vanished like a candle flame blown out in the cold wind of malevolence that swept over and through her the next minute.

Her office darkened, not so much as if the light faded but more as if it were being sucked out of the room. She had a sense, growing stronger every second, of *his* presence. She could all but see him in the corner there, his angry eyes devouring her.

CHAPTER TEN

"Mrs. Desmond?" Bill spoke her name from the doorway. For just a second, no more, he seemed to be backlit with a faint golden glow. As she blinked and looked at him again, it vanished. Or maybe it hadn't been there at all.

The blackness was gone too. She was still in her office, in the ordinary light of day and the glow from the overhead fluorescents.

"It's nothing." She managed a tremulous smile. "I just—I realized I had forgotten something important. Here, be an angel, won't you, and finish these up." She snatched some papers from her desk, hardly noticing what they were, and thrust them at him.

"Sure thing," he said. He gave her a queer look, but he took them and nodded and turned away.

His boss, he thought, was acting plenty weird these days. All in all, he guessed he couldn't blame her. He had always liked her, that quiet elegance that you couldn't pretend to have if you didn't. She was aloof, true. In the past she had kept a careful distance between them, but he had eventually come to see that it wasn't just him. He wasn't sure if anyone ever got really close to her.

She seemed to be loosening up these days, though, and he would like to have asked what had frightened her so a moment ago, but they weren't quite that chummy yet.

He looked at the papers she had handed him. Receipts, telephone memos, the odd clipping, even a catalog from Williams-Sonoma. "Now what on earth," he wondered, "Does she expect me to do with these?"

* * * * * * *

Alone in her office, Catherine sat down weakly at her desk. Her heart threatened to pound its way through her rib cage. She tried to think what had happened. She hadn't the slightest doubt who had visited her. But why? And more importantly, how?

Of their own accord, her eyes raked the corners of the room, as if he might still be there, leering at her, but the office was empty.

She shuddered. Had she somehow drawn him to her? She had thought after all that "traveling" to those two was going to be safe, so long as they couldn't see her. Now, in some inexplicable way, Yellow Beard was stalking her.

"Hey."

Catherine jumped and looked up to see Fermin Dean in her doorway. "Sorry, didn't mean to scare you," he said, "Are you all right? You look like you've seen a ghost."

She wondered briefly what he would think if she said she had. Probably, he would think she was losing her marbles. He might be right.

"Just a little on edge," she said.

"I'm buying some of the boys a Christmas drink at The Polo Lounge. Care to join us?"

She was on the verge of declining, still haunted by Yellow Beard's horrible presence, but she couldn't exactly explain that to Fermin. Anyway, she wasn't sure that she wanted to be alone just now. Maybe a room full of convivial people was what she needed.

"I would love to," she said instead. "If I really can be just one of the boys."

Fermin laughed. "Well, yes, but let it be said, you look lots better in a dress than the others."

* * * * * * *

Jack, who didn't much like parties to begin with, glanced for the umpteenth time at his watch and wondered yet again if it was still too early to leave. He would rather have not come at all, but when the station's owner rents a suite at the Beverly Hills Hotel for a Christmas party, one did have a degree of obligation. Particularly when Peter Weitman had specifically asked him to attend.

"The boss asked for you in particular," was how he had put it, which did make the obligation a bit weightier. Peter had given him his job, after all, and if he could repay the favor in some measure by sipping a weak Chivas and water and listening to some not-very-amusing banter, it seemed the least he could do.

"You wouldn't be thinking of slipping away, would you?" someone said beside him.

He turned toward the voice. Kitty Fane, the station's new weatherperson, regarded him with eyes both amused and speculative. They had been introduced briefly before and he had watched her initial performance on the monitor in his office. She was pretty, in a reedy way, though personally he liked his women with a little more substance than she carried on her slight frame. Her hair was auburn and the eyes gazing into his were green and large, made larger still by generous shading of brown and green. The hand she laid on his arm sported black fingernails. Why on earth, he wondered, would anyone want black fingernails? They made her otherwise lovely fingers look like talons.

"Because if you are," she said with a smile, "I do wish you would take me with you. This is a bit of a bore, isn't it?"

He smiled back, patiently. "You wouldn't want the old man to hear you say that," he cautioned.

She threw a quick look over her shoulder, but the nearest party guests were several feet away and engrossed in their own conversations.

She smiled back at Jack. "Well, were you?" she asked.

"Leaving?" He glanced again at his watch. "I think it's a bit early yet for that. And here he comes, by the way." Peter Weitman and Thaddeus Tremayne—the old man—were making their way through the cocktail party crowd that, like the Red Sea, parted before them, following a path that must inevitably bring them to where he and Kitty Fane were standing.

Kitty might try her wiles out on him, Jack thought with amusement, but she knew only too well where the main chance lay. She drew her shoulders back like a boxer entering the ring, making her small breasts more prominent in the shimmering emerald green dress she wore, and turned to greet the newcomers, her smile wide.

Weitman did the introductions. Kitty laid it on a bit thick, Jack thought. "I can't tell you what a thrill this is," she said, holding Tremayne's hand a trifle longer than was necessary and gazing up at him with something of Titian's Adoration in her expression.

Jack saw that Thaddeus Tremayne was no more immune to flattery from an attractive woman than any other man, but he had a solid reputation too as a hard-headed businessman, and after a few chatty remarks, he said, "I wanted to have a few words with this young man, if you'll excuse us."

Kitty made a moue of disappointment. "Of course, but I insist on equal time."

"Agreed." It looked as if she had scored a point with the owner, though it was said by experts that you could never know what was going on behind that polite mask Tremayne wore.

90

"I'll be waiting," she said. She flashed a coy smile and moved in the direction of the bar.

"Pretty." Tremayne watched her walk away from them, emerald-clad hips swaying provocatively.

When he turned his gaze to Jack, it was all business, however. "I told Peter I particularly wanted a chance to meet you. I wanted to tell you that we've been getting lots of really good feedback on the pieces you've done."

Behind him, Weitman wore a pleased-as-punch grin. Jack, after all, had been his find. He gave Jack a quick wink.

"I'm glad to hear it," Jack said, "but I hope you'll understand if I say I'd like to think some of it was negative. My goal is to get people thinking for themselves, and if they're all parroting my opinions, I'm not doing my job."

"Then I can tell you that there is enough disagreement to assure that your job is being done nicely, and no more than just enough. I especially liked that piece last week on the Middle East."

"That's one area, at least, where we don't have to worry about everyone's agreeing."

"Just so." Tremayne smiled benevolently and looked at someone over Jack's head, a signal that Jack took to mean their conversation was finished. "Keep up the good work. And I think you'll find a pleasant surprise in your next pay check."

Jack, who felt he was already exorbitantly paid for doing nothing more than spouting off his opinions, could only mutter a quick thanks, but Tremayne was already on his way with a brief dismissive nod. Weitman paused to clap Jack on the shoulder and whisper a hasty, "Good job."

His reason for coming having been accomplished, Jack thought it was probably safe to start planning his exit. He did a brief tour of the room, stopping here and there to chat with a colleague, and declining the offer of a fresh drink from a black-jacketed waiter with a tray. Within the half hour he was slipping into his well-traveled trench coat, but before he made it out the door, a hand grabbed his arm and he looked down at black fingernails.

"Do take me with you, please." Kitty glanced up at him with one of her most alluring smiles. "I so hate to be seen leaving a party alone."

"I'm sure there is not a man here who wouldn't happily solve that problem for you," he said gallantly, but he fetched her coat for her and helped her into it—sable, he noted, and very good sable, too.

Miss Fane was generous with herself. Or somebody was. "I thought you were going to have a conversation with the old man."

Her smile this time was conspiratorial and just a trifle smug, which told more clearly than words that it had been, in her terms, a successful conversation. "Mission accomplished," she said.

They exchanged nothing more than some desultory remarks as they rode the elevator down, but when they came out the lobby doors to the wide front steps, where he had supposed they would part, she held on to his arm. "I have a bottle of Moet Chandon in the fridge, if you'd like to stop by," she said. "And I'm practically just around the corner."

"I'll have to skip that corner this evening." As gently as he could, he freed his arm. "Previous engagement." She needn't know that it was with a Graham Green novel.

"One that can't be broken?" She arched an eyebrow but he gave her an apologetic grimace. "Then you'll have to take a rain check," she said with a weatherperson's undiminished cheeriness.

She handed him a scrap of paper from the pocket of her sable. He glanced and saw that she had already written her number on it. Miss Fane liked to be prepared, apparently, for any eventuality.

"Call me," The invitation in her eyes hinted at more than a glass of wine.

* * * * * * *

Pulling into the long, sweeping driveway of the Beverly Hills Hotel, Catherine wondered, not for the first time, how it was possible that all of the young valet parkers could be so movie-star gorgeous. The one dashing toward her Jaguar could have stepped right off the big screen.

She was half in, half out of the car, when she glanced toward the lobby doors, where the wide steps swept down to the driveway, and saw Jack McKenzie come out of the hotel with a stunning redhead on his arm. He turned so that his back was toward Catherine, but there was no mistaking the look the redhead slanted up at him.

Disappointment—and jealousy, no point pretending to oneself—stabbed at her. *Well, what did you expect*, she demanded angrily of herself, *it's not as if he's taken the vows or anything? He's a man, dammit. And trust him to pick a beautiful companion. Beautiful, if a trifle obvious.*

The towheaded valet held the door wide for her and gave her a smile that would have done a toothpaste commercial proud. She shook her head, biting her lip to avert the tears that threatened, fumbled in her purse for a twenty-dollar bill and thrust it into the waiting hand.

"Sorry, I've changed my mind." She gave her head a shake.

He glanced at the twenty and gave her another toothpaste commercial. "Please come again. My name's Larry, by the way." She had no doubt that he had sold his toothpaste to more than a few single ladies arriving at this fabled location.

"Mine's not," she said and was already driving forward by the time he swung the door closed for her. She kept her head turned, hoping that Jack wouldn't see her, until she was going down the other end of the curved driveway, and in a minute more she was merging into the traffic on Sunset Boulevard, and she could safely brush a tear away from her cheek.

* * * * * * *

Watching her taillights disappear, Jack cursed Kitty Fane, still smiling up at him, for her would-be seduction.

"Is something wrong? You looked so funny for a minute," she said.

No, that wasn't fair, it wasn't Kitty's fault, wasn't anyone fault, as far as that went. It was just damned bad luck was all.

"Sorry," he said apologetically. "I was just thinking of something."

"I hope you were reconsidering that champagne."

For a moment, meeting her eyes, he actually thought about changing his mind. Not that Kitty Fane looked any more appealing to him, but Graham Green somehow seemed less.

He flirted with that temptation only briefly, however. He had a notion that Kitty's charm, thin as it was already, would grow a lot thinner in the course of an evening. He wanted more from a woman than what she was so obviously offering, and he doubted very much that she had it to give.

"Sorry. Afraid it's not in the cards. Well, good night now," he said and was off down the steps, signaling for one of the valets, before she could offer any further enticements.

CHAPTER ELEVEN

Back in her apartment, Catherine changed into jeans and an oversized cashmere pullover, poured a glass of wine, and settled into a serious bout of floor pacing. She berated herself for a fool, for not having called Jack before this, raged at him for his infidelity—never mind that he had no reason to practice fidelity—found the world in general and all things upon it to be wanting. Had, in short, a wonderful session of feeling sorry for herself.

Having drained the wine glass and much of her emotion, she picked up the phone, found Jack's card and violently punched in his number.

He was surprised, certainly, to hear her voice. "Am I interrupting?" she asked a shade too sweetly. "You do have company, I take it?"

"In a manner of speaking." Was that amusement in his voice? Damn him, she was in no mood to be mocked.

"Then she will just have to listen. There are some things I want to say."

"That's not a problem. And it's a he, by the way."

"He?" She knew that there were drag queens who were very effective, but surely the redhead outside The Beverly Hills had been the real thing.

"Graham Greene," Jack said.

"Oh. But I thought...I saw...." Some of the wind went out of her sails.

"She was just a colleague," he said patiently. "We left the station bash—attendance obligatory or I wouldn't have been there at all—walked out together, and we parted company just about the time you escaped down the drive."

Her sails went utterly limp. She stared bleakly out the window for a moment, feeling like an utter fool, and blurted out the first thing that came into her mind.

"Have you had dinner?"

"I was just eyeing a can of tuna. Without much enthusiasm, I might add. Why don't I pick you up? I know a place I think you'll love."

"I'm in jeans."

"Perfect. So am I."

She had a fleeting memory of how he looked in jeans, and smiled into the telephone.

"And you can say all those things you wanted to say over dinner," he added.

* * * * * * *

She saved him the difficult chore of finding a parking place by saying she would wait for him at the curb. If he was surprised to hear that she was living at a new address, he saved his questions for later as well.

He was there in less than half an hour, a honk of his horn alerting her as the silver gray Porsche glided to a stop. She jumped in with a quick, nervous grin and fidgeted with her seat belt to give herself a moment's grace.

"I should explain," she began, but he interrupted her.

"Dinner, first. Explanations after. It makes for a much nicer evening. And I think we can treat ourselves to one of those, can't we?"

She breathed a sigh of relief. Why had she thought this would be so difficult? Nothing in the intervening years had felt more natural than that she should be sitting beside him in his car as they wound their way up Laurel Canyon, into the Valley, engine purring, Maxine Sullivan's honeyed voice insinuating itself into the comfortable silence. It had rained earlier, briefly and lightly, but the moon was splendid now. In her showy radiance and the gleam of headlights, the damp street was the silver of mackerel.

She was surprised to realize what a lovely evening it was.

* * * * * * *

It was the sort of Italian restaurant that had years ago already been a cliché: red and white checked tablecloths topped with half burned candles in fiascos, a fisherman's net on the wall, replete with glass markers, and on the facing wall a mural straight out of Cavalleria Rusticana.

Only two of the dozen or so tables were occupied. At one, a couple who might have stepped out of the mural shared a huge bowl of what looked to be fish stew, and a family noisily squabbled over an enormous platter of spaghetti at the other. In the corner an artificial Christmas tree twinkled rhythmically and near it a fire burned invitingly on a hearth.

"Trust an Italian restaurant where you see Italians eating," Jack said. "They'd rather eat at home, and if they eat out, it should be just like home."

An immense bosomed woman in a white apron came from behind a curtained doorway at the sound of their entrance. Her face lighted up when she saw who had come in. "Jack," she cried with obvious delight, and hurried around randomly placed tables to embrace him. *"Come sta?"*

"Bene, bene. E tu, Celestina?"

He introduced Catherine to Celestina, who gave her a quick once over even as she welcomed her to the restaurant. "But come, it is a cold night, you must sit over here by the fire." She led them to what was obviously the best table. "And a bottle of Barone, on the house. Sergio, where are you?"

A handsome young man in a red jacket appeared with glasses of water and a basket of bread still warm from the oven. "My grandson, Sergio," Celestina said proudly. "And the worry of my existence."

Sergio, all of seventeen at a guess, gave a little laugh at his grandmother's good-natured criticism and looked Catherine over in that instinctively flirtatious manner that Italian men apparently learned in the cradle.

The menus, large sheets of parchment, were already on the tables. Catherine picked hers up to read it, and Jack leaned across to take it gently out of her hand and put it back in its holder.

"I always let Celestina choose for me," he said. A thought occurred to him suddenly. "Lord, I hope you aren't on some kind of diet."

She crossed her fingers under the table and brightly laughed off that suggestion. "Not at all," she assured him.

"Because if you were, Celestina is the last person you'd want feeding you."

Celestina was back in a moment with three glasses and an opened bottle of wine, from which she filled theirs and poured just a splash of red into the third glass for herself. She raised her glass in a toast.

"To an old friend. And, I hope, a new one," she added with a shy but friendly look at Catherine. "Now, I shall fix a special dinner for you, yes?"

"Yes, indeed," Jack said. "Unless you want to pick...?" He looked innocently across at Catherine, who shook her head. She'd been given her cue already.

And was more than glad later that she had followed instructions. They started with little plates of antipasti: black olives in oil and garlic and a sprinkling of herbs—"from our own yard," Celestina informed them proudly—a dish of white beans flecked with anchovy, and paper-thin slices of salami, rolled into little cornets that exploded in the mouth with peppery flavor.

After that came a kind of curly edged pasta, obviously freshly made and dressed with nothing more than the most delicate olive oil, bits of tomato, and fresh basil, with a last minute squeeze of lemon.

By the time Catherine had used the crusty bread to clean her plate she was already thinking of adding an extra mile to her next run; and when she tasted the veal cutlet that appeared next, for which "ambrosial" would have been inadequate, she decided it would have to be two miles.

There was a bit of Gorgonzola and some figs to have with the last of the wine, and finally some tiny, not too sweet cookies to accompany the espresso.

"I don't know when I've eaten so well," Catherine said, sipping the espresso, and meant it. "Or so much," she added with an exaggerated groan.

"Celestina's a wonder." And when the proprietress appeared then to refill their cups, he said in a stage whisper, "I've asked her to run off and live in sin with me, but she says her husband would beat her."

Celestina giggled girlishly and left them alone. By now, the other diners were gone and Sergio was just cleaning the last table across the room where the family had made a happy mess of their spaghetti.

They had kept the conversation throughout dinner on a casual and safe level: anecdotes about his work and hers, the occasional asking after mutual acquaintances, and of course, the delicious food.

Now, Sergio having finished his chores and vanished discreetly behind the curtained doorway, they found themselves in sole possession of the dining room. The Christmas tree twinkled garishly. The candle sputtered in its straw-covered bottle. A cool breeze billowed the curtains and fanned the flames in the fireplace as a door was opened briefly in the kitchen, and closed again. There was a muted clatter of dishes being stacked.

Their conversation slowed and faltered. Catherine leaned across the table, her eyes on his, and took his hand.

"Jack," she began, and at the same moment, he said, "Catherine."

They laughed, dispelling that brief moment of tension, the first since she had climbed into his car. "You first," he said.

"I've left Walter," she blurted out, not at all the pretty speech she had rehearsed earlier.

He lifted an eyebrow and waited for her to go on, deciding that this probably wasn't the best time to start spouting his opinions.

"For good," she added. She fidgeted with her napkin and managed to drop it on the floor. Jack was up before she could reach it and handed it back to her.

"I'm such a nuisance," she said.

"The most beautiful nuisance I've ever seen."

She gave him a grateful smile and went silent again. If her mother could only see her now: self-possessed was she? She felt like a tongue-tied schoolgirl and there was Jack waiting so patiently, watching her so intently. And how was she supposed to have any clue what was going on right now in his mind. He probably thought she was bonkers.

She took a deep breath and began to talk, haltingly at first, trying each word out as she spoke it, and then in a rush that came spilling out faster than she could think.

"When I lost...when Becky died, the way she did, so horribly, it was like, I don't know exactly how to say this, I think, no, I *know* that for a time I lost my mind, in the most literal sense.

"In a way, though, when I began to recover, I realized that it had opened me up, to myself, to life, like I had never been before. All I could think about was all the time I hadn't spent with her, all the things that we hadn't done together, those things that you are always going to get around to, but never do. The words that never get said. And I saw how important these things might have been, and how unimportant were so many of the things I had done instead. How much of our time had been wasted, and how precious every moment can be.

"It was like I had been held to a scorching fire, as if everything extraneous in me, in my life, had been burned away, and all that was left were the things that really mattered, the truly important things:

Love, and people and connecting with them. That's hard, I'm having to learn, but I know that I must learn."

Her eyes were down as she said this, not so much watching the little fly that had discovered their cookie crumbs but more to avoid what she feared she might see in his expression, but now she looked up again into his face.

"You are one of the things that matter. I don't know after all these years how you feel. In a sense, *that* doesn't matter. I had to tell you anyway. I owed you, I owed myself, to tell you. I had to tell you that I love you. I've always loved you. I never stopped."

He needed a few seconds to collect his wits. He didn't know what he had expected to hear from her, but despite the hopes that never left him, this wasn't it.

"Lord, you do choose your moments, don't you?" he said.

Watching him, watching the expressions flitting across his face, she had a heart-sinking thought that she had goofed again, had scared him away. She knew that many men did not like for a woman to take the initiative, but she really had believed that he was different.

"I think this time the moment chose me," she said.

He took her hand again. "Catherine, you must know, surely you realize, that I've never stopped loving you either? How could I? You're so entwined in my heart it would kill me to tear you out. I know, I tried for years."

Tears glinted in her eyes. She tried to say something in reply and found the words simply wouldn't come. She shook her head, half laughing, half crying.

"The miracle," he said, "is discovering that you still love me."

The tears began to stream down her face. "Oh, my darling, till the day I die."

Celestina came in from the kitchen, and with one quick glance, backed through the curtained doorway out of sight. Neither of them had even noticed her.

Jack got up from his chair and came around to where Catherine sat, dropping on one knee to take her in his arms. "My darling," he said, and after that there were no words for long minutes.

He got up finally, brushing a speck of lint off his knee and surreptitiously rearranging the front of his trousers. "Well," he said, "Celestina is an old friend, but I do think maybe we had better take our leave before I put that friendship to the test."

They finished the last of the wine that Sergio poured into their glasses while Celestina wrote up their check.

"The wine is good, yes?" Sergio asked, smiling from one to the other of them, and Jack assured him that it had been excellent—though, truth to tell, he was sure plain tap water would have tasted like champagne on this occasion.

Celestina saw them to the door, her eyes shining with approval. "You must bring the beautiful signorina again," she said. "Too many these young ladies today, all skinny like boards, they pick, pick, pick, half the food is wasted. I like to see a woman enjoy her food."

"Which," Catherine said when they were back in the Porsche, "You have to admit, I did."

He started up the powerful engine and looked over at her in the dashboard's glow. "Are we in any hurry?"

"The night is ours," she said, suddenly shy.

"Good." He started the CD player. Perfect choice: Chopin's music surrounded them.

She leaned back into the soft leather and surrendered herself to the music, to the night, and the sensual vibrations of the car's movement. Again, there was little need for conversation. For the present they shared a magical place in which words mattered not at all.

Instead of turning toward West Hollywood, he pulled onto the freeway headed north. She didn't question him as the myriad lights of the Valley swept by. An endless stream of cars surrounded them on either side, but inside the Porsche there was only the glow of the moment and the glorious music that carried them along—and a hand that reached across the space between them to take hers.

After a while, they left the freeway and began to climb the two-lane road that ran through Topanga Canyon. It twisted and turned, this way and then that. He was a good driver and the car seemed to sense exactly what he expected of it.

They swooped over a ridge and down again, another hairpin curve and back up, gradually traveling higher and higher into the mountains, then making their way downhill, the car like a graceful bird in its descent. They came around a wide bend and the ocean spread out below them, a seemingly endless black slate in the pale moonlight, marbled with ribbons of glittering foam.

He turned south on Pacific Coast Highway and she knew then where they were headed, and her heart began to beat a little faster with the knowledge.

CHAPTER TWELVE

It was all too obviously a man's apartment, everything dark and crowded, and had the look of one that had been lived in, comfortably, for years. A threadbare brown sofa and a much more comfortable looking leather recliner with a reading lamp beside it, and a pile of books on a nearby table. Piles of books everywhere, in fact, and crowded shelves of them as well. A reading man's room. A workstation with a computer took up most of one wall and through an open doorway she could see a corner of a rumpled bed. She tried to ignore the suggestion that planted in her mind.

"You couldn't have just moved in here," she said.

"The last resident left pretty well most of it behind. A friend of Weitman's. He got an assignment in Berlin and took not much more than his clothes and a laptop. I just had to carry in a suitcase or two."

Faded blue drapes covered a pair of windows. "The beach view?" she asked. She walked to them and pulled the drapes aside.

"Want me to hold your feet while you look?" Despite the joking tone of his voice, she noticed that he kept a respectful distance, making no effort to approach her or initiate anything more than a sociable visit between friends. Cold feet? Or good manners?

His description of the view had been a bit of an exaggeration, if not too great a one. Over the tops of low-slung buildings one could see a patch of moonlit ocean, without the need of dangling from the window.

She turned, surveying the room again, and finally brought her eyes back to where he still stood just inside the door.

"Well." She left that word suspended between them.

"Catherine." He took a cautious step in her direction and halted again. "When you said you were divorcing Walter—is that a done deal?"

"There's no decree yet. I haven't even filed. But yes, it's over. I won't be going back. I don't think, frankly, he even wants me back."

The more fool he, Jack thought, and said aloud, "Because I'm not much of a one for poaching on another man's territory."

She had removed her wedding ring earlier, dropping it into her jewel box with a sense of finality, and she held out her hand now for him to see the white band of skin on her finger.

"In this case, I assure you, he has forfeited all title to it."

He hesitated for a moment longer. "I see," he said, and then, still sounding unsure of himself, "The question, of course, is, what are we going to do now?"

She, however, was done with waiting—and with being the lady. "This," she said simply, and crossed in three quick strides to where he was standing, threw her arms about him and, stretching slightly on tiptoe, kissed him.

She gave him full credit for losing whatever shyness had possessed him until now. He gave a little sigh that might have been a groan and kissed back, in earnest, crushing her to him.

Like a dam bursting, it flooded over her all at once, making her knees so weak that she could hardly stand and could only cling to him. Tremors of desire raced through her.

As if on cue, they moved toward the bedroom and, still locked together, fell across the unmade bed, trying to maintain their kiss and at the same time struggling with one another's clothing. She stripped his shirt over his head—that did require breaking the kiss, if only briefly, but they took advantage of that break to get her pullover off as well, and then it was jeans tugged down, hers somehow kicked off, and naked flesh ground against naked flesh.

She seemed to be swimming in a cloud of light, oddly like that other light, drifting upward, upward, ever upward. The room faded, even Jack had become only a multitude of sensations permeating her being, lifting her higher, filling her with rapture until she thought she must burst and then....

And then she did, bursting into the light that exploded within her.

* * * * * * *

Jack found himself humming an aria from Tosca in the shower. He turned off the water and stepped out of the stall. Catherine's damp towel hung neatly on the towel bar. Next time he'd suggest a shower *à deux*. He caught a glimpse of his grinning image in the bathroom mirror. All men happily in love must look like idiots, he thought, toweling himself briskly.

In the bedroom, Catherine stretched lazily, enjoying the feeling of happy satiation so long absent in her life. Absent—what was the point of kidding herself—since the last time she had been with Jack. She had only known one other man in that sense, and what had happened between her and Walter, so long ago and even then so rarely, had been so disappointingly different as to be a another experience all together.

She opened a closet door, looking for something more comfortable than her jeans and sweater, found a worn blue bathroom, and put it on.

Jack came in naked from the bathroom. He took her in his arms again, holding her close and kissing her tenderly. "I have something to ask you."

"No one but Walter. And not for years with him," she said.

He laughed, but she could see he liked that answer. "That wasn't the question, though. The question is, will you marry me?"

It was her turn to be surprised. "Really, you are the old fashioned sort, aren't you? You know, darling, today you don't have to marry the girl just because you slept with her."

"But I do. I do have to marry you. I've wanted that since the first day I laid eyes on you and nothing has changed since then, except that I have wasted far too many years without you in my life. It's what you were saying earlier: I don't want to waste any more of them either."

She shook her head and his heart sank. "You can't turn me down, Catherine. Say yes. You have to say yes."

"Yes," she said, and brought the grin back to his face. "But I suppose you have heard of something called bigamy?"

"As soon as you are free. The very moment the divorce is final. Although to tell the truth, I'd marry you today, tonight, and to hell with the consequences."

She hugged him tightly. "I don't think we need be that extreme. But marriage license or no, from this day forward, I am yours, I am your wife."

The bathrobe formed a blue puddle on the floor and they fell across the bed. This time, they made love more gently, more slowly, savoring each second, the almost mystical merging of not just their bodies but their very beings as well.

Later, wrapped in his warm embrace, she slept—and dreamed of evil, a blackness descending upon her like a cloud, enveloping her, taking the breath, the very life out of her.

She woke with a cry, sitting bolt upright in the bed. Instantly Jack sat up too, taking her in his arms. She clung to him, sobbing against his broad chest, struggling to get her heart to beat at its normal rate. He held her tightly, felt her shuddering in his arms, and murmured wordless sounds against her hair.

Finally, the sobs stopped, her breathing slowed. "Better?" he asked.

She sighed deeply. "Thanks. I'm sorry I woke you."

"Any excuse to hold you in my arms." He drew back slightly and looked down at her. "If that was a bad dream, it must have been a lulu."

She met his worried gaze and managed a tremulous smile. "There's something I have to tell you," she said.

"Something bad?"

She nodded. "It's quite a story, I'm afraid."

It took her several minutes to marshal her thoughts. He waited patiently. Finally, she said, "This is going to sound so bizarre."

She started with the tunnel of light when she had been shot, told him of the incidents in which she had seemed to travel to other locations, and ended with her experience with little Debbie and her mother in the shopping mall. He listened without interruption, heard her through to the end.

"Do you think I'm crazy?" she asked when she had finished her story. She tilted her head up to look into his face.

"No," he said firmly. "The story is crazy, I'll admit that. But I have one good reason to believe you. No, make that two, the first one being that I know you are not given to making up stories. You've always been too honest for your own good, as I see it."

"And the other reason?"

"I saw you. In my office, that day when you, what did you call it, traveled to see me. Just for a second. I thought I was going crazy, but I came in and there you were, only I could look right through you, and I blinked and you were gone." He paused thoughtfully. "And next thing I knew, I was sitting by you at a concert." He grinned suddenly and snapped his fingers. "You little devil, that wasn't a coincidence at all, was it?"

She smiled sheepishly. "All's fair in love and war, so they say." She grew quickly serious again. "Jack, there's something more. Just now, when I woke up so frightened—something like that happened to me in my office as well. I think that this man, Yellow Beard, is stalking me. I don't mean physically, I mean, on an astral level."

"Catherine, Of course, you're frightened," he said patiently. "Why wouldn't you be, after everything that's happened? But the two of you, sharing the same unique gift, traveling back and forth to one another? That really does stretch the imagination. What just happened to you was a nightmare, plain and simple."

"Maybe you're right," she said after a moment. She had to admit that what he said made sense—and the idea of Yellow Beard stalking her on an astral level certainly didn't, "But even so, that still leaves the big question: what am I to do? I can't bear it. Sometimes at night, I hear them—Becky, those other children, crying. It frightens me, terrifies me, but I must find these men. I must stop them. Surely that was why I was given this gift. Surely I have been given a mission."

"Maybe you've just given that mission to yourself. Look, okay, I buy this business of your traveling—I have to, I've seen it for myself. But that doesn't mean it's now your job, to track these men down. That's a job for professionals. And you aren't, my darling, wonderful though you are."

She was disappointed that he did not believe her. At the same time, though, she could see the logic of his arguments. It was just that, she felt so sure inside herself that she was right. How could she expect anyone else to understand that, though? She didn't understand it herself.

"All right, setting that aside, and I'm not saying I agree with you, there's still that, whatever you want to call it, that dream, that vision I had of Yellow Beard. You are willing to believe me, believe the astral travel business, anyway, and I am more grateful for that than you could imagine. But who else would? How could I go to Roby Chang and tell her about the changes in his appearance, without telling her I am seeing these men on an astral level?"

He frowned. "That is the problem, isn't it? How could she be expected to believe you?" He thought for a moment. "Maybe she wouldn't have to hear that part of it."

"I don't see how it could be avoided. If I say he's changed his appearance, she's going to ask me how I know that, isn't she?"

"She can't if she doesn't know who you are."

She gave him a puzzled look. "But how could I...?"

"There is such a thing as an anonymous tip. And I am a newsman; meaning, my sources are protected."

She considered that for a moment, and nodded her head. "Yes. I think that might work." She had been too close to the problem to see such an obvious solution. And what a relief, she was thinking, that she had decided to share the problem with him.

"Tomorrow. I'll call this Chang woman first thing." Which would, he thought but did not say, neatly turn matters over to the professionals, where they belonged; and leave Catherine safely out of it. "For now, however, I have a far better idea."

One which, as it happened, she liked too.

* * * * * * *

In a shabby cottage miles away, Lester Paterson sat up in bed, immediately awake, eyes staring into the darkness.

He had seen them, two of them, going at it. The bitch, and a man with her. He knew the man, too, or thought he did. His face was familiar.

Who were they? Was he a threat too, or just someone she'd gotten to bang her? Why did her face keep teasing him? Even now, he could see it just off at the edge of his mind.

She had been crying when he had seen her before, that thought popped into his head. Someone he'd raped? There'd been a few of those over the years. If he wanted something, he took it, and to hell with what they did or didn't want. And some criers among the ones that he hadn't exactly raped, all that shit that women put on to make a man feel bad when he could tell they were loving it as much as he was. Hell, that was the whole point for a woman, wasn't it, to make a man feel good?

Nearby, Colley snored and farted, snored and farted. What a pig! Paterson got out of bed and padded naked into the kitchen to get a beer from the refrigerator.

No, it hadn't been sex with the woman, he was sure of that. A woman might slip his mind but his pecker never forgot.

He thought briefly of the man. There'd been a few of them from time to time too. A hole was a hole as far as he was concerned. But, no he hadn't fucked him either, he was sure of that too. He was familiar, though, he'd seen that face somewhere. Maybe a movie? He had one actor on the hook already, that little pansy O'Dell. Maybe a friend of his?

He went into the living room and switched on the television, and a dark glow seemed to blossom from it and course through him as his hand touched the knob, like he had been sent a message. Only, he couldn't read the message. It faded away from him as he tried to grab hold of it.

What he needed was to track down that bitch, and find her he would. He didn't know what was going on, but he knew she was bad for him, and what was bad for him had to be eliminated. He closed his eyes and called her image to mind. If he worked at it, he could almost be there wherever she was, like they were spirits together. If he could only figure out what was the bond between them.

He had to kill her, of course. She was a threat to him, in some way he couldn't define. There was something else, though, that nagged at him. He almost felt as if they were related, the two of them. They weren't of course. He'd only had one sister, and she was dead. Still, it felt as if there were some *thread*—he didn't know what other word to use—tying them to one another.

Weird shit. Where had all this come from?

CHAPTER THIRTEEN

Roby Chang took her files with her and walked down the corridor to the office of her superior, Special Agent in Charge, Harold King—The King, to his agents, though they did not call him that to his face.

"He's waiting for you," The King's secretary motioned her in. Chang went through into his office.

King stood at the window with his back to her, surveying the traffic on the San Diego Freeway below. He heard the door and said, "Have a seat."

She took one of the hard wooden chairs facing his desk and waited while he took his own seat behind it and slipped a cigarette out of his pack. He put it between his lips but did not light it. The King had given up smoking a month ago. He had not yet given up the cigarettes, however. They had become a prop.

"Fill me in. Any progress on the kiddie snatchings?" he asked, the cigarette bobbing in one corner of his mouth.

She handed the files across to him. "Not much, sir. These seven appear to be the same perps. The descriptions we've gotten are vague, but they match pretty well with the Desmond case. The problem is, the kidnappings seem to be spontaneous events."

"Randoms," he said resignedly.

"Right. These appear to be crimes of opportunity—which means, unless a witness turns up, there's almost nothing to go on. Probably they have the getaway vehicle strategically placed, near an exit. A pick up in the Desmond case, but a van works better. Once you've got the kid inside, he or she won't be seen by any passers by. A van can become a prison on wheels.

"Apparently, though, the vehicle is about all that's set up in advance. As near as we can tell, they prowl around till they spot a kid momentarily separated from her parent, or maybe they create a distraction to separate them. It happens quickly. In a crowded mall, especially now, at Christmas time, when those places are pure bedlam, they can have a kid outside in a minute or two, and they're gone practically before anyone even notices the kid's missing."

"It's gutsy, but the risk is greater too," he said. "Dog jumps over the fence often enough, sooner or later he catches his balls on the barbed wire."

"Unfortunately, so far the barbed wire is clean," she said. "The luck's all been on their side. The closest was the Desmond thing, or we would know almost nothing, and that was only because they varied their M.O., snatched the kid out of the parking lot instead of in the mall."

"Any thoughts on that?" he asked.

She screwed up her face. "I doubt it was significant."

"Don't tell me any of your doubts, I've got enough doubts of my own. Tell me something you believe."

"I believe it was still a crime of opportunity, just the opportunity occurred in a different spot."

He gave a weary sigh. "And no leads since then?"

"We know that they have used at least a couple of the kids to produce movies and photographs. We've identified them in those pictures there." She indicated a small stack of photos.

He picked them up and leafed through them, grimacing in disgust. "Damn, I want these guys roasting on a spit." He tapped the pictures with one finger. "Okay, what about this end of it? The pigs feeding at the trough?"

"We've put the heat on there too. We've picked up a few customers, got lucky at a newsstand in Hollywood. And we've got a couple of suppliers staked out. should get busts in a few days. But so far no one has led us to these guys. There is one thing though." She waited for him to give her a go-ahead nod. "We got a tip one of the men has changed his appearance, rather drastically, we're told. I had Philips work on the earlier drawings."

She passed a pair of drawings across the desk. "This is the original, and this is what Philips did with it, based on the tip we got. The mole is gone, the nose is changed, maybe the chin, too. Plastic surgery, sounds like. We're checking around with clinics and hospitals. We may get something there, but more likely this was some fly-by-night operation. This guy wouldn't go to Cedars of Lebanon for a lift."

King studied the drawings intently. "Makes a big difference." He looked across at her again. "Let me guess: the tip was anonymous?"

She nodded. King was known for pursuing tipsters with nearly the same fervor that he pursued the criminals themselves. "They're almost always dipping out of the same pot. Find the tipster, you find the perp," was a mantra of his.

"How'd we get it?"

"From a newsman. Jack McKenzie, he does pol-op on Channel Three. We've checked him out. He's as clean as a whistle, not even a speeding ticket. Well-respected, impeccable credentials. I'd bet my retirement fund that he has nothing to do with the snatches."

King knew his agent, had worked with her on many cases and considered her the best of the best when it came to crimes against children. He watched her face intently and saw the smile that didn't quite make it to her lips. He leaned forward on his elbows, cigarette bobbing energetically. "Go on," he said. "You've got that look."

"That look, sir?"

"Like you just swallowed a five-pound canary. There's something you haven't told me."

She allowed herself just the hint of a smile. "It's not much."

"The doctor said that about my dick when I was born, but he underestimated. Let's have it."

"Well, a long time back, this McKenzie had a thing going with Catherine Desmond. Catherine Dodd, she was then."

He pursed his lips thoughtfully. "As in the little Desmond girl?"

"The same."

He leaned back in his chair. It gave a creak, like a sigh of relief. His cigarette went still.

"Of course, it could be coincidence," she said

He smiled wryly. "I want to know how he got this information. For all we know, he saw it in a dream. You'll let me know when you find the link with Desmond." He made it a statement and not a question.

"Yes, sir." She nodded. She agreed with him. There was a link to be found, she was sure of it, and she would find it. She had already placed Jack McKenzie under surveillance. If there were anything going on between him and Catherine Desmond, and she was willing to be money on it, she would know about it soon.

* * * * * * *

Time had weighed so heavily on her since she came home from the hospital, and now it rushed past at breakneck speed.

Each day seemed crowded, yet when Catherine looked back on them as she lay in the shelter of Jack's embrace at night, she could not see any of those momentous events by which one normally marked the calendar of one's life. Unless you counted her call to her attorney to begin the divorce proceedings, and one to Walter to tell him. If he felt any dismay, he kept it carefully under control.

"Whatever he needs me to sign," he said. "Have him give me a call."

She and Jack spent every spare moment with one another. They listened to Christmas carols while they trimmed her tree. They jogged together in Beverly Gardens, the long, narrow park that ran through Beverly Hills, an activity for which he had an evident and, to her, mysterious affection; and, more to her liking, strolled hand in hand on the beach at Santa Monica. They held hands in a rundown theater on the West side and marveled at Greta Garbo, never more beautiful, in *Camille*; and made love each night, often more than once a night.

In short, they did all the things that every other couple in love normally does in those initial weeks together. Of course, not every couple got to practice astral projection.

"I do need to bone up on this," she said. She was more determined than ever to master it, though she could not altogether shed her fear, either.

"We'll make a game of it, why don't we?" Jack said. "You pop in whenever and wherever you like, and try to keep me from spotting you, and I'll do my damndest to catch you at it."

Which was what they did. At first, he always caught at least a glimpse of her, though in all fairness, it was deliberate on one occasion, when she found him in conversation with the redhead from the hotel steps.

"It was purely business," he assured her afterward. "And thanks for not letting *her* see you, that would have been hard to explain."

By Friday, however, in the privacy of her office with the door closed, she projected herself into his office and stood for several minutes waiting for any sign that he saw her. When it became clear that he did not, she decided to brush up on yet another skill. She stood behind him and stared hard at the back of his head, willing him to telephone her.

For a long while, it seemed that she would be unsuccessful. Then, abruptly, he turned from his word processor, cast a glance around the room without spotting her, and picked up the phone. She waited just long enough to see that he was dialing her number, and was back at her desk in time to take his call.

"Tell me you didn't see me," she said when he came on the line.

"Just now? No, not a glimpse, you just popped into my head all of a sudden and I thought I ought to phone...oh. That was you, wasn't it?"

"Bingo."

"Hmm. I suppose it might be all right to know that you can drop by unseen whenever you wish, even, say when I might be taking a shower...."

"Now there's an idea."

"...But it's kind of scary to think that a woman can just plant an idea in a man's head whenever she chooses."

"Darling, women have been doing that since Eve looked up and saw a glimpse of red in an apple tree."

He laughed and she was grateful once again that he was self confident enough to be able to play this game with her.

Except, it wasn't exactly a game. Even now, traveling only to Jack, she was ever aware of that other presence. It seemed to hover just beyond the borders of her consciousness, Marley's ghost, waiting to catch her off guard.

But she did not mention that to Jack. He would tell her she was imagining it.

Maybe she was.

CHAPTER FOURTEEN

They ate together every night. On her night to "cook," it was Chinese take-out at her place. "If you thought you were getting a kitchen wench in the bargain," she told him, placing a container of cashew chicken on the table, "You made a bad deal. I can boil an egg and butter toast, and I make a hell of a pot of coffee and a great martini. After that, it's take-out, darling."

More often, dinner was at Celestina's. Young Sergio continued his clearly instinctive flirtation with Catherine, which they both took in stride.

"It would be a bit more flattering," she explained to Jack, "If I didn't see him practice the same wiles on every female who comes into the place, age and figure notwithstanding."

Celestina made her special meals for them and beamed at them as proudly as if she had stage-managed the whole business herself.

"So happy they are now," she told Sergio. "Not like that first night, when they both looked scared to death." At least, she thought, until they had eaten the beautiful meal she had cooked for them. It just proved what she had always known: a good dinner was the cure for most of life's woes.

"At this rate," Catherine said, finishing off a dish of chicken parmagiana, "I shall be as fat as a cow. A mad cow, I assure you."

"I promise you lots of exercise later." He gave her a lecherous wink.

It was more than the food, though, that made this particular dinner special. They were just finishing their coffee when he came around the table and, kneeling on one knee, slipped a diamond engagement ring on her finger.

"I wanted to make it official," he said. "That is, if you're still agreeable."

"Oh, darling, yes," she told him, tears in her eyes.

Celestina, already informed of Jack's plan, beamed from the kitchen doorway as they kissed.

* * * * * * *

After dinner, they drove into Beverly Hills for Christmas shopping. Rodeo Drive was crowded with chic shoppers, women in Donna Karen and Dior, men in Armani. Bored drivers leaned against waiting limos outside Saks and Neiman Marcus. Christmas trees and wreaths lined the streets and a band of carolers in Victorian costume fronted a crèche that might have graced an art museum and certainly bore little resemblance to the original manger of their song. "Oh, Come, All Ye Faithful...." they serenaded the passersby in sweet harmony.

Where the passersby were invited to come, apparently, were the high-end stores that beckoned at every hand, their windows glittering and flashing with every kind of luxury item imaginable. The neon lights that made the wet streets glisten highlighted satin and velvet as well and sparkled on jewels and perfumes in precious bottles.

Catherine set cynicism aside and let herself enjoy the music, the mad rush, the fabulous displays, all presented to make the shopper feel she or he had to have this or that particular treasure to make the holiday complete.

They were in Tiffany's, shopping for something for Peter Weitman, when a voice behind them said, "Jack McKenzie, hello."

They turned, and there was the redhead from the Beverly Hills Hotel. She looked utterly chic, Catherine thought, in tight black pants with a faux leopard jacket. A Kelly green scarf tied prettily at her throat showed off her pale skin and auburn hair to its best advantage. At her feet a white poodle with a matching green bow in his hair strained at his leash to sniff Jack's shoes.

"Maurice, do behave," Kitty scolded the poodle. She gave the leash a tug, and said brightly, "Isn't Christmas the most fun?" She looked from one to the other of them, and at the sales clerk behind the counter, on the surface addressing the whole group, but it was clear to Catherine that she had singled Jack from the herd as if she were a champion sheepdog at the field trials and he an errant lamb.

To his credit, the lamb feinted and tried to pretend he hadn't noticed the bitch's maneuver. "It certainly has been tonight," he said.

The sales clerk drifted tactfully away and Jack introduced the two women. On an impulse, Catherine shoved her hands into her pockets. It was tempting to show off her new ring, but better sense told her it was tasteless to flaunt one's happiness, and tempted the fates as well. For all her stylishness, Kitty Fane did not have the look of a happy woman.

Or, she chided herself, maybe I am just being mean. One could not indulge in sour grapes without leaving a bad taste in one's mouth.

"It's so good to meet you," Kitty said with a brittle smile.

"And you as well." Catherine wanted to mean it, but Kitty had already shifted her attention back to Jack, her smile infinitely warmer. "I hope you haven't forgotten our rain check."

"I had, as a matter of fact," he said. "I've been pretty occupied, I'm afraid."

"Well, it will keep." Kitty smiled brightly, seemingly not at all discouraged by what Catherine would have taken for a polite brush off. "And the champagne's still cold." As was the glance she gave Catherine. "Do take good care of him, he is very special. To us at the studio, I mean."

"And to me as well," Catherine said. "Goodbye now."

When they had left the store and were safely on the sidewalk outside, she said, "She's very pretty," and added in an almost inaudible voice, "for the type."

Jack found himself fascinated by a collection of ties in a passing shop window. He did, however, reach to clasp her hand in his, and held it tightly when she would have pulled it away. As for Kitty Fane, she had a habit of making acid remarks about their fellow workers at the station. He had no doubt that his back would make an equally attractive target, now that it was turned.

It wasn't his back, however, but Catherine's that Kitty was studying as she came out of Tiffany's. She saw Jack take her hand. Someone special, then, she wondered? There had been no scuttlebutt, and office gossip more often than not was pretty sharp on that sort of thing. Theirs was a news office, after all.

On the other hand, he had been sporting a schoolboy sort of excitement the past few days, like a man with a secret. She remembered a recent occasion when she had found an excuse to visit him at his desk and he had suddenly glanced over her shoulder with a chuckle that had made her look around.

"Just remembering a joke," was the explanation he gave, and certainly she had seen nothing that ought to have made him laugh. Thinking of his new lady friend, she pondered now?

She looked at Catherine's derriere with a critical eye. A little too fleshy for jeans, in Kitty's opinion. Some women ought to pay more attention to what they put on. Though she supposed some men might like that full figured look.

The poodle was making an enthusiastic inspection of a fire hydrant. "Don't be vulgar," she told him with a sharp tug at the leash. She started in the opposite direction from that taken by Jack and Catherine, but paused to glance at her reflection in Tiffany's window. She preened a little, and was pleased with what she saw. No excess poundage on her anywhere. She was careful about that.

The trouble was, men simply had no idea how hard a woman had to work to keep herself in tip-top shape. If they did, they would appreciate it more.

She had been on her way home, but somehow her empty apartment seemed less appealing to her. Thaddeus Tremayne had said he "might" call later, but that prospect was too slim to cheer her any. Even if he did come by, it was unlikely to be an exciting interlude. The dynamo of the boardroom, as he was known, had turned out to be a dud in the bedroom. As that type so often did.

When it came to sex, to sex for pure enjoyment and not as part of a business calculation, her taste ran more toward the working class: gardeners, garage mechanics, construction workers. Nothing too polished, too polite. Often when the sheets were down they turned into animals. Even a little roughness was exciting too, so long as she had the upper hand. You didn't very often get that with the business suits.

Her instincts had told her that Jack McKenzie was an exception and on that score her instincts were never wrong, but so far, he had given her no opportunity to prove them.

She thought about a drink at the Polo Lounge to see what stars were out tonight. No, not the Polo Lounge—that sort of dingy place in Westwood, where the jocks from U.C.L.A. liked to hang out, that was more the mood she was in.

Maurice shifted his attention to the trunk of a palm tree. "Come on," she said impatiently.

* * * * * * *

As if they both wanted to cement the shift in their relationship that the ring symbolized, they made love that night with a special intensity, a long, almost leisurely ballet of love that only in its final moments built to a frantic, bone-jarring crescendo that left them both spent and breathless. It seemed to her, impossibly, to be better each time.

Later, they watched *Casablanca* on the bedroom television. At least, she watched *Casablanca*. He was more interested in looking at her. He had all but forgotten the nearly foot-long scar that ran up the inside of one thigh, relic of a young girl's bicycle accident. Somehow, instead of diminishing her beauty, the scar that some men might see as a flaw was oddly endearing to him. Perfection was boring, wasn't it? He wanted a woman who was real, not some airbrushed centerfold—and not a dumb blonde type, either. Some men might turn on to that sort, but he found intelligence sexy. He traced the faint white line of her scar lovingly, first with his finger, and then with his tongue.

And somewhere between Paris and Morocco, *Casablanca* was forgotten.

* * * * * * *

He woke during the night to find her sitting up in bed, arms clasped about her knees. She came easily into his arms when he reached for her. "Another bad dream?"

"Not as bad as before. But I could feel him looking for me. It's like he is searching through space, trying to pin me down. And I'm so afraid that sooner or later he's going to find me."

He held her tight. He wanted to tell her he would protect her, but how did you protect someone from a phantasm? Particularly one that might only be in her mind. He chided himself for his disloyalty, but he could not rid himself of a suspicion that Catherine phantoms were a means of consoling herself.

Of one thing, he was certain: there was something more at play here than mere vengeance, something he could not yet put a name to. Even when she had gone back to sleep, resting comfortably in his arms, he found himself staring up at the ceiling, trying to understand the unease that nagged at him.

* * * * * * *

On Saturday morning, she took Jack with her to Becky's grave. He was the first person with whom she had shared that particular pilgrimage, something he seemed to understand tacitly and respect. It was amazing, she thought, how quickly and easily they had slipped back into the old rapport, things as often as not needing no explaining. Except, sadly, for that one area....

They said almost nothing at the gravesite. He stood patiently while she removed a few weeds and arranged fresh flowers around the headstone: yellow and purple glads, white mums—and some carnations dyed a hideous blue, like nothing in nature. They puzzled him, they were so unlike Catherine's usually impeccable taste, but he kept his questions to himself.

When she was satisfied with the result, she rose and he put one arm around her to hold her close and gave her all the time she needed in silent contemplation.

"She liked flowers, the more colorful the better," she said.

"I wish," he began and stopped himself. "I shouldn't say it, I think."

"You wish you had known her?"

"I wish she had been mine," he surprised her by saying.

Her eyes filled with tears, the gold and white and purple of the flowers blurring into a rainbow haze. She hugged him tightly. "Oh, Jack," she said in a voice that threatened to break. "So do I, my darling. So do I."

She shivered suddenly, and looked over her shoulder with frightened eyes.

"Something?" he asked. He had begun to recognize that frightened gesture.

There was nothing out of the ordinary to be seen: a funeral service just emptying from one of the chapels down the hill, mourners collecting in little puddles around shiny cars.

"Someone walking on my grave, I guess," she said, and shivered again.

He had again that worrisome sense of some doom pending, like taunting ghosts gathering around them. "The air's gotten cool," he said, taking her arm and steering her toward the Porsche.

She hated the thought of hurrying away from Becky's grave, but a dark cloud seemed to have descended upon her. She glanced up at the sky, and was surprised to see that it was still clear and blue.

* * * * * *

"But what are we doing here, Trash?" Colley asked, steering the van slowly up the winding drive of Forest Lawn Memorial Park. "How are we going to find any kids in a cemetery?"

"I don't know. It's just something I felt. Pull over," Paterson said, indicating a parking area next to a chapel. The doors of the chapel swung open as they parked and a group of mourners began to file out.

Paterson and Colley sat in silence, watching. A young girl appeared, grown men on either side of her. Father? Uncle? Brothers? She was pretty, as near as they could tell from the distance, thirteen, maybe fourteen, with that air peculiar to adolescent girls, veering from graceful to awkward and back again in the space of a heartbeat.

"We'd never get ahold of her and get out of here," Colley said.

Paterson opened the glove box, revealing the gun inside. His fingers itched to pick it up. He had an urge to, he wasn't sure what, to start shooting, somebody. Something. Why *were* they here? He had felt this hunch while they were on the freeway, and followed it blindly until it had led them into the cemetery, but now they were actually here, he had no clue what or who he was looking for.

He glanced around. There was nobody else to be seen: just the group from the chapel and up the hill there, a silver Porsche. As he looked, it began to move, disappearing around a curve of the driveway that would take it to the exit.

The mourners were getting into limousines and cars, a black-suited man directing traffic. The girl had disappeared. Colley was right: it would be suicide to try anything in this crowd, in broad daylight, and no quick way to escape. Anyway, whatever instinct had guided him to this place had faded into nothing. That tingling sensation he sometimes got was gone.

He slammed the glove box door shut. "Let's go," he said. "There ain't anything here for us."

But there had been. He was sure of it.

* * * * * * *

Without asking, Jack drove from Forest Lawn to San Marino, to the Huntington Museum, one of their favorite spots in the long ago past. Catherine had always considered the Huntington a gem. Unlike, say, Hearst Castle, which was, if one were frank, a showing-off place, the Huntington had clearly been designed as a home, in which one could actually imagine living, if on an admittedly grand scale.

There was the main art gallery too, with *Pinky* ("Too precious," she had pronounced it) and *Blue Boy* (better, "But he's an arrogant little brat, isn't he?" Jack opined) and Catherine's favorite, *Mrs. Siddons as The Tragic Muse*, all browns and golds and velvet folds that begged you to reach and touch them. The famous actress in her

119

over-dramatic and wonderfully self-absorbed pose was, as Catherine had once put it, an olden and artful version of the vanity license plate.

Today it was the gardens that drew them. The rain had fled, leaving a pale December sunshine, the air brisk and pleasant, the sky a Chamber of Commerce dream.

There were several gardens to choose from, all meticulously maintained, all worth contemplating: a Shakespeare garden, planted with the various herbs and flowers mentioned in his writings, each with its name plate to say what and where ("I know a bank whereon the wild thyme blows," *A Midsummer Night's Dream*). There was a desert garden, a meandering walk that led through large areas planted in cacti and other desert flora; and a little bamboo "forest" as well, and a long neatly clipped lawn lined with statuary.

They passed these by in silent agreement and took instead the arbor covered walk that led to the Japanese Tea Garden. In spring, clouds of lavender wisteria blossoms would mass overhead, their scent driving bumblebees and hummingbirds into a happy delirium, but for now the naked branches twisted and matted together like sticks dropped in some Giant child's game.

At the end of the walk a mother demonstrated a temple gong, a long thick wooden pole suspended by ropes in front of a bronze disc. While her two children watched fascinated, she pulled the pole back and released it. It struck the disc and a deep bass note echoed balefully.

"Ring it again," the little girl cried, and "Let me, let me," shouted the boy.

"Well, just once, and not too hard." The mother smiled an apology at the handsome couple strolling her way. Not that they would mind, she supposed. When you were in love like that, everything was wonderful, wasn't it?

Just past the temple gong, struck now with a determined ferocity by the little boy, wide steps led down to the postcard-perfect Tea Garden. Even in winter its little rolling hills were a vivid green. A stream, man made to look perfectly natural, meandered through them and in its dark water jewel-colored Koi darted among lotus leaves. A high arch of a bridge in glossy scarlet crossed the stream—for show only, there was a less spectacular span for actual stream-crossing—and on the opposite bank a path led to the farthest hillside where open shoji panels invited the eyes into a reproduction of a classical Japanese home.

It was an enchanting place that seemed to have been dreamt up and created especially for lovers. Hand in hand, they followed the stream's path, laughing at the Koi who swam into the shallows of the bank and mouthed their pleas for food, mindless of the signs that forbade their feeding.

They stopped at the foot of the scarlet bridge, roped off to bar trespassers. Catherine eyed the perilously steep ascent.

"You have to wonder how the geishas got up and down them in their sandals, don't you," she said. "And they did it so gracefully. I think I should have to crawl."

"Not exactly how one imagines Madame Butterfly's entrance," a voice said at her elbow.

She turned, and gasped. "What are you…?"

Roby Chang's penetrating glance swept over her and to Jack's puzzled expression, and back to Catherine again.

"We have to talk," she said.

CHAPTER FIFTEEN

They met by arrangement at a Big Boy restaurant in Burbank. By the time Jack and Catherine got there, Chang had already established claim to a large booth set apart in one corner and was fending off the efforts of the hostess to seat a family of four there instead.

They ordered breakfast. Just coffee for Catherine and Jack, and an astonishing order of food for Chang: pancakes (a full stack), eggs over easy, both bacon and sausage, and hash browns.

"All the basic food groups," Chang said. "Calories, caffeine, sugar, and grease."

They made small talk until the food came and the waitress had satisfied herself that these three wanted nothing more.

"Just a little privacy, if we may," Chang said, with a smile that took any sting out of the remark.

"Now," Chang said when the waitress had gone, "Who's first?"

Catherine had already decided on her way there that she would tell Chang everything. She began to talk, in a low voice that, Chang noted approvingly, wouldn't easily be heard at a neighboring table. Not that anyone appeared to be listening, but you could never be sure. And it wasn't a story that ought to be overheard.

The everydayness of their surroundings made Catherine's recital all the more fantastic. She told of astral spirits that soared through space and fiends that skulked in shadows, while around them a dissonance of voices rose and fell and dishes clattered. The scent of searing flesh, the aroma of fresh baked bread, wafted by them and a ghost of old grease haunted everything. At a nearby table a couple argued in sibilant whispers and at another a trio of children squealed and laughed in carefree delight. A baby cried. Against this backdrop of commonplace, the pages of Catherine's eerie story turned.

Chang ate as she listened without comment. She found herself thinking of The King. He would nail her to the cross on this one.

Astral projections? Angels with messages? And a pair of killers, molesting a little girl in a dream.

Yet that much, at least, was not fantasy. Really, none of it appeared to be, however bizarre it sounded. At least, when Catherine Desmond talked of those two, her anger was real, her sincerity evident. Certainly she believed the story she was telling. This was no made-up fantasy hatched in a morbid mind still grieving for a lost child.

But could *she* believe it? Grief did strange things to one's thinking. And why, she wondered, couldn't I get a nice, normal case with axe murders and incest and nothing bordering on the supernatural?

Catherine had finished. She sat waiting for the agent to respond. Chang hadn't interrupted once. Her expression had remained throughout one of guarded neutrality. Catherine and Jack exchanged glances. He shrugged.

Chang wiped up the last of the syrup and pushed her plate aside. "And that's all of it?" she asked. "I don't suppose you'd want to give me a demonstration of this, this gift of yours, would you?"

"It doesn't work quite like that. Physically, I would still be here, sitting right where I am."

"But your—what did you call it—your Ka, would be across town?"

"Yes, it's my Ka, my spirit, whatever you want to call it, that travels.

"But she'd look like she had simply fallen asleep," Jack said. "And, I have to tell you, I have seen her when she travels. She's appeared in my office, a couple of times, when she wasn't physically there."

"There is one thing I forgot to mention," Catherine said. "I don't know if it will make any sense."

"Nothing else has, what difference can it make?" Chang asked dryly. "Go on, let's hear it."

"When they were with that little girl, I heard the one I call The Bear, say, 'trash can.' It was such an odd thing to say, wasn't it?"

"Trash Can?" Chang's head came up, her eyes sharp on Catherine's face.

"Yes. Does that mean something?"

Chang smiled. At last something she could sink her teeth into. "Trash Can Paterson," she said. "I've been wanting to catch up to that bastard."

She motioned to the waitress for the check, and shook her head when Jack reached for his wallet, "No, this is on the bureau. At the least, my boss is going to find this fascinating. Let me talk to him."

And maybe get myself tossed out of his office; and out of a good job while I'm at it, she thought, but did not say aloud.

* * * * * * *

To her surprise, The King did not toss her out and did not laugh. He heard her through without a word and leaned so far back in his chair she thought it would surely overturn, his hands folded behind his head, eyes ceiling-ward, unlit cigarette dangling from the corner of his mouth. The silence was agonizingly long.

"You believe her?" he asked finally.

Chang took a deep breath. This was the plunge. She could laugh and tell him she thought Catherine Desmond was a nutcase and she was only passing the story on to keep him totally filled in. Or, she could put several years of hard-earned respect on the line.

"I do," she said. "I don't pretend to understand it, but I really think she's telling us the truth. And Trash Can Paterson is no fantasy, certainly. He's slipped out of two seemingly certain convictions, and has been out of sight since then. And this sounds like his sort of doings."

He continued to stare at the ceiling. She resisted an impulse to look up, though it had begun to seem as if she might as easily find her solution there as anywhere else. So far, it was the rare case with no arrows pointing her the direction to go.

"Gabronski," The King said after another painful silence.

"Sir?"

"Gabronski." His chair came down with a thud and he looked straight and hard at her, the way he did when he had made up his mind to something. But what, she wondered? "Never heard of him?"

"I don't think...oh, you mean *Doctor* Gabronski? The so-called L.A.P.D. psychic?"

"He's really not L.A.P.D., but he did help them with the Boulevard Strangler a couple of years back. Led them right to the scene of the crime, didn't he? Caught the bastard with his skivvies at half mast and the army at attention, the way I heard it."

"Yes, sure, that was the story at the time, though I have to admit I thought the media was hyping it up a bit. But anyway, that's kind of a marshy area, isn't it? Isn't Gabronski, well...?" She faltered.

"Christ, he's a fruit loop. That's no skin off our butts, is it?"

"No-o-o. But, are you suggesting…well, do you think…?" She picked her words carefully. "Would the Bureau actually use somebody like him in a case?"

"Has used. And not somebody like him. Him. A couple of times, as a matter of fact."

She was genuinely astonished. "I didn't know. Never heard."

He shrugged that off. "It was all very low key, no publicity. He didn't give us very much, a couple of leads, minor ones that helped a bit. It was kind of a draw for us. Which is why we never gave the story out."

"And you're suggesting," she said, tentatively, because she didn't want to come out of this conversation looking like a complete idiot, "maybe I should have him take a look at what we've got here."

"It couldn't hurt anything, could it? We've got a woman who says she's shipping herself through space, and landing on top of these bad guys. Right out of a Stephen King movie. Not my bag and not yours either. This Gabronski might have some ideas we can use. And it's kind of down his alley, isn't it?"

"Yes. That's certainly true." Her tone of voice was anything but convinced. She had her own reasons for disliking the suggestion but she kept them to herself. If the King noticed her lack of enthusiasm, he took no heed.

"Anyway, if we keep it quiet and it doesn't pan out, we're no worse off than we are now. Why don't you take this Desmond woman to see the good Doctor? Maybe the two of them together can pinpoint for you where this Paterson is, when he's not in outer space. And try not to let them both vaporize out of your sight, okay?"

"Where…?"

"See Renner, he handled the last case with the Doctor. In the meantime," he picked up the altered drawing of Trash Can Paterson, "send these pictures to Desmond, and the boyfriend, see how close Phillips came to what she thinks she saw, see if she wants to make any alterations."

"Are we going to use them?"

"I'll think about that," he said.

Chang recognized his tone. The session was over, the issue settled. She got up from her chair but before she could reach the door, he stopped her.

"You understand, Agent Chang, if you get a location, we're going to need something more than a psychic vision to convince a judge to sign a warrant."

125

"I understand, sir."

"Good. Just keep that in mind."

Great, she thought as she walked toward her own office, now I've got not one but two ghost chasers to deal with. Crapola.

CHAPTER SIXTEEN

"I thought you didn't believe in this stuff?" Jack had to shout to be heard over Bob Segar, singing "Old Time Rock 'n' Roll" at a considerable volume. They were in Chang's red Bronco on the freeway, heading at a thrilling speed toward Mission Hills, the roar of the traffic and the wind through the opened windows competing lustily with the music and rendering conversation difficult.

Chang slowed and aimed the Bronco at an off ramp. "It's one thing if a guy handles a piece of someone's clothing and thinks he can sense where that person is, which is what the doctor did with the Boulevard Strangler. It's a big leap from there to people popping in and out of the woodwork. And I don't know personally if there's really anything to this guy or not. I'm just saying, he may be able to give us some advice."

Catherine certainly hoped so. She was more convinced than ever that Paterson was stalking her on an astral level, but she knew that Jack was unconvinced. What was the point of arguing? Unless this Doctor Gabronski had something to offer, what on earth could anyone do about Paterson's stalking? If any help was to be forthcoming, it probably would not be of this earth—and that was as puzzling to her as everything else connected with this business.

They drove a mile or so on a curving side street, winding for several minutes up into gently rolling hills. Chang turned into a drive with an ivied gate and a sign reading Happy Acres. A button on the gatepost produced a muffled voice. Chang identified herself and after a pause, the gate swung open and closed quickly behind them.

"A rest home?" Catherine asked.

"Hospital. Very private, very expensive." The drive snaked past neatly manicured lawns to a massive faux Tudor house. Gravel crunched beneath their feet as they walked to the wide steps that led to a heavily carved wooden door.

A white-suited orderly, looking more like a football lineman than a nurse, opened the door a few inches, his thick body blocking the doorway. Chang flashed her badge. He stepped back without glancing at it and swung the door wider to let them in, and closed it carefully behind them, the lock snapping noisily into place. "This way," he said.

It might have been a private residence, though certainly a very grand one. The high-ceilinged hallway was a checkerboard of black and white marble. At nearly its midpoint a tall Christmas tree glittered, seemingly trimmed in ice that turned out to be, on closer inspection, scores of crystal ornaments: Bacarrat, Orrefors, Lalique. The landscapes on the walls would not have embarrassed The Huntington, and French tulips languished in ornate vases on mahogany tables, their perfume a vast distance away from the antiseptic smell of the ordinary hospital.

It all had the look of a stage set. Catherine half expected the actors to make their well rehearsed entrances from the doors on either side, set the drama in motion, but the hallway was empty, their footsteps echoing dully on the marble. Where, she wondered, were the patients?

Their guide opened a door and stepped aside. "Wait here," he said, and left them. Again there was the snap of a lock as the door closed. Elegant or not, the hospital was certainly security conscious.

It was a very pleasant room, at least. A profusion of green plants, hanging spiders and pots of dracaena and philodendron and houseleek softened what otherwise might have been an oppressive grandiosity. A small fire burned on the grate, and a table before it had been set with a silver Georgian tea service and cups Catherine guessed to be Crown Derby. The chairs grouped around the tea table were tufted leather and looked authentically antique and stiffly uncomfortable.

She walked to the leaded glass window in the far wall. It overlooked a sloping lawn and a perfectly maintained garden abloom, even in this winter season, with flowers. Citrus trees, lemon, she thought, or orange, lined a high wall that sheltered Happy Acres from any curious eyes.

Chang joined her at the window and noted the security cameras atop the wall. "How the other half lives," she said dryly.

They swung around as the door opened again and two men entered. The taller of them, rapier-thin, clean-shaven, came forward to shake hands. "I'm Doctor Ederle. And this is Doctor Gabronski," he said, introducing his companion.

Doctor Gabronski was a tiny, elfish man with long white side-burns and a beard that gave him a Santa-Claus look, an effect enhanced by the little round belly that strained at a snugly closed vest of red, and the lively, intelligent eyes that sparkled merrily at them through thick glasses.

"So very delighted you could come," he said, beaming around at them.

The introductions done, Doctor Ederle gave them a look, not quite wary, but weighing. He glanced again at Gabronski, and made to go. "I'll leave you to your chat. You'll call me, Doctor, if you need me?"

"Just so, just so, thank you." Doctor Gabronski's shiny baldpate bobbed up and down.

"I've had tea prepared," Doctor Ederle addressed their visitors, "And if you need anything else, or you have any difficulties, the bell is right there by the door." He nodded briefly once more in Gabronski's direction. "Doctor," he said, and took leave of them.

Gabronski had shown a marked deference for his colleague, but now he grinned with the glee of a child at a party and rubbed his hands together delightedly. "Well, well," he said. He gestured toward the waiting chairs and the highly polished tea service. "Shall we have some tea?"

Chang, who felt these days as if she had stumbled down a rabbit-hole, was tempted to ring the bell by the door and ask if she couldn't have a shot of Jack instead. She dismissed that idea as quickly as it had come, however. This was one case where she most definitely did not want any hints of unprofessionalism to pop up down the road. "Nothing for me," she said.

Catherine took tea, and Jack declined, and they sat in a semi-circle near the fire. It was a cozy setting, the chairs more comfortable than they had looked, and Catherine felt quickly at ease with their host, so that, when he grew serious and prompted her with, "Now then, I understand you have rather an unusual story. Suppose you tell it to me from the beginning," she found herself repeating her strange tale without hesitation.

Gabronski listened attentively, only nodding his head occasionally to encourage her. When she had finished, he graciously refilled her cup and contemplated the fire for a brief moment.

"And you've come to me," he said, his eyes going from face to face and settling on Chang's, "to see if I can give you any insight into this, what did you say his name was, Paterson?"

"Well, yes, that too," Chang said. "But, mostly, we wanted to see what you made of Mrs. Desmond's magic act."

"Oh, not magic, certainly," Catherine objected quickly. "Though I'm not quite sure what to call it either. Doctor, you don't think I'm crazy, do you?"

His eyes twinkled with amusement. "Crazy? No, absolutely not. But it is a singular story, isn't it? I don't think I've heard one like it before. Tell me, if you will, what do *you* think has happened? Is happening? You must have given it some thought."

Catherine nodded and thought for a minute. "First of all, I think that I did die when I was shot, or very nearly died, at least. And I think I was sent back by someone—some*thing*—to try to stop these men. What I don't understand is, why me? I'm no kind of hero and I haven't any weapons to use against them. Even the astral projection, it doesn't accomplish much, does it? I mean, yes, I was able to interfere on one occasion, but there must surely have been others I didn't even witness. And when I am there, I have no physical presence. What I mean is, why was I picked for this? Why not a man, someone physically strong? Or a police person? Why not Agent Chang here?"

"Agent Chang would have had herself committed before this point," Chang said, and added quickly, "Sorry, Doctor, I don't mean to be flippant."

"The point is, why did she choose me?" Catherine persisted.

"By 'she'," Gabronski said. "I take it you mean this individual who appeared to you, first at the hospital, and later, you think, in a flower shop."

"It was a woman, both times. At least, she appeared as a woman. But I have sort of thought...well, do you think...might she be an angel?" She couldn't help feeling a little silly asking such a question, and she was aware that Chang stiffened slightly when she heard that word, but the Doctor took it in stride.

"An angel?" He spread his hands. "I couldn't say. That's a fairly modern concept, in any case, that of the sweet-voiced angel, the smiling cherub. The Old Testament angels were warriors, mostly, quite fierce and not at all sweet. When Abraham's angel revealed itself, Abraham swooned in terror. And the cherubim were set outside Eden like a swarm of wasps to guard against Adam and Eve's returning. As for Lucifer, well, we need only recall that he was an angel himself before he fell from grace. Nothing cute about any of them. I shouldn't think your visitor was anything like those. But, spirit, yes, someone from beyond this existence, I think that's evident. Someone, it would have to be, very concerned, someone who loved you very much on this plane, and carried that love, that concern, through to the other side."

Catherine took a sip of tea that had grown cold and thought about what he had said. "A woman who…," she started to say, but he interrupted her.

"Not necessarily, that's the point I was getting to. You are here before me at this moment, a woman, a young woman. If I may be permitted, a beautiful woman. But your soul is neither woman nor man, young nor old, beautiful nor ugly. Those are perceptions of our senses. We live in a physical world and it is our senses that make that world what we call 'real' to us, but this visitor is not a sensory reality, she is only an illusion projected to you by, as I say, someone who carried great love for you into the beyond, or someone with a powerful need to see these crimes redressed." He thought a moment. "Is your mother alive?"

"Very much so," she said with a smile.

"Father, then?"

"No, he passed away about ten years ago." She had a sudden, bitingly vivid memory of her father, sitting with her in a little boat on a summer afternoon, fishing without any great purpose, and telling her stories of his wartime adventures—mostly fictitious, as it turned out, but entertaining nonetheless. Yes, there had been a great love there, back and forth. She could see that he might well come from beyond to guide and protect.

She frowned. "But, if my father wished to come to me, to give me messages, help, why not simply project the image of himself?"

The Professor shrugged. "Perhaps to make it easier for you to accept initially what he had to say. If your dead father had appeared to you, you would have been sure immediately you were hallucinating, you would have rejected out of hand whatever he had to say, attributed it to your injury, or the drugs you were being administered. That he was real, that his message was real, was probably the last thing you would have credited.

"But a woman…we tend to trust women more, I think, than we do men, logically or not. And a doctor…well, we put confidence in what a doctor tells us, don't we? If I were making a visit from the other side, and wanted you to take me seriously, I think I might very well have chosen the same appearance. Mind you, I can't know. I can only offer what seems to me an explanation."

"All very interesting," Chang said, "But I can't see that this helps us any, other than your endorsement of Mrs. Desmond's experience. The question is, what do we do now? How do we make use of this…well, what would you call it, this gift she's been given. I'm not saying I buy it altogether, but if you're both right, then it had to have been given to her for a purpose, to use. But how?"

Gabronski studied Catherine carefully. "I think I should like to see you do a projection."

Catherine's throat went dry. "If you feel it will help," she said. "But, I can't always do it at will. It sort of comes and goes."

"I was thinking…." He hesitated. "I wonder if under hypnosis… if you would not object?"

"I'm not sure that's wise," Jack said quickly. He did not voice what was really troubling him: if Catherine's phantom stalker were really only a figment of her imagination, what might it wreak upon her in a hypnotic trance, the conscious mind and its protective capabilities lulled to sleep?

"You're concerned for her well-being, of course, as I am also. The advantage of hypnosis is, if there is any kind of threat to Mrs. Desmond, I can simply and immediately bring her back. Safer, I think, than what you have been doing. And there are some suggestions I can plant, for making this easier to do in the future, for instance. And most especially, for protecting herself."

"In that case, yes," Catherine said with determination, swallowing her anxiety.

"Catherine," Jack started to say, his personal fears not at all lessened, but she shook her head firmly.

"Let's do it," she said.

Jack bit his tongue. More and more he felt as if he were on the sidelines in a game he little understood, with rules unknown to him.

His heart ached for Catherine; he wanted to take her away from this whole business, so far away that it could never reach her again, help her to mend, to forget the past. Only—and this thought came unbidden to mock his fears—he knew perfectly well that she would not go. And that, he thought, was where the real problem lay. There was something not altogether innocent in Catherine's alleged connection to Paterson; a passion beyond what was altogether rational, something that instinct told him was dangerous.

Gabronski took a few minutes to set the stage. He closed heavy draperies over the windows and dimmed the already dim lights further, and brought a footstool for Catherine's feet. "No need to lie down, the chair will be fine. So long as you're comfortable?" He lifted an eyebrow.

"Quite."

"What about us?" Chang asked. "Do we hold hands and concentrate, like at a séance? Or what?"

He smiled tolerantly. "Just move your chairs back a bit, there, that's fine," he said. "And try to remain quiet, please."

At the Doctor's instructions, Catherine closed her eyes and began to breathe deeply. His voice was low and coaxing. She found herself going under easily, naturally, her tension fading.

"You will cloak yourself in the light," his murmuring voice told her, "The light will protect you. And you will remain invisible to all eyes. You will be only a witness. You will see, and remain unseen, safe within the shielding light."

She drew the light around herself as he instructed, felt its protective comfort invade her, relieving her anxieties. Her breathing deepened.

"In the future, you will do this yourself whenever you choose, easily, naturally…in the light…."

Help me, help me…the cries came from a great distance; not just Becky's voice, an entire chorus of young voices calling to her: *Help me…help…help….*

"…Cloak yourself in the light…."

She slipped effortlessly downward—and found herself standing in a playground. In the distance, two young boys tossed a baseball back and forth, but closer to where she stood, the small carousel, the teeter-totter, the swings, were all empty of children. There were only two men nearby, seated on a bench, watching the boys play, and… her heart skipped a beat. The two men were Paterson and The Bear. For a moment she hung back, her fear resurfacing and then she heard the Doctor's voice within her, and did as he instructed, reaching again for the light as if she had known all along how to do this, wrapping it once more about herself.

"Here he comes now," The Bear said. They looked at her. No, she realized, through her, at someone approaching from behind. For a moment, though, she thought Paterson looked directly into her eyes.

She shrank away from him, and was back in the Doctor's cozy room, the fire crackling beside her, that moment of terror like a scent lingering in her senses.

The sudden opening of her eyes gave Gabronski a shock. He had been in control, fully expecting to bring her back in due time on his instructions. It was rare, almost unheard of for a subject to awaken on her own. That, more than anything else, told him how frightened this woman really was, far more frightened than she had admitted or shown. He ought to have realized that, he scolded himself.

"You are fine, you are safe," he told her quickly, and reached to take one of her hands in his. It was ice cold.

"*Are* you okay?" Jack demanded, kneeling by her chair and turning her face toward him.

"Yes. I...." She hesitated, still disoriented, trying to collect her thoughts. "It was them: Paterson and The Bear. They were in a park, a children's playground, watching two little boys play, and waiting for someone. The Bear said, 'here he comes,' and then I woke up back here."

"Did they see you?" Gabronski asked, still distressed, and puzzled, by her sudden awakening.

"I...I don't know. I thought not, but, then, Paterson looked at me, as if he were looking into my eyes. It...it startled me. I'm sorry. I panicked. That's what brought me back."

"That third person you said you sensed," Chang said in an excited voice. "Did you see who he was?"

Catherine shook her head. "No. He was approaching from behind me. They looked toward him, looked through me I thought, only, as I said, Paterson might have glimpsed me, or maybe he only sensed me. He seems to do that."

Chang jumped up from her chair, clenching her fists. "We need to know who they were meeting."

"I'll go back," Catherine said, but her voice was tremulous, without conviction.

"No. You can't," Jack said firmly. He understood how Chang and Gabronski felt; but Catherine's safety was his first concern. When she looked as if she might argue, he appealed to the others. "Look at her, she's white as a ghost. I'm not going to let her go there again."

Catherine started to reply, but Gabronski gave his head a vehement shake. "I think he may be right," he said. "There's something else: I've been thinking about this, and I don't like it. You say that this person has only recently begun to, as you put it, to stalk you? And that he has quickly grown stronger at it, his presence more real with each occasion?"

"Yes. At first, it was only a vague feeling, but each time it gets worse. Even now, wrapped in the light as you instructed me, I had this sense that he knew I was there, that he could step right up to me, could take me in a stranglehold...." She gasped with the memory and buried her face in her hands. "It's horrible, I can't describe it."

Gabronski nodded. He at least seemed to have quite accepted Catherine's stalker as real. After a moment, Jack asked, "If it is true, if he really is stalking her on some invisible level, what can we do about it?"

Gabronski's jolly demeanor of a little while before was gone entirely. He frowned while he considered the question, and was silent for so long that Jack was about to ask it again, when finally he spoke. "I have an idea that perhaps this individual, this Paterson, that perhaps he too has psychic abilities, abilities that may even have been heretofore untapped. He might have been totally unaware of them until recently, though probably he used them from time to time without thinking about it, or maybe he simply considered them hunches. Many people have these gifts, even use them, without being consciously aware of them."

He looked directly into Catherine's face. "But there is some powerful link between the two of you, on the astral plane. I very much fear that your visits to him may have been what awakened whatever gifts he possesses, may even be feeding them."

"You mean, every time I see him, I am making him stronger, leading him to me?"

"It would appear so. I think to visit this individual again may be to place yourself in grave danger."

"But I can't stop, don't you see?" Catherine said in a plaintive voice. "If this is what I was sent back for, I have to see it through."

"Catherine, you don't even know that you were 'sent back' for any purpose," Jack said angrily. "At best that's just a guess on your part. And for what purpose? You said these voices told you there was something only you could do? How could that mean catching these two monsters? That's what the police are for, isn't it, people like Chang, here? How can you imagine that you're the one, the only one, who could do that?"

"I don't know," she admitted with a shrug. "I don't know what it is that only I can do. I only know I have no choice but to continue down this road." Her voice dropped to a near-whisper. "This life that I was given back, it isn't really mine to own, is it? It was only lent to me, as I see it. And maybe that's the point: that I was killed, and the very worst that could happen to me is that I'll end up back where I was when Paterson shot me."

Jack wanted to say, that's the very worst thing that could happen to me, too, but her eyes pleaded with him for understanding. Understanding that he did not have to give. He swallowed his frustration and said nothing.

"Anyway," she said into his silence, "Whether I was given some heavenly mission or not, now that I know who and what he is, I could never rest until I see him brought to justice. I owe Becky that. I owe it to all those weeping children."

Chang shot Gabronski a quick look, but he only shook his head sadly. "Yes, I can understand that," he said softly. He folded his hands across his belly. "It's intriguing, isn't it? You speak of an angel, but really, doesn't it seem that you have two angels, the bright one, and a dark one? You are wed to both of them, I think, for reasons that we cannot yet perceive."

"Is there no way to protect myself from that dark angel?" Catherine asked.

He sighed. "Only the light. It was the light, your bright angel, who sent you on this mission. We have to believe she will protect you. Of one thing I am certain. I know evil of this magnitude, I have experienced it before—and nothing on this mortal plane could protect you from it. There are no crosses, no silver bullets, no wooden stakes to kill such demons when they are within you."

* * * * * * *

They were quiet on the way back to Los Angeles. For once, Chang did not even turn on her rock and roll music. After a time, to relieve the somber mood, Jack said, "A charming man, that Gabronski."

"Yes, he's a darling," Catherine agreed with him, glad to be diverted from her morbid thoughts of Paterson. "Is he the chief of the hospital?"

"That's Ederle," Chang said, "He's the chief. He runs Happy Acres."

"In any case, the patients must adore Doctor Gabronski."

Chang started to say something, but on her left, a huge semi tried to bully itself into a too-small opening in front of them. She put a hand down on the horn and her foot on the gas. They shot past his bumper with a hair's breadth to spare.

"Doctor Gabronski is a patient at Happy Acres," Chang said. In the wake of their astonished silence, she negotiated her way past a slow moving Toyota.

"A patient?" Catherine finally managed to ask. "Not a Doctor?"

"He's a Doctor, yes, or at least he was." She changed lanes with a blast of her horn and focused for a few seconds on the heavy freeway traffic.

136

"You're both too young to remember, of course," she said after a moment. "I don't personally remember it myself. It happened thirty or more years ago, but it's something of a Bureau legend. Gabronski murdered a string of children. Five, I think, before he turned himself in. Claimed he'd been possessed by a demon. They found him insane, naturally. He's lived at Happy Acres ever since. It's a mental hospital, a very discreet one. He's a model patient, they tell me."

CHAPTER SEVENTEEN

Chang dropped them at Catherine's apartment. On an impulse, Jack suggested a drive to Laguna Beach. "You need to get away from everything," he said. "Forget all this business for one evening, at least."

The suggestion was a good one. The weather had turned warm, as it could do in the California winter and, off-season, Laguna was mostly empty of the tourists that in summer packed its sidewalks and restaurants. Except for an occasional roller skater, they had the Promenade that snaked along the beachfront to themselves. The turquoise water deepened to blue black where it stretched toward the hump of Santa Catalina Island just visible on the misty horizon.

Closer, the surf washed in rivulets over the sand and formed little tidal pools in the rocks that dotted the shore below the ragged bluffs. They scrambled over the rocks and examined the miniature aquariums with their brilliant anemones, purple urchins, huge sea slugs and skittish crabs.

The daylight faded and they abandoned the slippery rocks. They had dinner at Dizz's As Is, an intimate shingled house whose walls sported a photo gallery of the in crowd of Hollywood's glamour hey-day. Judy Garland, Clark Gable, Lana Turner and myriad others smiled their approval down on the vermouths they sipped and the rack of lamb that followed. As if by common agreement they spoke not at all of Gabronski or Chang or Trash Can Paterson. Jack was happy to see that by the time she was sipping an espresso, Catherine's face had lost that haunted look she had worn for the last several days.

It was late by the time they settled into the Porsche again and headed north on the San Diego Freeway, a lustrous pewter moon winking off and on through patches of cloud overhead. Catherine leaned against the soft leather upholstery, one hand in Jack's, and savored the feeling of deep relaxation. Somewhere between Los

Angeles International Airport and Santa Monica Boulevard, relaxation became sleep.

Glancing over at her in the dashboard's pale luminance, Jack felt himself engulfed in a tide of emotions: love, concern, protectiveness. He could not bear the thought of what she was suffering, and the possibility that anything could happen to her, could take her away from him again, was unthinkable.

Her suggestion that life had only been lent to her this time around for one specific purpose and one purpose only would not bear his contemplating. He was sure that, if she really had been "sent back," it was as much to share life with him as to ferret out a pair of admittedly evil child molesters.

He still thought that her belief that she had been given a mission might be nothing more than self-delusion, fed by her desire to avenge her daughter's death. One thing that he had come to realize: if Paterson was stalking her, as she believed, Catherine was stalking him, as well. In some bizarre psychic way, they were each of them feeding a need in the other.

Anyway, hadn't she told him that she had heard him call to her when she was hovering between life and death? That clinched it as far as he was concerned, and though she might think it treasonous, he was determined that their love for one another would take precedence over anything else, Paterson included.

So, as he backed the car into a parking place near Catherine's apartment, it was with no great happiness that he saw Chang's now familiar red Bronco parked just outside the front door.

She was waiting for them on the sidewalk as they walked up. "Chang," he said before either of the women could speak, "I know how important this case is to you, but you've got to see that this is tearing Catherine apart."

Chang gave him a measuring look, and a longer one at Catherine. "Yes, you're right," she said with a sigh. "I know that you are, only...." She hesitated.

"Only?" Catherine prompted her, already sure what she was going to hear.

"There's been another one. A boy this time, snatched from a playground. I suspect the very playground where you saw them earlier today."

Catherine fumbled in her purse for her keys. "Come up. I'll make coffee."

* * * * * * *

They sipped coffee in Catherine's living room while Chang gave them the details. They could faintly hear the hum and clang of Santa Monica's traffic even through the closed balcony door. A fire on the grate offered a welcome respite from the cool December air.

The discussion grew heated as well. For all the dread that it bred within her, Catherine felt more strongly than ever that she had to find Paterson and his companion, before they did more of their evil. Perhaps if she had after all gone back to that playground a second time when she was with Gabronski, she might have found some way to prevent this latest kidnapping. That was a suggestion, however, with which Jack disagreed heartily.

"It's too dangerous for you," he insisted.

Chang was torn. She cared about Catherine, cared about both of them. Jack was right, of course: it was dangerous. She understood how he felt. Probably, in his shoes, she would feel the same way.

The bottom line remained the same for her, however. She had some bad guys to catch, really bad guys. And so far, Catherine was her best shot—hell, her only shot—at catching them.

"But it doesn't have to be dangerous, does it?" she argued, wanting to convince herself as well as them. "Gabronski talked about wrapping yourself in the light, so they don't see you. It's that simple, isn't it? You hide yourself in the Heavenly glow, you find them, you go outside…you can go outside, can't you?"

"I don't know," Catherine said thoughtfully. "I wouldn't be able to turn a door knob, that requires some physicality and I haven't mastered that yet. But, since I have no body, I suppose I could just pass through a door. I've never tried."

"Well, then, that's what we need. If you can go outside, you can get me an address. A house number, a street name. Anything. That's all. Then you come home. You won't have to put yourself at any kind of risk."

"Won't she?" Jack said. His stomach churned at the very idea. "Gabronski also told us he thought every time she visited Paterson she was making him stronger, bringing him closer to finding her."

Catherine sighed. "Don't worry, darling, I will be careful. I'll do what Chang says, pop in just long enough to see them, and back out again. And I do think I can manage to remain unseen. Maybe if he doesn't see me, he won't know that I'm there."

Jack remained unconvinced, but he already knew the futility of arguing. He swallowed his frustration. "Can you just do this now at will?" he asked instead.

She shrugged. "I can try. Gabronski gave me that suggestion when he put me under earlier, didn't he? It's as good a time to find out as any."

She slipped off her shoes and stretched out on the sofa, plumping up a pillow for her head. Jack sat on the floor by the sofa. Chang got up to dim the lights. By the time she sat down again in her chair, Catherine's eyes were already closed, her breathing slow and deep.

* * * * * * *

"It's a thousand bucks," Paterson said, and when the man seated opposite him hesitated, he added quickly, "It's the best one yet, worth every penny, I promise you. This kid's cute as a bug. You can watch some of it if you want to."

"No, that's okay, you're cool." Danny O'Dell took out his wallet and peeled off ten one hundred dollar bills, laying them neatly on the filthy tabletop. The place was a pigpen, he thought. It even smelled like one. He wrinkled his fastidious nose. Well, what could he expect? When you lay down with dogs....

Paterson did not so much as glance at the money. "You hear that, Colley, we are coo-ol?" He made two syllables of it. "Cool, I like that. Have another line, bro." He indicated the cracked mirror on the tabletop with its mound of cocaine. "Colley, get our friend a beer."

"Thanks, but I have to go." O'Dell slipped the DVD into an inside pocket of his jacket and jiggled his keys as if to leave, but he lingered for a moment.

"Do you...?" he started to ask, and paused hesitantly, before he screwed up his courage to ask the question that had puzzled him for some time. "Do you guys ever feel bad? You know, guilty about any of this?"

Paterson's look was at once amused and darkened underneath like clouds before a storm. "Guilty?" he echoed. "What are you talking about, guilty? You some kind of puritan, are you, thinks sex is evil? I notice you're quick enough to run here when I tell you I've got a new movie for you. Are *you* feeling guilty?"

The actor showed a trace of embarrassment. "No, you're probably right," he said. He looked away from Paterson's ferocious glower.

"Course I am. Say, you want to try some for yourself? The real stuff, I mean, not just movies of it. We can set that up for you, too, you know."

O'Dell swallowed. He didn't really like talking about this sort of thing. Watching it, yes, imagining it—but until Paterson, he had never actually confessed his special interests to anyone. How had Paterson wormed it out of him, anyway? He didn't actually remember. They had been doing drugs, drinking—somehow, they ended up watching a movie, one of the special ones. Paterson had reeled him in like a fish on a line.

"How about I fix you up with the next one?" Paterson said, so offhanded, he might have been discussing a deal on a used car. "Cost you, say, five thousand."

For a moment O'Dell actually considered the offer. The money didn't deter him. He could afford that. It was the idea that frightened him, though. It even sickened him a little when, as now, he considered it.

He knew himself well enough, though, to know that he would feel no such shame when he arrived home and immediately put the new DVD into his player, locked his bedroom door, and watched it through to its end. Then, he would be filled with fantasies of the very thing Paterson was offering to arrange for him, and would berate himself as a fool for not taking up the offer.

Now, though, with these two watching like a pair of vipers getting ready to strike, he hadn't the courage to say yes. "I'd better not," he said with a roll of his eyes that would have been entirely familiar to his television audience. "Too risky. What if I was recognized?"

"We can put a mask on you. I don't guess anyone would recognize your pecker, would they. That's not famous, is it?"

Paterson laughed again, but suddenly his eyes narrowed and he shot a look around the room as if someone had entered it, peering into every corner.

""What is it, Trash?" Colley glanced around too, puzzled and concerned at the same time.

Paterson's sudden look of alarm spooked O'Dell. "Did you hear something?" he asked, genuinely frightened. Just being found here, with the drugs and the movies, would ruin his career. Nobody was going to sponsor a children's television show hosted by an actor arrested for drugs and kiddie porn.

I must be crazy, coming here, he thought. In the future, he would make arrangements to meet somewhere. Or maybe there oughtn't to be a future. He had half a dozen movies, surely he didn't need more. What more was there to see?

Except—a new face, a different body. A new fantasy. That was what it was, yes. He lived in a world of fantasies, they were his stock in trade, that was what excited him, not the reality. He would never really do what Paterson suggested. That was sick. He only wanted to watch, not even in the flesh, but at a remove, on his television screen. That was the difference between him and them.

Paterson shook his head and looked calmer, but there was an underlying anxiety that didn't quite leave his eyes. "Nah. I just like keeping an ear tuned, is all."

"I'd better go." This time O'Dell did get up, a little too quickly. He patted the pocket with the DVD in it, slipped his hat on his head and the dark glasses over his eyes. "I'll let myself out."

When the door had closed behind him, Paterson strode quickly across to lock it "I'll let myself out," he mimicked in a falsetto voice. "Pansy."

Colley took a long sip of his beer. "You know, Trash," he said speaking slowly, "There was one of those kids at least didn't have any fun."

Paterson wheeled on him. "What are you talking about? You bringing that up again?" He grabbed an ashtray off a table and flung it at Colley, ashes and cigarette butts leaving a trail across the dirty carpet. The glass ashtray caught Colley on the shoulder.

"Ouch, damn it, Trash, that hurt."

"Don't you be throwing that business up to me," Paterson railed at him, "You know damn well it wasn't my fault what happened."

Colley wilted in the face of his harangue. "You're right, Trash." He rubbed his bruised arm meekly.

"Listen, you don't like what we're doing, you just take your butt out that door, you go on and quit right this minute. Maybe prissy little TV host will give you a job."

"I didn't say I wanted to quit, Trash." Colley's voice had become a whine.

"Cause there's plenty of guys would like to be getting what you're getting and get paid for it too," Paterson said, pacing back and forth in long, quick strides.

"Shit, I know that, I wasn't complaining."

"Well, don't you be, and don't you be talking about her, it wasn't my fault. Damn, that makes me sore."

"I'm sorry, Trash, I didn't mean nothing, I was just running my mouth, you know what I'm like. I'm not as smart as you."

"You got that right," Paterson said more calmly, mollified. "And don't you forget it either."

Colley clamped his lips tightly together and turned on the TV news. Paterson was about to tell him to turn the damned thing off when he remembered something: a man on the television screen, not this man, another one, working his yap about something: the Mid East maybe, blah, blah, blah.

TV. Shit, that was it. That was where he had seen the bitch's boyfriend, the man he had seen in the sack with her. He was some kind of news reporter.

He sat down in a chair in front of the screen, staring at it, hardly even noticing what he saw. He knew who she was, too.

Catherine Desmond. Why hadn't he tumbled onto it sooner? And she had been here, just minutes ago. Maybe not in the flesh, but her ghost, her something.

He was sure of it.

* * * * * * *

Going through the door had been as easy as pie after all, the wood no more substantial to her than a wisp of a cloud. Outside, Catherine looked back at the house she had just left, a fake New England cottage that years ago had probably been charming. Once white paint was now dingy and peeling, dark green shutters hung askew. A curdle of shrubs, overgrown and badly in need of a trim, lined the walk and a bamboo fence, eight feet high, blocked the view from the street.

A rusty van and an Oldsmobile of questionable vintage sat in the drive, both license plates splattered with mud so that all but one or two of the numbers were illegible.

Chang needed an address. The house numbers too had been disguised, but the paint that had been daubed over them had not quite covered them. Three seventeen, she thought, or maybe fourteen. All she needed, then, was a street name.

Moving along the drive was oddly like walking, she could almost feel her steps making contact with the cement, though she knew that wasn't possible. Or was she gaining physicality?

No sidewalks here, only a narrow strip of weedy grass. A rusty mailbox tilted starboard on a bare wooden post. She reached for the mailbox door, thinking there might be letters inside, but her hand went right through the metal latch. So much for physicality.

She heard the familiar growl of a car's engine and the whine of tires going fast on pavement. The headlights of a car shot past an intersection maybe fifty yards away.

Of course, even in the country, even where people made it clear they wanted to be left alone, streets and roads were marked, weren't they? She moved in that direction, found it easy to hurry; found, in fact, that she could move as fast as she wished, virtually flying.

Yes, there was a street sign: Morning View Road. And the cross street...she came closer to the sign, and found the scene before her fading rapidly, growing paler. She paused, took a step back. Her sight grew slightly clearer.

She thought about that for a moment. It was Paterson to whom she traveled, to whom she was linked, and apparently, she could only travel so far away from him before the link began to weaken.

She tried again to get close enough to read the next sign. She made out a letter A. Au. Or was it Av? Yes, Av, Avalon, she was sure of it, but when she moved closer still, wanting to confirm, it faded into oblivion, and she felt the solidity of her sofa beneath her. She was back in her apartment, Jack leaning over her anxiously, Chang watching from her chair.

"Are you all right?" Jack asked.

"Yes," she said after a moment of mental inventory. "Yes, I'm fine." She even managed a smile. "And they didn't see me, I'm sure," she added. It had been a relief to find that she could indeed conceal herself from Paterson. She need not be so frightened of him, then, surely. "And, I saw our 'third person' at last. Danny O'Dell, he was there with them."

"The children's show, the little twirpy guy with the checked suits?" Chang said. "And you're saying he's actually Danny the Diddler? Crap, that is disgusting, isn't it? Are you sure he was into this kiddie stuff with them? There could be all kinds of reasons why he was there. Maybe he sells Tupperware on the side?"

"No, he was buying a movie," Catherine said. "Paterson talked about the kid on it, a little boy, and O'Dell paid him a thousand dollars."

Chang whistled. "A thousand bucks. For sure that was no travel video. Jeez, that's a great lead. I can have this O'Dell creep put under surveillance. If he's actively into this filth, we'll get him."

"There's more, too," Catherine added triumphantly, "I heard Paterson call his friend—the one I called The Bear—he called him Collie. Like the dog."

Chang made a note. "If he's got any kind of record, we can find him in the computer. What about an address? Did you get that?"

"Three seventeen, or it might have been three fourteen, Morning View Road, cross street, Avalon, I think. It's the first house down

Morning View, maybe a quarter of a mile. And, it's out in the country, very rural, a large open field across the way, no houses close around that I could see."

"That should do it," Chang said. but there was an odd hesitation in her manner.

Jack sensed it. "That's enough for a warrant, surely, isn't it?" he asked.

Chang was thinking that maybe she was going too fast, asking for a warrant, with nothing more to support it than Catherine's astral visit. She was still having a hard time getting her teeth into this ghost business. And King wanted something concrete, not just visions.

On the other hand, they couldn't take a chance on Paterson slipping out of their hands, could they?

"I'll see my boss tomorrow," she said aloud. "And ask for the warrant."

CHAPTER EIGHTEEN

Jack found himself staring at the two images of Trash Can Paterson on his computer screen, trying to read the expression in the eyes of what were, after all, only an artist's renderings: the original and the revised one that Chang had sent them.

He looked from the computer to the photo of Catherine on his desk. She smiled fondly at him from within its silver frame. It had been taken at the marina one evening, her hair blowing in the wind. You could just glimpse, if you knew to look for it, of the scar at her temple.

It was almost as if Paterson had branded her with that bullet, he thought, marked her as his own. The two of them were linked, maybe, as Catherine believed, on some supernatural level. Even if it were only in her mind, though, the result was the same, wasn't it?

He thought, not for the first time, that what he was fighting was not Paterson, but something within Catherine herself, something more than just the need to avenge her daughter. The two of them, she and Paterson, were on a collision course, racing toward one another with an equal and frightening determination.

When the collision finally came, what then?

Or would it end, as Catherine seemed to think, with Paterson's arrest? Today, assuming Chang got her warrant.

He stood and got his jacket and left the office for a scheduled meeting with the big brass. Not until he was in the elevator and ascending swiftly did he remember that he had left the sketches of Paterson on the computer screen. He considered going back and closing the file—but, really, even if someone saw them, what harm could it do? They were just drawings of a man whom certainly no one here at the studio could know.

* * * * * * *

Kitty came out of her own office, only half reading the letter from her sister Doris back in Cleveland. It didn't require careful perusal. She could have rattled it off almost by rote. The usual insincere expressions of affection, sugar coating for the unsavory taste of the letter's real message: send money. Nothing quite that blunt, of course. It was always about their father's deteriorating condition, the medical expense, the pills, the trips to and from the doctors.

That little man with his always dirty fingernails ("he's a gardener, of course his hands are dirty," her mother used to argue) and his poker-stiff back, spent his hours now huddled in a leather wing chair in their front room, carefully placed so that he could see out the front window, though there was no evidence that he was at all conscious of what lay beyond the glass.

Yet, even in the convalescence of his Alzheimer's, even unable to remember his name or know clearly where he was, Roger Fane still managed to tyrannize his remaining daughter. Just as he'd always done, just as he used to tyrannize his wife, just as he tyrannized Kitty herself as a girl, with his muted but nonetheless potent sadism. He had been their jailer, the three of them his prisoners. Her mother escaped from that unhappy life by dying. At her funeral, looking down into her mother's coffin, it seemed to Kitty that her mother wore a faint smile of satisfaction, of relief.

Thank God she had managed to escape, too, and not by that means. There had been a man. Looking back, she supposed he hadn't been the nicest of men, but he was excited enough by her beauty, and eager enough to despoil her fifteen year old innocence, that he was agreeable, if a trifle reluctantly, to meet the demands she'd made: not marriage, she hadn't cared for that prospect either, not with him, but she wanted an apartment of her own, money, new clothes. The means to remake herself.

She took all that he would give, and gave as little as possible in return, and wasted no time trading in her reluctant lover for a newer, and more agreeable model—and by choosing carefully from among what quickly proved to be a long list of candidates, had carefully and steadily improved her place in the world.

The only difficulty was when Roger Fane tracked her down and tried to use her age to make her return home. She countered by using the trump card he had dealt her the first time he crept down the hallway at night to her bedroom. In the end, he saw the wisdom of acquiescing in her freedom.

Of course, he had never stopped resenting her, and she had no doubt that her escape had made things all the more difficult for

Doris, whose bed had surely replaced hers and who was stuck in the bargain with caring for him now, changing his soiled clothes, feeding him with a spoon—and wishing him dead, Kitty had no doubt.

Well, he was to her, at any rate. She had tried many times over the years, for her own sake, not for his, to think of something good about him, something she could say in his favor. The best she had ever been able to manage was: he grew lovely roses.

She stuffed the letter back into its envelope. She would send money. She always did. It was a small enough price to pay to assuage any guilt she felt at leaving Doris stuck with the burden she herself had so happily chucked.

She was on her way to the cafeteria, but she suddenly found the thought of a cup of coffee alone less than appealing—she had no friends among the women on the staff, and the men would be reluctant to be seen socializing with her. Not that she minded; she had no interest in worker bees. She had learned her lesson early—aim for the ones at the top of the heap. They were the ones who could do her the most good.

Jack McKenzie popped into her mind. If he was not quite at the top of the heap, he gave every indication that he one day would be. Of course, there was his lady friend, but in her experience, lady friends came and went, and they did not often mean a man wasn't amenable to the right approach from the right woman. A quiet lunch a deux couldn't hurt, surely, maybe at that little bar cum restaurant on Vermont, where no one from the studio would be likely to see them and fuel studio gossip?

Thinking that it couldn't hurt to ask, she detoured in the direction of Jack's office. His secretary was on the phone. Kitty finger-waved at her as she went by. The secretary started to say something, but the other line flashed just then, and she answered that as Kitty disappeared through the door.

She was disappointed that he was not there, was about to turn around and leave, but some instinct made her change her mind. She was a newsperson, after all, and curiosity was a newsperson's greatest asset. And, if she were to make any progress with Jack, she needed all the ammunition she could gather. So long as she was here and, for the moment, at least, unhindered, why not see what there was to see.

Which was, unfortunately, not much. The top of his desk was as clean as a whistle, no papers, no scribbled notes, no clues as to what might have been on his mind before he left—only a pen set in its marble holder, and the picture of his lady friend, Catherine. She picked that up and looked at it. Not terribly pretty, she thought, hardly the sort she would have expected to catch Jack McKenzie's fancy.

She put the picture back and as she did so, jostled the mouse to his computer, and the dead gray screen came to life. She had intended to take a quick peek inside the desk drawers, but she found herself instead staring at the computer screen, at drawings of two men.

No, she corrected herself quickly, one man, in two different renderings. She looked from one to the other. One of the pictures looked familiar, teasing her memory. She had seen it before—but when, where?

She glanced around the room, as if she might find the answer somewhere nearby, and her eyes fell on the silver framed photo on the desk.

Catherine. Catherine Desmond. The name popped into her head, and with it came the memory of the newspaper brouhaha months ago, the child kidnapped, found murdered, and the drawings of the perpetrators aired for hopeful identification.

The drawing on the computer screen, the one on the left, was one of those—and the other was clearly a redrawing of the same face. Yes, the broken nose, fixed. The mole removed. The hair cut short, and darkened.

He'd changed his appearance, and this was what he looked like now. Only, she had not seen this picture publicized. Jack had it, on his computer. Which meant Catherine Desmond almost certainly did too, and the police, the F.B.I.

And nobody else. It would seem that so far the updated picture had not been released to the press. It came to her in a flash that what she was looking at was not just a pair of drawings. She realized with a sense of exultation that she was looking at a news scoop. Maybe, even, a promotion from weather-person to reporter, if she played her cards right. And she had the top dealer in that game in her pocket, so to speak—Thaddeus Tremayne.

She typed her e-mail address into Jack's computer, selected the drawings, and hit the send button. Safer to print them out in the privacy of her own office—or Tremayne's.

Jack's secretary, her expression peevish, was just on her way to Jack's door when Kitty came out. "You might have told me he wasn't there," Kitty said as she went past her.

* * * * * * *

It was a win-some lose-some sort of case, as Chang saw it. The King agreed to the search warrant for the Morning View house, not without some reluctance.

"She saw this in a dream, right?" he asked and gave her a cautious look. "You know, don't you, if this turns out to be a fiasco, we're going to have a lot of egg on our faces."

"In an astral projection, yes," Chang said, and added, "I believe her, sir."

"Well, let's go with it," he said with a resigned sigh. "We should have the warrant this afternoon, this evening at the latest. Assemble a team. Take all the guys you want. We don't want anybody getting away over a back fence. You'll have to include the L.A.P.D., this Conners, obviously. And the locals. It's county, right? Sheriff's deputies, then."

For a moment she came close to urging him to move the warrant along, try to get it right away. Already time had passed since Catherine paid them her astral visit during the night. If Paterson had any inkling…but she dismissed her impatience as needless stewing. Paterson had no clue. Catherine was convinced of that. There was no reason to worry about his slipping out on them. She let that slide.

"What about this Danny O'Dell?" she asked instead. "What about a warrant to search his place. Desmond says she saw him with Paterson."

"Another of Mrs. Desmond's visions?" He snorted. "Could be imagination. Could be indigestion. Hell, if Desmond has a mean period we could be staking out Mrs. Butterworth. The guy's a TV star. My kids watch him. I don't want them kicking my butt because I made a false bust on their idol. And all we've got to charge him with is this dream thing of Desmond's. That's about as substantial as a fart in a whirlwind."

"She saw him buy a movie."

"She says. Could be *The Sound of Music*."

"A thousand bucks? That's porn for sure. Special porn."

"Hell, then it could be a bunch of nuns balling the pope. We need the goods. You want a warrant, get me the goods. I want you on him like flies on dog poop. If he's diddling the kiddies on the sly, I want to know. I want to know what he eats, when he sleeps and whether he hangs to the left or the right. For the moment, what we've got on him is squat. Squat doesn't buy warrants. Especially psychic squat."

"And the picture? The reworked drawing?"

"Don't need it now, and it would only freak Paterson if he saw his face on television. Anyway, by the time we got it out there, we'll already have him, won't we?"

* * * * * * *

Paterson's pictures hit the noon news. Chang was wolfing down a sandwich at a favorite bar when she saw it, and nearly choked. Mere seconds later, her cell phone rang. She needed no special intuition to tell her it was the King.

"Damn and hell fire," The King swore when she entered his office less than twenty minutes later. "How did this happen?"

"Reporters," was all Chang could say. "Someone got nosey. I'll look around, but it may be hard to pin down. Desmond let something slip, maybe, or the boyfriend."

"So, what's your read on this?"

"It might spook him," Chang said dejectedly. "He could run."

He thought about that. "But, would he? You get your picture on the TV, would you run, or hide? This place of his, you said it was totally isolated? No neighbors anywhere close?"

"Yes," Chang agreed reluctantly.

He lifted an eyebrow. "Well, there's no way he could know we've tumbled to his hiding place, right? Desmond was sure they didn't see her, you said."

"Yes, she was sure, but…."

"But?"

And what was bothering her, anyway, she asked herself? Paterson hadn't known she was there. Catherine had been sure of that. That was the point, really, the key to how Paterson would react. The King was right. So long as he thought his lair was safe, Paterson was far more likely to lay low. If only she didn't have these doubts—if only she believed wholeheartedly in Catherine's astral projections….but this was no time to share those doubts with The King, not after she had persuaded him to go ahead with a warrant. For sure he'd tear her a new one now if she said she wasn't sure…

"No, he doesn't know we know where he is."

"Then, he thinks he's safe there. He'll go to ground. He's got this partner, the Collie, to run errands. All he's got to do is sit tight till things die down. He'd be a fool to make a run for it, which only ups the chances of his being seen, and he doesn't strike me as a fool. What's your time on the bust?"

"We thought we'd go in late tonight," Chang said. "The idea was to catch them in bed asleep."

"Move it up. How soon can you put it together?"

Chang thought for a moment. She could most likely get a team together in an hour, two at the most, but she wanted this to go down perfectly. Rushing things was an invitation to mistakes. "Five thirty?" she said, making a question of it.

He nodded. "Do it. And let's hope he doesn't watch a lot of television."

* * * * * * *

It took them less than an hour to strip the place. "Get everything in the van," Paterson ordered the minute he saw his face on the television screen. "And make it quick. We got to get out of here."

"Probably nobody around here even saw you," Colley said, already loading up his arms with their possessions. "You almost never go out in the daytime, and when you do you're in the van or that Olds you stole. And I go to the store for us. Anyways, there ain't nobody nearer to us than half a mile or more. Who'd see you? And they's no way anybody would find this place unless somebody did spot you going. Hell, we're in the middle of nowhere."

"Someone might've seen me, and I ain't waiting around here to find out. Besides, she knows where I am. I'd bet money on it. She was here, I knew it, damned bitch. I can just about smell her. Cops could be on their way here this minute. Put all them DVDs in a box, we ain't leaving them behind, not after what we did to make them."

He snatched up the phone and dialed a number. Lit a cigarette while he waited. The voice had barely answered before he said, "I need money, fast."

There was a pause. The voice said, plaintively, "I don't have it, Paterson. I told you, I'm broke as it is. I'll have money in a month or so maybe, but…."

"I can't wait a month or so. I need five grand now. The cops are hot on my tail, and if I get caught, you'll go down with me. You get the money and I'll call you and tell you where to meet me."

He hung up and immediately dialed another number. This time he said, "I need to talk to O'Dell. Tell him it's his friend Mike. Tell him it's important."

He fidgeted while he waited. That damn pansy had better not try to put him off. He was in no mood.

"You aren't supposed to call here," O'Dell said in a peeved voice.

"Yeah, well your cell phone was turned off or something. Listen, I need some money, five, six thousand, at least. And that place of yours up in the mountains, I got to borrow it for a while."

"That's not a good idea. A friend of mine was going to use it next weekend. Besides...."

"I don't give a rat's ass about any besides, nor any friend of yours either, you can put them off somehow. I'm telling you, I need it, I got to save my ass, and yours too, you dumb punk, this is serious. Meet me in the Laurel Plaza parking lot at eight, bring me the cash, all you can get your hands on, and the keys. And a map to the cabin in case I get lost trying to find it."

He hung up before O'Dell could argue any further. That faggot would do what he was told. He'd be too scared not to. You started fooling around with kid stuff, you couldn't afford to take any chances.

"You got that shit packed up yet?" he demanded, whirling about. "Damn it, Colley, get a move on." He ground his cigarette out in a dirty saucer.

The place had been rented in another name, rent paid in cash to a man who also got certain other benefits from the deal and wasn't likely to give the cops any help. Paterson made sure of that with another phone call just before they left, to say they were leaving and to deliver a veiled warning, just in case.

They abandoned his stolen car several miles away, carefully cleaned of any fingerprints.

"You cleaned the prints off everything at the house?" Paterson asked for the fourth time.

"Course I did," Colley said. A thought flashed through his mind: had he remembered the empty beer bottles on the kitchen counter? They had been in such a hurry. He thought he had. He squinted, trying to remember. He'd done the bedroom, he was sure of that, and the living room, and he remembered wiping off the stove and refrigerator.

I must have done the bottles, he told himself. Anyway, far better not to mention his uncertainty to Paterson, not the mood he was in.

They rocketed onto the 14 Freeway at high speed, the van careening briefly. Colley drove. Paterson was thinking about Catherine Desmond, about the way she seemed to pop in wherever he was.

How the hell does she do that, he wondered? He closed his eyes, seeing her in his mind....

* * * * * * *

They were at Catherine's apartment. Jack was kneeling, just laying a fire in the fireplace. Catherine had taken a platter from the cupboard, meaning to put the take-out lo mein on it. The chardonnay was poured. As much as possible, they were trying to make this an ordinary evening together, trying not to think, let alone talk, about what was about to happen out in Canyon Country. They both of them assiduously avoided looking at the clock on the wall.

And, out of nowhere, Paterson was there, standing just in front of her, grinning wickedly.

"Jesus," Jack swore, rocking back on his heels. Catherine dropped the platter, scarcely aware of the crash, the broken crockery that scattered at her feet.

"You bastard," Jack said. He grabbed up a log and leaped to his feet, swinging it at Paterson—and it went right through him.

He's only a projection, Catherine thought. *He's no more physical than I am when I project. I have only to break his concentration....*

She lunged at him, hands up as if to ward off a blow, and as quickly, as easily as that, he was gone—but she had forgotten to avoid his eyes, they locked on hers even as she moved, and it was like a bullet exploding in her head all over again, she cried aloud in pain, and fell in a heap to the floor.

* * * * * * *

Paterson and Collie were gone. "Crapola," Chang swore aloud. Even without a search, she could see they had fled. Drawers were yanked out and upended, contents scattered on the floor, empty closets stood open, shelves were stripped bare: all the evidence of a hasty flight.

Somehow, Paterson had known. Spooked by the likeness on TV? Picked it up from Desmond's wavelengths? Maybe there was something to this psychic business. She looked around for anything that might salvage the day.

"They didn't waste much energy on decorating," Conners said in a despondent voice.

"Or cleaning." The place smelled of sweat and urine and rotting food. A ratty sofa, a couple of chairs, linoleum floors with most of the pattern worn off. A cheap blonde with silicone boobs leered at them from a wall calendar, the sole concession to art. The bedroom was littered with dirty clothes, the twisted sheets on the bed filthy with stains she didn't want to contemplate. Dishes in the kitchen sink, a trio of empty Rolling Rock bottles on the counter. Maybe something there? A faint wisp of smoke drifted from a cigarette in a saucer.

"Check those bottles. Check everything for fingerprints," Chang said. "And get samples of anything that looks like blood or semen. Dirty Kleenex, too, toilet paper. Hairs. Bag it all. They might have left us a souvenir. Get that cigarette, too. And the sheets."

While they others went through the motions of searching the house, she thought about Paterson. The obvious thing would be for him to get out of Los Angeles as quick and as far as he could go, but criminals sometimes had their own brand of logic. The really logical thing would have been for him to stay where he was, in Canyon Country, and he hadn't done that, either.

The windows behind her suddenly lit up with a flash of lightning—rare in the California winter, and there hadn't been any hint a moment earlier of an impending storm. It made her think of Catherine. If Paterson was still in the city, it was because he was looking for her.

Just at the moment, her cell phone rang. She answered, heard Jack's voice, frantic with worry. She listened to what he had to say, and said, simply, "Pack. You're moving."

* * * * * * *

Chang's safe house was a little cottage on a side street in Hollywood, inconspicuous and obviously chosen with safety in mind. There were grates over the windows and the front door had been wired with motion sensors that would provide early notice of any approach.

Chang went in first, pulling heavy draperies closed before she turned on the light, and gave the four rooms—living room, kitchen, bedroom, bath—a quick but sharp once over. Satisfied, she motioned them in.

The interior was Spartan but adequate: in the living room, a television with rabbit ears, a faded green corduroy sofa and a matching chair; an antiquated gas stove in the kitchen, and a dripping faucet that had left a permanent rust stain in the sink; but everything was clean and the bed in the bedroom was surprisingly comfortable when Jack tested it.

"I've slept in worse," he said.

"Home sweet home," Catherine said wryly.

"I'll sleep outside for the night," Chang said, "In the Bronco. Just to be sure."

"Wouldn't you be more comfortable on the sofa?" Catherine asked.

Chang gave the sofa a dubious look. "On that thing? Never fear, I've slept in the Bronco plenty. Anyway, I don't want to wait till someone's standing by the sofa with a gun at my head before I know they're coming. Always get them before they get inside if you can."

They had stopped on the way to pick up a pizza and some cokes. They ate in a dispirited silence, watching the evening news with Paterson's picture now on every channel, and the story of the unsuccessful raid on the house in Canyon Country.

The pizza tasted like cardboard. Jack managed only a few bites before it stuck in his throat. Catherine had no more appetite than he did, but Chang ate half, looked at what was left and mimed a question at the other two.

"Be my guest," Catherine said and Jack shrugged. Chang finished the pizza, drained the last of the Coke from her glass, and left them getting ready for bed. She was careful to be sure the door locked securely behind her. Like that was going to do any good, she thought, people passing through walls the way they did. She had never had to deal with anything like this before.

She settled into the Bronco, put her coat over her for a blanket. The rain had stopped and a pale moon cast a watery light. She slid the seat back as far as it would go, tried to find a comfortable position, gave up finally and sat upright, wishing she had a beer.

She had goofed. She had let Paterson and Colley get away. She should have known his picture on TV would send him running.

But had it? King was right: the smart thing would have been for him to stay put where he was. He couldn't know they had found his hideout. Running around in public with your face plastered all over TV wasn't the sensible thing to do. And she had a notion that this guy was smart enough all right, animal cunning at least. Protective cunning.

It hadn't looked like they had been gone from Morning View more than a little while. One of the beer bottles had still been on the cool side. That cigarette in the ashtray wasn't altogether out either, had been smoldering for a bit. If she had gotten there just a little faster. Why hadn't she pushed King for the warrant, moved the bust up even an hour or two?

She didn't like the answer that came to her.

* * * * * * *

Mommy, Mommy, help me.... Catherine woke in terror, sweat drenched, heart pounding. For a moment she couldn't think where she was. It came back to her then: Chang's safe house. Beside her, Jack snored softly.

Even awake, the nightmare haunted her. She saw the truck, Becky struggling, Paterson grabbing the gun.

Where was he now? She had to know. She slipped quietly from the bed and went to the living room. Despite the risk she knew she was taking, she sat on the sofa, closed her eyes, and willed herself into space.

At first she thought she had failed to find him. Then she saw him a short distance away—or, barely saw him, the image was far fainter than anything she had seen before, fading in and out like a bad phone connection. A dark shadowy location, no city lights, no neon, only the faintest moonlight.

She looked around, tried to find some physical clues, but the scene faded altogether and she was back in the living room of the little cottage, Chang watching her from the doorway.

"I saw the light go on," Chang said. "Just checking. You okay?"

"I tried to find him, but wherever he is, it's a long way from here. I saw a dirt street and a house; a shack, really. Not much more than that."

"Mexico, maybe Tijuana," Chang said. "Which makes sense. If you're on the lam, that's a good bet. You can always pay off the locals there, if you've got the bucks. What it tells me is that you're not in any immediate danger. It's a good two to three hours from here to the border. You can sleep without worrying."

She couldn't, though. Back in bed, she tossed and turned. Jack slept fitfully beside her but she could not stop thinking about Paterson. The gray light of dawn was tinting the blinds at the window before she finally did slip into a deep, dreamless sleep.

CHAPTER NINETEEN

It was weird, but Chang felt almost like she had been cheating on Conners. He was her partner. They had to be able to trust one another to work together. That was one of the basic laws of their business. In their line of work, your relationship with your partner was closer than your relationship with family, friends, husbands, lovers. Your life depended on it.

So far, though, she had told him nothing at all about the astral part of their case. However nutty it might sound, she owed him the truth, the whole story. Hiding information from your partner was bad karma…and dangerous to boot.

"I need to talk to you," she told him on the phone. "Someplace good and private."

There was a pause on the line. "I live on Hancock. I was just making a fresh pot of coffee."

She hesitated. In her mind, she had a vision of those cute little buns of his. The smart thing would be to keep things totally businesslike between them. The last thing she needed in her life was any complication, and the way he had made the suggestion sounded suspiciously to her like he was considering complications.

"What's the address?"

* * * * * * *

Jess Conners stood for a long moment looking at the phone, thinking about Chang. What did this mean, her coming by? He knew what he would like it to mean. That thought started a tingling in his groin.

"Down, boy," he said aloud. He did not think it would be a good idea to open the door for her with a boner on display.

He made coffee and while it was brewing he smoothed out the non-existent wrinkles on the coverlet of his bed. He took a shower, even though he had showered less than an hour earlier, brushed his teeth, flossed, ran a razor over his baby smooth face, smoothed the coverlet on the bed.

He slipped on a plain tee shirt and a pair of walking shorts. Quick to take off, he thought, and scolded himself. Best not think along those lines. Not till he saw where things were headed.

He poured himself some coffee, considered a shelf of compact discs, loaded Frank Sinatra into the player, turning the volume down to a mellow level. He smoothed the coverlet on the bed and paused to look at the picture of his father on the wall.

"Hey, Pop, wish me luck," he said aloud.

He idolized his father. His father had been a cop. That was what had ultimately decided him on a career in law enforcement, but the decision hadn't been an easy one. What he had wanted, really, was to be a singer, like Sinatra or Tony Bennet. About as opposite to law enforcement as you could get.

He'd talked about it with his parents. They were the kind of parents it was easy to talk to. His dad said little; just nodded and said, "Whatever you want to do is fine with me," but his disappointment showed through his accepting demeanor.

"That kind of singing is out of fashion," his mother pointed out to him. "The kind you like to do. I doubt if Frankie could make it today. It's all rock and roll." She did not mention his father's disappointment, either, but her concern showed through as well.

She was right, of course. Besides, he didn't actually think he had the kind of talent that was needed to make it as a singer. In the end, he'd done what they both hoped he would do. Mostly, he wasn't sorry. He kept it a secret that he sometimes dropped in at a Karaoke bar out in the valley, where he was unlikely to run into anyone from the station, and savored the applause he invariably got. Otherwise, he sang for himself, in the shower, around the apartment. He had an idea he'd like to sing for Roby Chang but, unlike in the movies, you couldn't just burst into song without looking like a dork.

He took a sip of his coffee, changed his mind and poured it into the sink, rinsed the cup carefully and placed in on the dish rack, and took a Corona from the refrigerator instead.

The doorbell rang. He took a long swallow of cold beer, ran a quick hand over the coverlet, and reached down inside his shorts to tug everything over to the right side, which someone had told him made a better showing. On an impulse, he stripped off the tee, hid it under a cushion on the sofa, and went to answer the door.

* * * * * * *

His apartment turned out to be a pleasant little studio, neat as a pin. Either he was a good housekeeper, or he had done one hell of a job putting it together in the thirty minutes since her call. Or, it came to her mind unbidden, he had someone who cleaned for him. Or someones. Like, girlfriends.

Well, gee, Chang, she chided herself, like this guy wouldn't have women crawling all over him, especially if they saw him like this, with his shirt off, and why did he answer the door without a shirt, if it wasn't to show off some great pecs and washboard abs? Fortunately, she was not a crawler. Fortunate for her. Unfortunate for him.

"Nice," she said, glancing around. The bed was even made. She never made her bed. What was the point? As soon as you crawled under the covers it was messed up again, wasn't it?

More surprising than the neatness of the apartment, which if she had thought about it, she would probably have expected, were the furnishings. The work out equipment in the far corner was no surprise. You could see he was a work out kind of guy.

Most everything else, though, was Scandinavian modern, spare, light colored wood, stylish. One wall was taken up with shelves of books, many of them looking old, and more than a few leather bound. A reader, then, but that wasn't much of a surprise either.

What to make, though, of the odd curios that occupied almost every available space? She wouldn't have pegged him for the sort to need the illusion of permanence that such relics provided. A child's toy horn, with a red bulb on one end, the kind you made honking noises with; a pair of enormous shoes dominated another table, too big, surely, even for his ample feet; a parasol, opened and attached to one wall. Playbills, too far away for her to read. It was one thing to find a spinster with a collection of china birds, but she couldn't see Conners in this odd assortment of miscellany.

And, Jesus, who was that singing, Perry Como? She felt like she had stepped through the television screen, right into the middle of *Leave It to Beaver.* Any minute now, June would spin out of the kitchen—or was that Loretta Young?

She slipped off her jacket, shed the shoulder holster too and laid them all across the single chair. "You clean for yourself?" she asked. "My place is always a dump. Sanitation people threaten to close me down all the time."

"I train my wenches," he said with a self-deprecating grin. "They take turns coming in to clean for me."

"Hah. Sure it isn't the guy by the pool with the pink toenails? He gave me a dirty look when he saw where I was headed."

"Dickie? He gives all females dirty looks. He bakes cookies for me though. Chocolate chip. Really good. Want coffee?"

He held a half-finished Corona in his hand. For courage? "I'll have one of those," she said.

He got her a beer, mimed a wedge of lime. She nodded and he brought the beer with the lime stuck in the neck. It was cold and wet, and she took a quick swig. For courage.

The wall opposite the bookshelves was lined with framed photographs. She paused in front of the largest, a picture of a man in clown costume: baggy pants, bright red suspenders, fright wig, but without the makeup. That would explain the honking horn, and the oversized shoes, and probably the parasol as well. She leaned closer. The face grinning at the camera looked familiar.

"That's my dad," Conners said, standing behind her, close enough that she fancied she could feel the heat from his body. "He's a clown. Well, retired cop, really, but he does kid's parties, store openings, stuff like that. Weird, huh, a clown for a dad?"

"You call that weird? I've got an Aunt Tessa who thinks she's a Manchu princess. Whiteface, foot-long fingernails, the works. Only time I could bring any kids home from school was Halloween."

He grinned. "Is she? A Manchu princess, I mean."

"She was born in Sacramento, same as my dad." She took another swig of the Corona, wondered if he would think she was an alky if she asked for a shot of Jack with it and decided against it. She took the plunge: "Have you ever heard of astral projection?" she asked.

"Out of body, you mean. Sure."

"You up on this stuff?" She was surprised. She had expected to have to sell him on the story.

"Not really. A little, I guess. My dad's a clown, you already know that. Mom reads the tarot cards. My sister does feng shui and horoscopes. You're a Scorpio, right?" She gave him a withering look. He shrugged. "Just your average new-agers, is what I'm saying. Hey, this is Los Angeles."

Chang sighed. "Maybe I should have become a dog groomer."

"Oh, yeah, my sister does horoscopes for dogs, too."

"Cut the shit," she snapped. "I've got serious stuff to talk about here."

"Okay, so talk. Have a seat." He went to the sofa and dropped into it. In the middle. If she sat on the sofa she would have to sit practically on top of him. The only other seating was the chair over which she had tossed her jacket. She'd look like an ass, she thought, moving it so she could sit there. That left the neatly made bed. No way was she going anywhere near that.

She sat beside him on the sofa, as far away as she could get, at the end, and set her beer on the table next to it. Thought better, picked it up and wiped a ring of moisture off the wood with her sleeve, set the bottle instead atop a *TV Guide*. Stalling, she acknowledged with an interior grimace.

"What's up?" he asked.

"You remember when Catherine Desmond was shot? When her kid was snatched? She says...well, she says she died. Out of body, like you call it."

"The tunnel, the white light, that sort of thing?"

"Exactly." She sighed. "You *are* up on this. Maybe it will be easier for you to get a handle on. It kind of blew me away. So, yeah, anyway, when she got back from, well, from wherever she was, that tunnel, she started hopping to and fro. She says she travels. In space, I mean." She gave him a doubtful look.

"Well, sure," he said, "Doesn't everybody."

She let that pass. "Mostly, where she traveled was to Paterson. Wherever he was at the moment. Seems like she somehow ended up linked together with him. She's convinced she was sent back to nail his ass."

"And that's how we ended up at Morning View Road," he said. "I kind of wondered. I mean, that anonymous sighting sounded kind of flimsy."

She was relieved to find him taking this so easily, had half expected him to think she was nuts. Though why she should care about his opinion she couldn't imagine. "Exactly."

"But, if she's tied to him on an astral level, why haven't we been able to catch up with him?"

The question hit a raw nerve. It had been bugging her since their failure on Morning View the day before. She jumped to her feet and began to pace, hitting her fist into her open palm.

"It's my fault, is why. I wasn't quick enough. From the beginning. I believed her, and at the same time I didn't. It was just too far out for me. While I was waiting to be convinced they got away from us."

"Come on, we were plenty fast getting there."

"Just not fast enough. Think about it. If I had gotten to that house an hour sooner, maybe even just a few minutes, we'd have had him. She did her part, she told me where he was. If I had just been quicker out of the gate."

"Hey, you're beating up on yourself unfairly." He stood and came to her. She stopped in her pacing, looking into his face. "You can second guess anything," he said. "Maybe we'd have gotten him an hour earlier, maybe not. The reality is, he gave us the slip. It happens. We'll get him. I know we will. *You'll* get him. You're the best, everyone knows that."

"I dragged my butt."

"You didn't drag your butt." He paused, and gave her a sheepish look. "Believe me, I'd have noticed. I've had my eyes on your butt."

His smile was reassuring. And very sexy. His eyes positively smoldered with desire. In some corner of her mind, she warned herself that this couldn't go any further. She was Roby Chang. She didn't need any man, and she especially didn't need this man.

Her body called her a liar. He put his arms around her and brought his mouth down to hers. It was like an electric contact. She could feel the heat flame up between them. She made a funny squeaking sound in her throat. Her arms lifted around him of their own accord.

The kiss seemed to go on forever, their bodies grinding together, his hardness crushed against her belly, a potent promise of what was in store for her. After an eternity, he ended the kiss, kept his arms around her as he guided her to the bed against the far wall. They paused there, his fingers stroking her shoulders, her arms, her breasts. His lips went to her throat, her ears, her mouth again, and she felt fingers fumbling with the buttons of her blouse.

Oh, hell. She pushed his hand away, undid the buttons herself, stripped naked in mere seconds, aware of him undressing too—he was quicker, but, crap, he had less to take off. She refused to look. *Well, just a teensy glance.*

She squeezed her eyes shut and fell onto the bed, felt him drop beside her. He touched her thighs, and she reached for him and took hold of him. It was big, not enormous, just nice, rock hard, slick to the touch. It felt good. It felt wonderful. It had been a long time. Her blood simmered in her veins, reached the boiling point....

It was violent, it was frantic, and it was fast. Or it seemed to be, she couldn't really tell, time had stopped. She was overwhelmed, filled up in every sense with him. She ran her hands down his strain-ing back, felt his butt. Definitely prime beef.

"Oh," she gasped again. "Oh." He was driving her out of her mind, it had never been like this, she…she…she….

She shot to the moon, did a couple of orbits, and came crashing back down to the bed, gasping for air. After a few minutes he rolled off of her. They lay side by side, regaining their breath. He reached for her, tried to take her into another embrace.

She shoved his hand away, sat up violently. "Damn," she swore aloud. She jumped to her feet.

"What's wrong?" he asked, bewildered.

"What's wrong?" Chang snapped, struggling into bra and the men's boxer shorts she wore for panties. "Are you fucking crazy? This is wrong. The whole damn thing. I must have been out of my mind."

He got up too, still half hard, she was annoyed to see, and gave her a grin that only infuriated her further. "I thought it was pretty good. I thought it was great, actually." She snorted disdainfully. "Oh, come on," he said, "Don't try to pretend you didn't get off. That was a Mount Saint Helen's orgasm you had."

She reddened and stuffed her leg into trousers. "Oh, sure, and that makes it all right? Look, that was it, okay, let's just both of us forget this ever happened. I know *I* am going to forget it happened."

"Well, I'm not. For Christ's sake, you act like we just commit-ted some mortal sin. I'm a man. You're a woman. Boom, boom, boom. That's what men and women do together. It's just most of them don't have it as good as we just did. Honest. I know. I've done it before. A couple of times anyway. Not the same. Definitely not the same."

"Did you ever hear of 'don't get your bread where you get your meat'? How about, 'Don't shit where you eat'?" She strapped on her shoulder holster, slid the Glock into it. Thought momentarily of shooting him.

"My mother says the adage is the last refuge of the losing ar-gument."

"Great, I should have slept with your mother." He opened his mouth to say something. She stuck a finger in his face. "Don't say it. Don't even think it. And don't think I haven't heard it before, I know what the guys say about me. Any woman doesn't fall on her back with legs open has to be a dike, right?"

He grinned again, which did nothing to lessen her anger. "Hell, I'll scotch that rumor, I'll spread the word if it'll make you happy."

"What will make me happy," she wagged her finger in his face again, "Will be for you to keep your big mouth shut. And your fly, too, at least around me."

"Shit," he swore loudly.

"My sentiments exactly." She bent down for her shoes.

"Hey."

"What?"

He gave her a naughty schoolboy grin and winked. "One more for the road?"

She threw a shoe at him.

* * * * * * *

Even with the books and some work from the office, Catherine's day dragged on. She fixed an omelet for lunch and picked at it desultorily. She peeked at a couple of soaps, found it impossible to fathom what was going on, and to whom.

Out of morbid curiosity, she tuned in Daffy Danny's Alley. He was entertaining—one presumed you could consider it that—his young studio audience with hand puppets. She studied him, his exaggerated expressions, the rolling eyes, the gear-shifting of his voice from normal baritone to falsetto that sent the youngsters into paroxysms of laughter for some reason. To her mind he was a bad imitation of Pee Wee, who at least had been genuinely funny.

Was O'Dell a child molester, an accessory, however inadvertent, to kidnapping and murder? Was he looking his little guests over while he entertained them, committing vile acts upon them in his imagination, or even planning them in reality?

Chang came in while the show was on. Catherine glanced at her and saw the fierce jut of her chin and her eyes dark with anger.

"What's wrong?" she asked.

"Nothing," Chang said sharply and added, nearly under her breath. "Men are such assholes."

Which probably did not require an answer, Catherine thought. She looked back at the television. Chang crossed her arms over her chest, leaned against the wall, and watched the end of the show with her. She made a grimace when O'Dell, giving two of his little friends enthusiastic hugs, blew a kiss at the screen.

"Daffy Danny bye-bye," he squealed in tremulous falsetto.

Catherine punched the off button on the remote. "Now there's a man I can certainly agree is an asshole. I can't watch him without

166

getting angry. Those little girls he was holding just now, I kept thinking, what if…it sickens me."

Chang was thoughtful for a moment, her anger with Conners—even more, with herself—giving way to her detective instincts. "You know," she said, "I think maybe it's time we talked to that little creep in person."

CHAPTER TWENTY

O'Dell lived in the high rent end of Encino behind electronic gates that, to Chang's surprise, stood open. A short driveway curved around neat lawns and planters of geraniums, shockingly red in the December weather, to some architect's fevered dream of a Mediterranean villa that shouted nouveau-riche.

"I'll do the talking," Chang said. "All I want you to do is take a good hard look at him, and assure yourself that this really is the guy you saw with Paterson out on Morning View. We don't want to find out later that the snapshots didn't develop right on that particular trip." And King would tear her a new one if she landed them in hot water with this visit, but she kept that to herself.

Bronze doors offered Biblical scenes and a choice of an enormous knocker that would have had her spanking Eve's derriere—take that, you naughty apple pusher—or a more conventional doorbell. Chang chose the latter. Chimes somewhere within did an impressive imitation of Big Ben. After only a brief pause (had their arrival been announced, despite the open gate?) an olive-skinned young man in tight black silk trousers and a white linen tunic opened it and looked them up and down with limpid eyes that seemed not at all pleased with what they saw.

Chang flashed her badge. "F.B.I. We'd like to talk to Mister O'Dell."

"I'll see," he said, making a question mark of it, and closed the door in their faces.

The wait grew lengthy. Chang was about to ring again—maybe this time she would give Eve a smack—when he returned, holding the door wide for them. "This way," he said with a slight sniff. He sounded altogether disappointed that he hadn't been ordered to shoo them away like pesky flies.

They followed him down a wide corridor that split the house in half. The rooms they glimpsed on either side reinforced Catherine's impression of lots of money and less taste. Too much overdone furniture, too many too large pillows in too many colors. A white-flocked Christmas tree was trimmed all in lavender ornaments, and surrounded by a mountain of packages, all silver and lavender.

Silk clad hips swayed their way through doors at the far end of the central hallway and onto a Spanish tiled patio with more planters of geraniums. Enormous banana plants in terra cotta pots screened a pool that glittered blue and inviting in the afternoon sunlight. A faint mist of steam rose from its heated surface. Glowing grids on poles kept the chill of winter air at bay. It was December. Even in Los Angeles December wasn't exactly swimming pool weather, unless you were rich enough to take charge of nature.

Danny O'Dell was draped languidly under one of the radial heaters. Television, with its makeup, its filters and careful lighting, had been kind to him, making him appear a good ten or fifteen years younger than he looked in person. His eyes were puffy, his skin had an unhealthy yellowish pallor, and his gray-brown hair was thin and limp.

He had swapped his nerdy television suit for bathing trunks—not the string bikini she would have guessed, but white baggies with the grinning likeness of Sponge Bob Squarepants. Empathizing with his young audience members, she speculated, just one of the kids? The legs sticking out of the trunks were skinny and white. Sunglasses and a book lay on a table close at hand, along with a tall glass of what looked to her practiced eye like bourbon. A lot of it, hold the ice.

"Please, sit down," he said, and gestured toward a pair of chairs next to the table. "Some refreshments? A cocktail, perhaps, or there's iced tea if you prefer?"

"Tea, I think," Chang said, and Catherine nodded her agreement.

"Sergio, do be a dear and fetch the ladies some tea." He fluttered one hand vaguely in the direction of the house and Sergio bustled away. "Now, then, Sergio said you were police officers?"

"F.B.I.," Chang corrected him. "We just wanted to ask your help with a case we're working on."

He looked long and hard at her. A faint sheen of sweat glistened on his brow, more than would seem justified from the heater above them.

"Anything I can do, of course." He reached for his glass and took a long, noisy swallow from it. Chang caught a whiff of bourbon.

"I wonder if you've ever heard of anyone called Paterson," she said.

His eyes blinked rapidly several times. He screwed up his mouth and made a show of thinking. "Paterson? Is he an actor?"

"In a manner of speaking."

More thinking. "I knew a Waldo Paterson, I think. Or was that Peterson? Oh, and there's a Theresa Paterson at the station, big woman, blonde, works in publicity, I believe."

"This is a Lester Paterson. Sometimes goes by the name of Trash Can."

The eyes did their flutter routine again. He shook his head, Adam's apple bobbing. "What a cute nickname, I wonder how that came about. No, no I'm sure I would remember anyone who called himself Trash Bag."

Chang took a folder from her briefcase and handed him the two different pictures of Paterson. He barely glanced at them.

"Are there two of them? Oh, is this really the same person? How striking, I'd love to know who his surgeon is. One day soon I'm going to have to do something about these eyes." He rolled them at her, a gesture that never failed to delight the children in his studio audience. Chang kept her face carefully bland.

Watching him silently Catherine was thinking of the scene on Morning View Road. There was no doubt in her mind that this was the man she had seen there. She was equally certain he was lying now. Even if she hadn't seen him with Paterson with her own eyes, she would have been convinced of that. However entertaining he might be to children, he was no actor.

"You know," O'Dell said thoughtfully, "Now that I think of it, he does look familiar. He's on television, isn't he? Oh, wait, you're here about a case you said. Yes, that's it, of course. His face *was* on television, on the news. One of those if-you-see-this-man-call-the-police things. This is who you're looking for? But what on earth made you think I would know him?"

"It's routine. You're name came up in some paperwork."

"My name? How peculiar. Or maybe not. I am a television personality, after all." He favored her with what was meant to be a humble smile. She had unnerved him, this odd looking little woman with the frizzy red hair. And the other one, silent as a Buddha, watching him and sipping her tea as if it were the blood of her enemies.

"You think he might be one of your fans?" Chang looked skeptical.

He laughed unconvincingly and handed the pictures back to her. "You would be surprised some of the people I hear from. Fans. You'd think that would be the most wonderful thing for an entertainer, but it's a two-handed puppet, isn't it? Needy little creatures, always trying to get a piece of your flesh, wanting to stand in your light. Mostly I try to keep a distance from them. These days, you can't be too careful, can you? Since the Manson business, and the Jodie Foster thing, you just don't know. And those eyes, he does look a mean one, doesn't he? But, no, I'm sure I've never met him. Positive. But that's not to say I mightn't have a stalker. Stars have to worry about that sort of thing."

Chang thought of the gates at the entrance, left carelessly open. Apparently he had no real concern about the possibility of a stalker, any more than she did. It was hard to imagine one of his young fans, average age seven or so, tailing him with malicious intent, though she could certainly imagine a parent or two thinking evil thoughts.

He was talking too much and too fast and was obviously grateful when Sergio arrived with a tray holding two tall, frosted glasses which he offered to Chang and Catherine. Catherine held hers in both hands to keep from flinging it into O'Dell's face and took a sip. It tasted of bile.

"Perhaps Sergio…?" O'Dell held the pictures up for the houseboy's inspection. "Does he look familiar? They think he might be a stalker. Maybe a delivery person, or someone hanging around? A would-be gate-crasher?"

Sergio barely glanced in the direction of the pictures, gave a quick shake of his head, and hurried away, practically running.

"Or, he might have written me," O'Dell said. He took another long swig of his drink, nearly emptying it, and looked wistfully after his houseboy. "Sometimes they write wanting pictures for their children. At least they say it's for their children, though I often think they just don't want to admit it's for themselves. You can check my mail, if you'd like."

Chang took a picture of Catherine's daughter from the folder and handed it to O'Dell. "Recognize her?" she asked.

This time his denial seemed sincere. "No." He shook his head, looking puzzled.

"Or him?" She handed him a picture of Steve Madison, the boy who had disappeared a few days earlier from the park. He glanced at it and looked away almost instantly.

"No," he said, too quickly. The picture shook. Catherine's glass broke in her hand, startling them all.

"Sergio," O'Dell bellowed.

"It's all right," Catherine said, standing and dabbing at the spilled tea with her napkin. She had gotten nothing more than a small cut on one finger. She put it to her mouth and sucked the blood from it, carefully avoided looking at their host.

"I can't imagine how that happened," O'Dell said. "I shall have to flay that boy for bringing you a cracked glass." He gave the picture back to Chang, put a hand over his eyes as if the sun was in them and reached for the sunglasses on the table. "Really," he sighed, "I'm afraid I'm quite weary. Is that all?"

Chang stuffed the pictures back into her briefcase. "You're certain about this Paterson? You've never met him? Maybe at a party? In a bar?"

"I don't do bars," he said coolly. "And I'm quite sure I have never met the gentleman."

"He's not a gentleman." Chang stood abruptly.

"Sergio," he called again.

"Don't bother, we can find our own way out," Chang said.

"Sergio," louder this time, "Please see the ladies to the front door. And bring me a drink, this one is practically tepid."

* * * * * * *

"He's lying through his teeth," Catherine said when they had been escorted carefully out of the house, the door closed solidly, almost slammed, behind them.

"I'm going to love nailing that little weasel's butt," Chang muttered.

* * * * * * *

O'Dell hurried along the hall, drinking so greedily that the bourbon sloshed over the rim and puddled unnoticed on the tile floor. He locked the bedroom door after himself. The good stuff was in a locked armoire that he opened with shaking hands. He pulled out a little teak chest inlaid with mother of pearl and opened it with a key from a dresser drawer.

He'd get rid of everything, put it in a plastic bag and dump it into the ocean. He should never have had it in the first place. It was too dangerous. How had he ever let himself get dragged into this? It was all Paterson's fault.

172

He snatched up the DVDs lying on top. Just underneath them was a stack of photographs. He looked at the first one, a pretty young boy, the same boy whose picture that crazy looking F.B.I. agent had shown him just minutes ago, leaning back on a sofa, apparently asleep. Or was he drugged? He wouldn't put that past Paterson. He wouldn't put anything past Paterson. The man was a monster.

He knew that sofa all too well, too. Paterson had been sitting on it the last time he had seen him. If the picture were found in his possession, it would link him definitely with Paterson.

He picked up the picture, was about to crumple it, but his eyes fell on the one beneath it. A different boy, this one's wide eyes staring at the camera as if surprised to see it there.

O'Dell put the DVDs aside and lifted the stack of photos out of the box, sank back on the bed with its silk duvet and lilac Frette linens, and began to go through the pictures, savoring them one by one.

Maybe it was silly to think of getting rid of them. Those women hadn't accused him of anything. It was Paterson they were looking for. No reason to think they really suspected him. That fool Paterson must have had his name written somewhere, but that proved nothing. He was a star. Lots of people must have his name written down.

The Sponge Bob trunks slipped to the floor. The silk whispered faint insinuations.

CHAPTER TWENTY-ONE

Conners. Chang couldn't stop thinking of him, and what had happened between them. He was like a big boulder in the road, couldn't get over him, couldn't get around him.

She got up extra early in the morning and pulled her groggy self together, picked out a pair of lacy pink, never worn panties, slipped into them, and was about to put on her jeans when she saw herself in the mirror.

"Ugh." She grimaced in disgust, stripped off the panties and tossed them in the overflowing wastebasket, and switched to her usual boxers.

She stopped on the way to pick up a box of Krispy Kremes, because she had never heard of a cop who didn't scarf them up at any opportunity. Plus, she was inordinately fond of them herself, and she thought she might need to fuel her resistance.

Thus armed, she knocked on Conners' door, hoping as she waited that he didn't have company. Hoped he had a shirt on this time. And that he didn't answer in his skivvies. Or worse yet, in a towel. Towels came off way too easily.

To her relief, he was fully dressed, face clean scrubbed, hair still wet from the shower. And as perky as ever. Jesus, it was ten after eight in the morning. How could anybody be perky? One more strike against him in her book.

"Breakfast," she said, flaunting the doughnuts. "Got any coffee?"

"Just made," he said. He looked glad to see her, and wary at the same time. "Come on in." He stepped aside for her, but gave her plenty of room. He was thinking of those stories about de-balling men. For sure they were apocryphal. On the other hand....

His apartment was just as neat and clean as it had been the last time. That, she thought, was truly disgusting. You had only to look around the planet to see that some disorder was part of the Godly plan.

In the tidy little kitchen, he filled a Wiley Coyote mug for her and set a sugar bowl by it. She added three spoons to the cup, contemplated it a moment, added another and took a tentative sip. Just the way she liked it—hot as hell, sweet and strong enough to melt tin.

There was a just-rinsed bowl on the drain board and a box of granola on the kitchen table. She hated that stuff. "Nuts and twigs?" She gave him a scornful look.

He shrugged. "Healthy. But I love Krispys too," he added quickly. He took one and nibbled decorously at an edge. She bit off half of hers, chewed vigorously, and washed it down with coffee. The perfect breakfast. She cleared her throat.

"Look," she said, "I just wanted to say, well, I'm sorry I tore into you the way I did the other day. It was uncalled for. It wasn't like you grabbed me by the hair and dragged me to the bed."

"We could do that scenario, if it works better for you." He grinned a little tentatively. "I'm really flexible."

"Jesus, are you always so cheerful? Cops are supposed to be pricks."

He nodded eagerly. "I can do that, too. After what happened, I'm willing...."

"What happened, Conners, was just a fluke."

"Roby, see...."

"The guys call me Chang."

"Look, Roby, now that we're involved...."

"We are not—I repeat, not—involved," she fairly shouted at him. "We fucked, damn it."

"We fucked great. We fucked fabulous. Fabulous fucking qualifies as involved. I looked it up. It's in the regs."

She sighed and spread her hands. "You are hopeless. You know that?"

He grinned again, less tentatively. She wanted to punch him. Or something.

"I guess you're going to have to whip me into line. What the hell, I'm open minded," he said. "Look, tell me the gospel truth, didn't you like it too?"

She slapped a hand over her eyes. "Damn it. All right, yes, it was good."

"Just good?" He looked dismayed. It exasperated her. It also did something funny inside her where her heart would have been if she'd had one. Which she didn't. She had traded that in for a Glock and a shoulder holster.

"It was great, then, dammit, it was, what did you say, fabulous, okay, does that make you feel better?"

"Lots. Honestly. Because I'm hoping we're going to do it again. Oh," he put his hands up to forestall her and added quickly, "It doesn't have to be right now. I mean, we can wait fifteen, twenty minutes." She glowered. "Okay, a couple of days. Whatever. You set the pace. It's just, well, we are going to do it again, aren't we? Cause it would be a crying shame if we didn't. I mean, I've waited forty years for it to happen like that."

"You're only thirty-eight, for crap's sake," she snapped.

"I heard about you when I was out there in the ether. Projecting. I was waiting for the right time to tell you about that. See, the projectiles, that's what we call ourselves, they sat me down one day and they promised me this was going to happen. And it was just like they said it would be, the red hair, the sparks bouncing off the ceiling, everything. I just want to know if it's going to happen again in this lifetime, or if I have to wait for another go-round. Because if it's not till the next life, I'm going to hurry this one along, no sense wasting my time."

She sighed again and rubbed her eyes. This would be a lot easier if he wasn't so damned cute. She hated cute guys. Most of all, she hated cute cops. And she absolutely loathed cute cops who made her nipples get hard remembering what they were like in the sack.

Plus this man was impossible. You couldn't get him to be serious. Just her luck, she would have to link up with a Looney-Tunes. Why couldn't she have gotten some good old-fashioned psycho? She could simply have shot him after they got off. No jury would convict her.

"I don't know," she said. "I…I just don't know. Conners, I am not good at this shit. I'm married to the Bureau. You know that. That's the only love life I have. It's all I want. It's all I can handle."

"Okay." He sighed and said in a voice of infinite patience, "Then, tell me something: how did you get so married to the Bureau? What made you get into it the way you are? There's got to be a story there."

There was. She had never shared it with anyone before. "You don't want to hear it," she said.

"Yes, I do," he said, and for once he was absolutely serious. "Really. Tell me. Please."

Out of the blue, to her own surprise, she began to talk to him about it in a barely audible voice. She couldn't imagine why—now, here, with him. Maybe it was just time. Maybe because he looked so sincere. The words just seemed to come of their own accord and for the first time in her life she didn't try to stifle them.

"I had a sister," she said." The words came out slowly, unevenly, as if they were sticking in her throat.

"I didn't know that," he said.

"We were twins. Rachel and Roby. Little girls. We were eight years old and we had been to the store for ice cream bars. It was just a block and a half down the street, a nice quiet little residential neighborhood with a Mom-and-Pop at the corner. It should have been safe enough for two little girls." She paused for a long moment.

The anguish on her face tore at him. "Look, I'm sorry, if this is too hard for you to tell, it's okay," he said. "I didn't mean to push."

"No. I want you to hear it. I want you to understand. Don't ask me why, I don't know myself." She paused again, then went on: "There was this guy, sitting at the curb in a van, motor running. He tried to ask us for directions to some place and we ignored him. That's what Mom had always told us to do.

"All of a sudden, he jumps out of the van, starts toward us. 'Run,' Rachel said, and we did, we ran like hell toward home. But, all of a sudden, I realized Rachel wasn't with me, and when I stopped to look back, he was dragging her into the van. He threw her inside and he looked at me again and I took off. I ran."

She was breathing hard, talking fast, words running together, remembering it the way it had unfolded, memories she had kept at bay for years. She looked at him, with an eight year old girl's look of horror and pain. "I left her there, alone."

"Roby," he started to say, but she cut him off.

"They found her a week later in Griffith Park. The coyotes had eaten most of her face off. They had to identify her by her dental records. She was dead and I was alive because I ran." She paused.

"That's when I joined the Bureau. I mean, I didn't sign up till years later, but that's when I knew I was going to live my life catching people like him. I go after the shitbags, Conners, the real shitbags. These guys make your ordinary killers look like choirboys. I can't afford feelings. If I ever started having feelings, it would kill me."

"Jesus, Roby, you were a little girl," Conners said. "You did the right thing by running. You know that. That's exactly what you would tell a little girl to do today."

"I could have fought him. Even then I was a tough kid, I could beat the shit out of boys twice my age. I let him take her." Her voice broke. She turned away from him.

"Roby, listen, I can see why this was so hard for you, what happened between us. I'm sorry. If I had known, I'd have taken it slower, given you more time. But, Baby, you can't live without feelings, nobody can. And we can't just pretend it didn't happen either. I can be patient. I joke too much, I know, but, seriously, I can wait till you're ready. I just don't want to wait without any hope. Just tell me there's that. Just tell me maybe."

She turned to look long and hard at him—and saw, in the back of those warm brown eyes studying her so hopefully, what she had seen in the eyes of so many homicide cops, and hadn't seen in his until now: the virus that ate at them, a virus they caught from the evil they dealt with, nurtured by grief and bloodshed and anger and guilt. None of them escaped it. Some of them weathered it and survived. Some of them were broken and fell to pieces.

Conner's jokes, the college boy façade, the determined cheerfulness, were just his defenses against his vulnerability. She could see that. It broke her heart. It shouldn't be a bad thing to be a good guy.

"Okay. Maybe," she said.

He breathed a sigh of relief. "I'm not on duty for forty minutes. I think we could work it in."

"You are the most disgustingly sex obsessed man I have ever met." She went toward the door.

"That's the first really sweet thing you've said to me since you got here."

She snorted, but she did not move away when he came to her and put a tentative hand on her arm. He turned her toward him, very gently, searched her face for a long moment, and lowered his mouth to hers. It was a surprisingly chaste kiss, and brief—the kind friends might share without embarrassment.

She was a little disappointed at the brevity. She put her arms up around him, pulled him down to her, and went for something a bit more interesting.

He glanced over her shoulder at the watch he wasn't wearing and said, "Thirty-seven minutes."

She punched him in the gut and left before he could change her mind.

* * * * * * *

Catherine and Jack did finally have the quarrel that had been threatening.

"Catherine," he said after a mostly silent evening at the safe house, "I want you to listen to me, really listen. We have to go away. I mean, from Los Angeles."

She started to say something but he put up a hand to forestall her. He had rehearsed this spiel all day at work, wanted to get it said before she had a chance to argue. "Paterson can't reach you over a distance, you said, right? Then let's make it a real distance. Chicago. Or New York. I can get a job in either city, I'm sure of it. And New York is full of publishing houses, so you could surely find something as well. We'll start a new life where he can't reach us."

"And what if he learns to bridge the distance, what if he gets strong enough to find me there?" she asked. "What then? We run to London? South America? The moon?"

"If we have to. We'll go wherever he can't find us."

She shook her head. "It's no use. The answer is to see him brought to justice. In prison, if not dead."

"Catherine, you're just one woman, a stubborn one and a wonderful one, but there are limits to what you can do alone, and the time may have come for you to face them," Jack said angrily.

"I'm not alone," she snapped, and was immediately sorry that she had been so sharp. It was evidence of the strain she was feeling but it was no good taking it out on him. That was simply taking it out on *them*. "Besides, wherever we go," she said more patiently, "he will find us eventually. He will never quit now that he knows who I am and how to project himself."

"There must be someplace," he said in frustration.

"Darling," she said, pleading now, "Sooner or later, he'll reach me wherever I am. He's getting stronger all the time. I'll never be free of him so long as he's out there, searching for me."

"Which makes it all the more imperative that we put you out of harm's way. All right, maybe in time he could find you, but it's only an astral projection, right? Even if he learned that you were in New York, he couldn't do anything to you without going there physically. And getting away from here does buy us time. He could be caught and in prison before he gets strong enough to track us down. Catherine, if you love me...."

Despite the tension of the moment, she laughed. "That line, darling, is positively Paleolithic. Next thing you'll be asking me to bind my feet."

He laughed too, but begrudgingly. "Wrong era, but, okay, point taken. But, damn it Catherine," he strode back and forth, fists clenched, "That is what this is all about. I love you...."

"And I love you, but, damn it yourself, Jack, this, this thing that I have to do, it's a part of me now, maybe the major part. I'm not an apple tree, you can't just pick the fruit you want to eat and throw the rest to the hogs. If you want to make a pie, you have to take the whole tree."

He smiled glumly. "For a woman who edits books, you make a lousy metaphor."

"You think that's lousy, wait till you try my meatloaf."

They regarded one another grimly for a long moment. Jack felt as if he were struggling through a quagmire, torn between his love for her and his fear of what her obsession was doing to her, to them. If she were ill, physically ill, if she had cancer, he would never leave her, would nurture and succor her in any way that he could.

This was something else though, something he couldn't ameliorate for her, this fixation with Paterson. *That* was her cancer, and it was as malignant, as insidious, as anything that might have corrupted her body. It was poisoning her. Poisoning them, feeding a gulf that seemed to grow ever wider and deeper between them.

"Can't you see," she began, but he said, sharply, "What I see, Catherine, is that you're married to him, in some psychic way."

"Don't be dense," she snapped. "I just want to see his evil ended."

"That's not your job, Catherine. And it's not just his evil anymore. Somehow, it's become yours, it's imbedded in your soul. It's destroying you. I can't bear to watch it any longer. Every time he goes after you, every time you go after him, it's like some evil test of wills between the two of you, and I am left to stand helplessly aside and watch. It's killing me."

"There's something I haven't told you," she said in little more than a whisper. "I haven't told anyone. I can barely bear to face it myself: it's my fault Becky died."

"Catherine, that's ridiculous. Your daughter was murdered, by those two monsters. They kidnapped her...."

"I could have stopped it," she said in an agonized voice. "I should have stopped it. I should have been there, only...." She turned tear-brimmed eyes to him, "Only, I stopped to look at a magazine, one of those trashy gossip things. I stood there reading about some Hollywood bimbo for two, maybe three minutes. While they were dragging Becky from our car."

"There were two men. Armed men. Even if you had gotten there two minutes sooner, what could you have done?"

She shook her head, her voice rising in near hysteria. "They wouldn't have taken her if I had been there."

"You can't know that, darling, they might just have shot you that much sooner. They might have killed you."

"You can die and go on living."

"Catherine, I beg you...."

She turned away from him, her heart aching. How could she make him understand? She hardly understood it herself. Why had she even been given this gift? Gift? It was more of a curse, wasn't it? Yet she had been given it: *there is something only you can do....*

"It's no use," she said. "I understand how you feel...."

"Do you?" he asked, and now there was an unmistakable note of bitterness in his voice. He was convinced she had no idea how he felt. Worse, he believed she did not because she did not want to. That, more than anything else, tore at him like a demon ripping his guts out of him. Nothing, no one, was as important to her now as Paterson. Second fiddle was not a happy instrument to play.

"...But I can't," Catherine was still speaking, "I won't give up now, not until I've seen it through. Don't you see, Jack, those children, the ones he's damaged already, and the ones he means to steal. I'm all they have."

"Can't you see, you're all I have?" he asked. "Catherine, you can't bring Becky back to life."

For a long moment she stood frozen in place, clenching her teeth, her fists tight, trying to control the anger that flared up within her.

"Damn it, Jack, that's not fair," she swore finally, and whirled to face him—but he had gone, the door closing softly in his wake.

She stared at it, part of her wanting to run after him, to beg him to stay. She even, for a brief moment, wondered if he could be right, if she should give up her pursuit of Paterson and just run away, run so far that he couldn't ever find her.

There was no distance that great, however. In her heart, she knew that, and she knew, too, that she could never quit so long as he was still out there, still free to do evil. Sadly, she knew something else as well: she would never be able to make anyone, not even Jack, understand what this meant for her.

She stared about at the dreary little cottage with its tawdry furnishings. She was alone. When you got down to it, she had always borne this burden alone, and always would.

Oh, hell, she thought, that is too bleak. Tomorrow, the day after, she'd be ready to tackle things again. Ready to tackle Paterson somehow. Ready to patch things up with Jack. She knew that she had to do that. She couldn't allow this quarrel to continue.

But she still wouldn't be able really to share. Talk about it, yes, but the burden remained hers alone.

Well, then, somehow the means to do it must be shown to her as well, mustn't it? And hadn't the guidance she needed so often come to her in the past? She would just have to trust that it would again.

She walked into the bedroom, threw herself across the bed, and began to cry.

* * * * * * *

It was morning before she slept, and nearly noon by the time she woke, feeling scarcely rested, and utterly weary with living like a fugitive.

And for what, she asked herself for the umpteenth time? Paterson was gone, in Mexico probably, a hundred miles and at least two hours away. She even took the chance of trying fleetingly to find him on the astral level and got only a dim image that told her clearly he was nowhere near.

To make matters worse, she had picked up a bug, had woken nauseous and barely made it to the bathroom before she lost last night's dinner. Or maybe it was the stress of her quarrel with Jack.

In any case, it was one misery too many. She made up her mind that Paterson could not be allowed to steal her life from her by default. He might win after all in the end, but she was not going to give up everything for his sake.

She called Jack at the station and was told he was in a meeting. "Would you like his voice mail?" his secretary asked.

Catherine hesitated. Her feelings were such a muddle: frustration, anger with him for not understanding, anger and guilt with herself because at least a part of her suspected he was right. How could she say all that on his voice mail?

"No, I'll call him later," she said instead.

* * * * * * *

Chang waved her way past King's secretary and entered his office without knocking. He looked up, surprised. In all the time they had worked together, this was a first. And they weren't on the best of terms at the moment; since her unauthorized visit to Danny O'Dell, of which he had definitely not approved.

"Colley, sir," she said without preamble. "J. D. Colley. As in John David."

The King gave her a blank look and waited for explanation.

"We picked up some prints at the Morning View house. Paterson's. And his partner's. J. D. Colley. He had a couple of priors for molestation, pled down, got off. That's why he was hard to find. And the description matches." She dropped a mug shot on his desk.

"There's more," she said while he picked up the photos and looked hard at them. "We got some other prints, too. That actor's. O'Dell." She suppressed any temptation to say or even look I-told-you-so. "He lied to us when he said he didn't know Paterson. Plus, we got a man from O'Dell's television studio says there was an incident a while back, some kid said O'Dell came on to him in the john, tried to feel him up. It was all hushed up, big bucks shelled out probably, but the guy says he's willing to swear to it, even has the name of the kid."

King nodded his head and started to scribble on a piece of paper. "It's enough for a warrant. I want that house taken apart. If he's got any shit there, we'll nail him to the wall." He glanced up at her and paused, and raised both eyebrows. "Chang, you look like a cat that just inherited a fish farm."

She allowed herself a grin. "Not a farm, sir, a cabin. O'Dell owns a cabin, out in the woods. At Big Bear."

King grinned back at her, a rare occurrence. He leaned back in his chair and made a tent of his fingers. "Does he now? Tell me one thing more, agent. Does he hang left or right?"

"Right, sir. Definitely."

* * * * * * *

Despite everything, Catherine found that it astonishingly good just to be outside, in her car, moving with the traffic on the L.A. streets. It had rained early, but the rain had stopped and an erratic wind seemed determined to drive the remaining clouds away. Her spirits lifting, she promised herself that she would call Jack later in the afternoon and mend things with him. She meant to pick up the reins of her life again, instead of surrendering them to Paterson. What a fool she had been.

She drove straight to the office in Century City. She wanted work, catharsis, a chance to stretch her mental muscles.

She started with the mountain of mail that had accumulated in the few days she had been off. Bills, book proposals, letters. She sorted them into piles and, armed with letter opener, started with the financial stack. She had half opened a bank statement before she took a second look at the envelope and realized it wasn't her bank.

Fidelity Bank and Trust. It was another moment before she registered that this was the bank where Walter kept their joint account. She looked again at the address. Yes, it had been sent to the house and, both their names listed, Walter's first. Somehow this had mistakenly been forwarded with her mail.

She started to write "forward" on the envelope and then, remembering that it was half opened, decided instead she would drop it by the house. There were one or two things she had been meaning to pick up anyway.

She had no more than set the envelope aside than her phone rang and to her surprise, it was Walter on the line.

"What a coincidence," she said, meaning to mention the statement to him, but he began to talk in a hurry, his voice anxious, stressed.

"Catherine, I…I'm embarrassed to ask, but, I need some money. Some unexpected expenses at the restaurant. I wondered if…." He paused expectantly.

"Of course," she said, surprised. Walter had always been so meticulous in handling money, she could hardly imagine him running short. Finances had never been an issue between them, however. If anything, she supposed he had been overly generous with her. "How much do you need?"

"Five thousand." He blurted it out.

The figure was another surprise. She expected him to say a few hundred. It left her briefly speechless.

He misread the pause. "I can pay it back out of the money from the house," he said quickly. "With interest. I wouldn't ask if it weren't…."

"No, no, that's all right, interest won't be necessary, and I'm not worried about your paying it back. It's only, I don't think I have that much in my account."

"Can you spare two?"

She did a quick mental calculation. "Yes, I think I can. I'll have to stop by the bank a little later. Did you want me to drop it off at the restaurant?"

"I'll come pick it up at your office. If that's all right? And, Catherine, you are a peach, you don't know how much I appreciate this."

"Don't give it a thought," she assured him. It was not until he had rung off that she realized that she had forgotten to mention the bank statement.

Well, no matter, she thought, looking at it once again. He could pick that up with the cash.

She was still staring at the envelope, puzzling at the strangeness of Walter's behavior, when the phone rang again. This time it was a woman's voice, one she didn't recognize. "I'm calling from Fidelity Bank and Trust," she said.

Another coincidence? "Yes?"

"There seems to be a slight problem with your account. It's a bit overdrawn. We wondered if you could take care of that at your earliest convenience?"

"You must mean the joint account that my husband and I keep," Catherine said.

"Yes. That would be the one." She rattled off an account number. Catherine jotted it down. "It's only a few hundred, you understand. But we do like to stay on top of these things."

For a long moment Catherine contemplated what she had just been told. It was even more incredible to her that Walter could have allowed a bank account to be overdrawn. "I don't understand," she said, more to herself than to the woman on the phone.

"Well, there have been some rather large checks drawn on the account of late. Perhaps your husband wrote them, but you have seen the statement, I presume. Or if you haven't, I could send you another copy, if you like."

The statement? "No, that won't be necessary. I'll...."

"You really should review the charges," the voice said, and then there was a change on the line and she was listening to a syrupy orchestral arrangement of Eric Clapton's "Layla." After a few seconds, the line changed again and a woman's voice, a different voice, said, "This is Miss Frazier, thank you for holding. How may I help you?"

"I was talking to someone else," Catherine said, "Just a moment earlier. Another woman."

After a pause, Miss Frazier asked, "Do you recall her name?"

"I...I don't think she gave me one."

"I see." Miss Frazier took a moment to consider. "Perhaps I can help you. What seems to be your problem?"

"Our account appears to be overdrawn." She gave Miss Frazier the account number she had jotted down.

"Let me pull up that account." Miss Frazier left her to listen to more of "Layla." It was all legato strings, sweeping crescendos, muted rhythm. Only the melody was recognizable. She hoped for his sake Eric Clapton never heard it.

Miss Frazier came back on the line. Catherine was not surprised when she said, "I don't find anything wrong on that account. Are you sure of the number?"

"Yes, that's quite all right, never mind," Catherine said. "I'm sorry to have bothered you."

"Not at all. We at Fidelity Bank and Trust are always happy to serve our customers. Can I help you with anything else?"

"No. Wait. Yes. Please do something about the music. It's dreadful."

She hung up the phone and picked up the bank statement instead and considered. In all the years she had been married to Walter, she had never even glanced at one of these statements, had always left that account entirely up to him. She'd never had any reason to distrust him in that way. Now, contemplating looking at the statement, as that voice on the phone had advised her to do, she felt guilty, disloyal even, as though she were sticking her nose into Walter's business.

But, surely, it was what that disembodied voice wanted her to do, and who could that have been if not her intervening angel, once more prodding her to action. Anyway, the bank account was her business too, wasn't it? They had both always made regular deposits to it throughout the years of their marriage.

Her mother's hints flashed into her mind, that Walter might have a drug problem. That, too, seemed incredible. Yet, it did happen to people, she knew that much, to ordinary decent people whose descent into drug addiction started with one, seemingly harmless step. Certainly he had been through a period of great stress—without, she had to add, having the great good fortune that she had in linking up with Jack.

She snatched up her letter opener again and took a vicious stab at the flap on the envelope, fairly ripping it open, and took out the two precisely folded sheets within.

Her own bank didn't bother with checks at all anymore, only listed the check numbers and amounts, as she thought most banks did today, but Fidelity Bank and Trust still included both a listing of the amounts and, on a second sheet, photocopies of the checks themselves in miniature.

She looked at the debit amounts first. For the most part, they were routine. Property taxes, electric bill, water bill, gas…and there, in the middle, three debits of nine thousand dollars each.

Twenty-seven thousand dollars. She looked at the second sheet, at the reproductions of the checks. There they were, three checks written to the same payee: Harvard Beerman Health Clinic.

Walter was ill, then, and had said nothing to her about it, perhaps thinking that she would have put off her decision to leave—as she would have, surely. You couldn't walk out on a sick man, a sick husband, could you, not knowing that he was ill, not even if you were in love with another man?

She must confront him on this, make him tell her what was wrong. It wasn't the money that mattered. If he were ill, then she surely owed it to him, to their years of marriage, to contribute whatever she could to his care.

Only—and with this thought came once more that nagging sense of doubt, of something else amiss—Walter had health insurance, excellent and almost total coverage. They both did. There was almost nothing their insurance did not cover.

Drugs? Again that popped into her mind. Perhaps Walter did have a problem, and had already faced it, had already started rehabilitation. Did their insurance cover drug treatment? She couldn't remember.

She had never heard of the Harvard Beerman Health Clinic, but that of itself meant nothing. There were scores, maybe hundreds of private clinics throughout the city. What if this was some kind of a rehab center? Was rehab that expensive? She had no idea, really, but it certainly did sound like a lot of money.

She looked in her desk drawers for a phone book, and was eyeing the shelves along the wall when Bill came in with some manuscripts.

"Looking for something?" he asked.

"A phone book. Would you find…no, wait. Here," she wrote the name of the clinic on a piece of paper and handed it to him. "I've got to run to my bank. See if you can find out what this place is, what kind of clinic, I mean. If they do, well, any specialized kind of treatment, or just general medicine."

The bank was only a few blocks from her Century City office. She walked, hurrying against a chilling winter wind, worried thoughts blowing through her mind as she went.

It didn't matter that she didn't love Walter in any romantic sense, or that they were no longer together. Clearly, there was some sort of trouble in his life, and she owed it to him to do what she could to help. The money was the least of it. If it were drugs, say, then she must convince him to get treatment if he hadn't already.

She cashed a check for two thousand dollars and hurried back to her office. Bill was there before she had finished hanging up her coat.

"Harvard Beerman Health Clinic is not particularly forthcoming about their practice," he said. "They wanted to know what kind of problem I had, and whether I had been referred to them by anyone. That seemed to matter a lot. I don't think they take patients except by referral. But I did get you a phone number and an address." He handed those to her. "Are you all right? I have a friend who's a doctor, if you need one."

"No, that's all right, thank you," she said. She puzzled over the information when he had gone, and studied the address he had written down. Her Thomas' map of Los Angeles confirmed what she had already guessed, that the address was in Compton. Compton was a ghetto neighborhood, notoriously dangerous. Drugs, gangs, rampant crime. Not the sort of address she would have expected Walter to visit. Certainly not where you would expect to find an expensive clinic.

On the spur of the moment, she called Fermin to tell him she was taking the rest of the day off. She put the two thousand dollars for Walter into an envelope and sealed it, wrote his name on the front, and left it with Bill.

"My husband will be stopping by," she said, "See that he gets this."

The bank statement she put in the drawer of her desk. There would be time enough to forward that to him later. She picked up the phone, intending to call Jack, and hesitated. He would try to talk her out of what she planned to do. They would surely quarrel again.

She put the receiver back on its cradle, donned her coat again, changed from heels to walking shoes, and took the elevator to the garage.

CHAPTER TWENTY-TWO

Paterson had grown restless, not used to living cooped up with only Colley's company. A good enough partner in his way, he mostly did as he was told and he could be surprisingly inventive when the situation called for it. Still, having him underfoot full time could get old quickly.

Most especially, he was not used to going for long without sexual relief. And certainly Colley was no help there. Sooner fuck one of those wild burros that had wandered by in a pack the day before, was how he felt.

His thoughts kept circling back to her: the bitch. He wanted her dead, he wouldn't rest till he had managed that, but not until he had heard her beg. Beg for his cock, like they all did, before he finished screwing her. After that, she would beg for death. When he finally killed her, he would be doing her a favor. He wanted that so bad he could taste it.

Even those daydreams didn't satisfy him today, though. The cabin, primitive and not very big to begin with, got smaller by the hour. Christ, couldn't that television fag afford something better? He had called it his "little shack in the country," and Paterson had just supposed he was being cute, but shit, this really was a shack. The best you could say for it was that it was a long ways from anywhere. Or anybody. No other houses along this road, nothing more than a dirt track, and that ended a short distance beyond O'Dell's shack, just petered out at a steep, wooded hillside that attracted not even the more adventurous hikers. Since they had been here he hadn't heard or seen a trace of anybody except for the distant buzz of a chainsaw somewhere beyond the hill behind them, someone cutting firewood, and that had sounded at least a couple of miles away.

Today, there was not even that to break the silence, only a tuneless humming from Colley while he fiddle-farted around in the kitchen space, not really a separate room, just some counters along one wall with a stove and a fridge, and some cupboards overhead.

Outside a woodpecker drilled at a tree and the wind made ghostly noises in the pines. Shit. It was like being in prison.

Besides, something was gnawing at Paterson. Something to do with *her*, only he didn't know what, couldn't put his finger on it. He had been wet-your-pants happy that time he had popped in on her, just the way she had with him. Scared the shit out of her, he could see that, and once again, he was the one in control.

Only, he didn't know how he had done it. It was like, he was thinking about her, thinking hard, and all of a sudden, there he was. He had tried since, though, had given himself a headache thinking about her, and gotten nothing for his trouble. A couple of times he almost thought he could see her, in a distance, like she was out there in a deep fog, but he couldn't reach her.

He gave a snort of disgust and jumped up from the sofa where he was sitting, watching a grainy image on the little black and white television. One lousy channel, was all that the rooftop antenna brought in, and half the time you couldn't even watch that it was so bad.

"Get your coat," he said, "Let's go for a ride."

Colley stopped his humming—that was something to be thankful for—and glanced at the pale light struggling through the closed curtains over the windows. "Now?" he asked.

"No, I thought we'd put on our coats and sit in the van for an hour or two before we went anywhere. Course I mean now, you dumb ass."

"It's still daylight, Trash. Suppose someone sees us?"

"Who, one of those wild donkeys? They was the last ones to mosey by? Besides, the sun's mostly down. By the time we hit L.A., it'll be dark."

"L.A.? We're going into L.A."

"We got to get the rest of our money, I don't mean to leave that asshole off the hook."

"Sure, but ain't it dangerous…." Colley started to argue.

"Anyone tries to look too close, I'll slide down in the seat. It's my face plastered on T. V. No one's looking for you, are they? Let's go. You drive."

It was snowing lightly. "If it gets snowing hard we might not be able to get back," Colley said.

"Snow's barely falling," Paterson said. "If it looks like it's going to turn nasty we can come back, can't we?"

* * * * * * *

At one time Compton had been an upper middle class bedroom community for Los Angeles proper, a California stew of architecture: Victorians, Spanish bungalows, ranch, saltboxes. A tide of immigrants had built for themselves imitations of the homes they had left behind.

That had been several decades ago. In the intervening years the once proud looking bungalows and ranches had mostly disappeared or morphed into gas stations, thrift stores, groceries. The Victorians and the saltboxes were apartment buildings and boarding houses, with graffiti stained storefronts at the street level. More than a few of them were boarded up and empty.

Her Jaguar was decidedly conspicuous in the hood. Knots of idlers on street corners smoked and watched with undisguised curiosity as she drove by.. A wino slept in a doorway and a ragged looking creature of indeterminate sex pushed a heavily laden shopping cart.

Even here, however, not everything was utterly bleak. The occasional Christmas lights sparkled valiantly in windows, too, and she passed a middle-aged woman bustling her young daughter home from holiday shopping, arms filled with packages. Surprisingly, here and there was the evidence of someone's attempts at gentrification: a flower shop, a bookstore. A café that appeared altogether new and wouldn't have looked out of place in West L.A. sat incongruously three doors down from an adult video store.

She nearly missed The Harvard Beerman Medical Clinic. It sat behind stone walls and a heavy wire gate that presumably closed at night, already approaching. She was surprised by how quickly it fell now, as if she had never experienced a December evening before. The sky was a child's finger painting, smudges of color streaked among sooty clouds.

The clinic itself was a one-story stucco, faded pink, with glass brick windows. The ghosts of graffiti had bled through the thin coating of paint that had been daubed over it. Some straggly bushes lined the front on either side of an entrance door and a conspicuously unswept parking lot ran along one side, ending at an alley. A black cat, scrawny and wary, slipped around the corner of the building and disappeared into the bushes.

A gray Honda Civic and a big black Mercedes Sedan, altogether too conspicuous for Compton, sat side by side at the nearer end of the parking lot, and at the far end, like a social outcast, was a dirty white Toyota.

She parked in the middle. If anyone came shopping for wheels they would hopefully find one of the other cars more attractive than her Jaguar.

She entered a waiting room that belied the expensive treatment that Walter must have gotten here: the sooty walls badly needed a fresh coat of paint. A chipped plastic table strewn with tattered and outdated magazines sat between a pair of sagging chairs and the floor was covered with well-worn linoleum.

A buzzer rang as she came in and a frosted glass panel slid open in the wall facing the door. A receptionist in a pink uniform looked her over quickly and thoroughly, and a young woman standing behind her paused in her filing to stare in undisguised curiosity. Walk-ins were apparently not common here.

"Yes?" The woman in pink asked. The monosyllable was carefully neutral. A placard on the desk identified her as Miss Griff.

"I'd like to see the doctor," Catherine said.

"Are you a patient?" The tone said clearly that Miss Griff did not think so.

"No," Catherine said, and before she could explain further, the receptionist said, "We aren't taking any new patients," and started to slide the glass panel shut.

"Wait." Catherine put a hand on the pane to stop it. "I wanted to talk about my husband. He *is* a patient, I believe."

"Name?"

"Desmond. Walter Desmond."

She saw something register in the woman's eyes before she gave her head an emphatic shake and said, "Sorry, we don't have a patient by that name."

"Desmond," the girl at the file cabinet said, "Wasn't that…?"

"We don't have a patient by that name," the receptionist repeated firmly. She snatched up some papers from her desk and thrust them at the girl. "Donna, give these to Doctor Beerman. And then you can take your dinner break." This time the glass panel shut fully and firmly.

* * * * * * *

Sitting in the parking lot, twilight settling around the car like a fog, Catherine tried to make sense of what had just taken place. She understood that doctors needed to be concerned about patient confidentiality, but this seemed to have gone far beyond that. She was certain the receptionist had lied. There had been that flicker of recognition before she insisted that Walter was not a patient. And surely the filing clerk, Donna, had started to say something entirely different.

As if Catherine's thoughts had conjured her up, Donna came out a side door in the clinic and hurried head down to the Toyota at the far end of the lot. The light mounted high on one clinic wall cast a feeble glow in a small orange circle just outside the door and left the rest of the lot in growing darkness. Donna did not seem even to notice the Jaguar parked forty feet away. A moment later the Toyota's engine sputtered, coughed a time or two, and finally caught. Donna backed the car out of its space, turned, and drove into the alley.

Catherine started the Jaguar and followed her, down the alley and out onto a busy street. Evening traffic was thick and she wondered if she would be able to keep the Toyota in sight, but fortunately the drive was a short one. Three blocks away, Donna turned into the parking lot of El Palacio, an anything but palatial looking Mexican restaurant.

Catherine parked a few spaces away from her. She waited for Donna to go inside, gave her time enough to order. The lot was mostly empty. A homeless man dumpster-diving at the far end remained oblivious to her presence. She opened her purse and counted out five twenty dollar bills, folded them into a neat little rectangle, and thrust that into her pocket where she could reach it quickly and easily. She was careful to lock her car's door and gave the badly lighted lot a quick look around. The dumpster-diver still hadn't noticed her. Or didn't care. When you were hungry enough nothing else mattered. She walked briskly past steam-frosted windows to the entrance and went in.

The small dining room was damp and overheated, with a smell of old grease and exuberant spices. A long window opened to a kitchen where several women sweated and worked energetically, hardly paying any attention to her entrance. A jeans-clad waitress with ketchup-colored antlers on her head looked her over and made a motion with her hands that Catherine took to mean, sit anywhere.

Donna was at a small table along one wall, reading a paperback novel and sipping a beer. Catherine took a breath and approached her quickly. She had slipped into the chair opposite before Donna even noticed her.

"I'm sorry to intrude," Catherine said. "But, I wonder if you could spare me a minute?"

Donna gaped, startled. Her round face with its Cupid's bow mouth might have looked cherubic, if cherubs had spots and hard looking, too-narrow eyes that blinked when they saw her and then narrowed still further.

"You're that woman, like, at the clinic," she said.

"Yes and I…I do apologize for sneaking up on you like this, it's just…well, it's very important."

Donna clamped her mouth shut and closed her paperback novel. "Excuse me," she said and started to get up, chair scraping.

"No, wait, please." Catherine put a hand over the one with the book. "I won't take but a moment, I promise. And I would be ever so grateful if you would just talk to me." With her other hand, she took the twenties out of her pocket and laid them atop the table, her fingers not quite covering them. Donna's eyes flicked to the money and stayed there. She sat back down and took another sip of her beer. It left a faint ring of foam around her mouth. She licked it off.

The waitress approached and set a plate of chicken with rice in front of Donna, her eyes briefly registering the money under Catherine's fingers. "Anything else?" she asked, eyes sliding from Donna's face to Catherine's and back to the money. The felt antlers drooped and bobbed.

"Just coffee for me," Catherine said. Donna shook her head. At least, Catherine thought, I've got her attention. She waited until the waitress left before continuing.

"It's just that," she said, dropping her voice to a conspiratorial level, "well, I thought that the other woman back there at the clinic, the nurse…."

"Miss Griff? She's a bitch." Donna's eyes remained glued to the money on the table. "And she's not a nurse either, not a real one."

Catherine smiled faintly and nudged the bills a little further across the table with the tips of her fingers. "I'm sure she had her reasons for shunting me off. Her orders, probably. But I'm just so worried, about my husband, I mean. I'm afraid he's seriously ill, and he won't talk to me about it. I thought if I could talk to his doctor, but, well…." She let her voice trail off.

"It isn't like that," Donna said. "Your husband wasn't even, like, the patient. He just came in with his brother, it was his brother that was the patient. But it was, you know, your husband who paid for him."

"His brother?"

"Mike Something. He was like his half brother, I think, anyway, I remember they didn't have the same last name. They didn't look alike, either. But, you know, half brothers don't, do they?" She shrugged and pulled her eyes up at last to Catherine's face. As if of

194

their own accord, her hand with its chewed nails rested on the table top, moved slightly in the direction of the bundle of twenties.

Walter had no brother, half or otherwise. They had often talked of the fact that they had both been only children.

"And was he, this brother, was he very ill?" she asked.

A shake of the head. "Not at all. It was, you know, he had some work done. Like, cosmetic work, that's what they do there, the doctors at the clinic. Mostly cheap boob jobs, collagen, nose jobs. They fixed his nose, I remember. Not, like, a nose job, I mean, not a regular nose job. Just, when he came in it was all bent to the side, you know, like it had been broken or something. And they took a mole off his chin. I don't know exactly what all, I wasn't...are you all right?"

"Yes, I'm fine," Catherine managed to say and fought the dizziness that had swept over her, making the room tilt and sway. The background noise of the restaurant, the voices from the kitchen, the clatter of pans and china, faded into a distant murmur.

"'Cause you looked like you were about to pass out. Look, let me get you some water or something." Donna started to get up again and, remembering, paused to snatch up the money and shove it into a pocket of her jacket.

Catherine got to her feet, almost colliding with the waitress bringing her coffee. "No, thank you, I have to go." She tossed a couple of ones on the table for the coffee, and added, for Donna's benefit, "and thank you, thank you so much for talking to me."

She walked quickly away, out of the restaurant, heart pounding.

The waitress stared after her. "What was that all about?" she asked.

Donna took the money from her pocket and unfolded it. Five of them. A hundred bucks. Not bad. She shrugged and said, "Some society bitch slumming, who knows."

* * * * * * *

In her car Catherine sat and stared into the darkness. Walter and Paterson? It wasn't possible, surely? The man who had kidnapped his daughter? She couldn't believe it.

Was there some other connection? She thought of Walter hiding something in that space under the floor in his office. Once again, drugs came into her mind. Maybe the answer was there.

At the first stoplight, she called Walter on his cell phone and, when he answered, asked if he had gotten the money she had left for him.

"Yes, Catherine, thank you so much, I'll pay you back, I promise."

"I'm glad I could help. Sorry I missed you, but something came up." There were kitchen noises in the background, telling her he was at the restaurant. That was her real reason for phoning him, and no need now to ask. The house was empty. That was what she wanted to know.

She caught the Santa Monica Freeway west, glad to be out of Compton, took Westwood Boulevard off the freeway and drove north: toward the house that she had shared for so many years with Walter. The house where, she hoped, her questions would be answered.

* * * * * *

Something was wrong. From the moment he had stepped into his office after his meeting, from the moment the lights seemed to flicker, casting an eerie yellow glow briefly over the room, alarms bells had gone off in Jack's mind.

His first thought was of Catherine. He had agonized the remainder of the night over their quarrel, desperately trying to find some middle ground that they could settle in, and finding himself inevitably back at the same stalemate.

He had started to call her before leaving for work, and put it off. He told himself that it was consideration for the fact that she might be sleeping in, but it was sheer cowardice. He was afraid she might not want to talk to him, might never want to talk to him again. Cowardice and frustration, because he still had no argument that would convince her to give up her pursuit of Trash Can Paterson. He put the call off, hoping that some inspiration would come to him.

Now, however, the warning bells were too loud to ignore. He called the number at the safe house, but there was no answer. He listened in mounting frustration as the phone rang again and again. On a hunch, he called her apartment. Nothing. He hung up and checked his voice mail. Nothing there either. He tried her office, and when she wasn't in, asked to talk to Bill.

"She was here," Bill said. "She left a couple of hours ago."

"Did she say anything about where she was going?"

"Not really. She asked me to look up a clinic in Compton. The, let me think, The Harvard Beerman Clinic. She might have gone there."

Jack hung up the phone, more puzzled and worried than ever. Compton? Catherine's doctor had offices in Century City, not far from where she worked. Why would she go to a clinic in Compton, of all places?

Still—a medical problem. Maybe a different doctor? You couldn't hold the location against someone. And no real evidence that she had gone there anyway, that might have been mere coincidence, or something to do with a book. More than likely, Catherine had given in to the frustration and boredom of being confined, and her unhappiness over their spat, and had simply gone out for a breather.

That strange yellow light, like lightning, flickered again.

He dialed Chang's number.

* * * * * * *

Sitting at a stoplight in Hollywood, Chang listened with a growing sense of unease to Jack's worried explanation. She had been about to call both of them with her good news: O'Dell had completely caved when they had showed up with their warrant, had tearfully told them everything, had fingered Paterson as his supplier, both for drugs and for kid-porn.

"He's evil," he blubbered while the uniforms bagged and cataloged his collection. "I should never have gotten mixed up with him."

Amen to that, Chang had thought, but she could find no sympathy in her heart for O'Dell. He had been an all too willing participant, as far as she could see. Without the collusion of people like him, the Patersons and his ilk would be out of business before they started.

She had left Conners to book the actor and was on her way back to her office, to coordinate with the King for a warrant to enter the Big Bear cabin, when she got the call from Jack.

Now, the news that Catherine had disappeared—into Compton?—took precedence over warrants. Paterson thought he was safe in Big Bear. He would stay on ice for a few more hours. Catherine AWOL was another matter. "She's not at the safe house?" she asked.

"She doesn't answer the phone," he said. "I haven't actually been, yet." He paused briefly. "We had a quarrel. A stupid one."

"Meet me there," she said. The quarrel wasn't any of her business; Catherine's whereabouts were. The light had turned green and the driver behind her began to honk insistently.

She gave him the bird and hung a right at the next corner, already punching numbers into her cell phone.

"Shoot out at the O.K. Corral," she said when Conners answered.

* * * * * * *

Walter had no sooner ended his call with Catherine than his cell phone rang again. It was the voice he dreaded. He prayed each time that this would be the last, and knew in his heart that it would never end.

"I'm on the freeway, heading into town," Paterson said. In the background Walter could hear the roar of engines, horns honking, the whoosh of thousands of tires on pavement. "I need that five grand."

"I haven't got that much, Trash." He hated himself for the whine that crept into his voice. "Like I told you, I'm all tapped out. When the house gets sold, then I can...."

"I can't wait for no frigging house to sell, I need some money now. How much have you got?"

"Two thousand. That's all I could get. I'm broke, I tell you. And something else, Trash...." He hesitated, fearing the reaction he would get, but he forced himself to say it anyway. "I've been thinking about this long and hard. I'm giving it up."

Paterson's voice was sharp. "What do you mean, giving it up? Giving what up?"

"All of it." Walter's voice broke in a sob. One of the grill cooks glanced in his direction. Walter sniffled loudly and got himself under control. "I'll give you the two thousand," he said in a lowered voice, "and then I'm getting rid of all my stuff, I'm going to burn it. It's sick, man. *I'm* sick. I can't live with myself any more. I can't live with what I've done. I'm going to burn everything, and then I'm turning myself in. To the police."

"The police? Are you fucking crazy? What about me? Hell, here I have been nothing but a friend to you all this time, anything you wanted, nothing was too good for you, and you're talking about turning on me, turning me over to the cops? What kind of shit is that?"

"Not you," Walter insisted. "I won't say a word about you or Colley, I swear it, I wouldn't ever do that. I just…I got to do it, man, I've got to get this off my conscience. It's killing me, I'm dying from inside."

"Look, first place, you can't burn DVDs, they won't melt." He had no idea if that was true or not, but it sounded right, and anyway, Desmond was a dumb shit, he wouldn't know any better. "Okay, so say you don't want the stuff around any more, I'll take it off your hands, you just hand it all over to me and it's gone. Hell, I'll even get you some of your money back. Not all of it, but some."

"I don't care about the money."

"Well, you turn yourself in to the police, you're going to need money for a lawyer, that's for sure, lots of money. Look, where are you now?"

"I'm at the restaurant, but I'm just getting ready to go home. I'm going to do it now, before I turn chicken."

"Okay, calm down, calm down, listen, I'll meet you there, at your place. We'll talk about all this. Don't do anything till I get there, okay?" Walter hesitated. "Okay?" Paterson insisted.

Walter ran the back of his hand across his runny nose. "Okay. And, Trash, I mean it, I'm not going to say anything to the cops about you, not a word."

Paterson ended the call. "You got that right, you dumb fuck," he said. "Head for Desmond's place," he told Colley, "quick like a rabbit." His mood was ferocious. Everything had gone wrong, and he knew exactly who was to blame. But he couldn't have her husband screwing things up either. Going to the cops? What kind of shit was that?

"What are you going to do, Trash?" Colley asked, automatically picking up speed.

"What the hell do you think I'm going to do?" Paterson reached into the glove box and took out the .38, checking to make sure it was loaded. "He's dead meat. And good riddance, far as I'm concerned."

CHAPTER TWENTY-THREE

Catherine called the house on her way, to see if by any chance Walter had left the restaurant after her call and come home. Even when she was there, when she had driven past the realtor's For Sale sign and parked the car half in, half out of the garage, she called yet again on her cell phone. She could actually hear the kitchen phone ringing inside the house.

She thought about calling Jack, or Chang. Certainly she would have been glad to have either of them with her, or both. She was no hero. Her heart turned to ice when she thought of what she was about to do, but it was simply something else she had to do herself. She had to know, had to be certain; but the suspicions clamoring inside her head were so horrible that she could not share them with anyone while there remained the slightest possibility that Walter was innocent of them. Once a man had been tarred with that sort of accusation he could never be entirely free of it.

She owed him that much, at least. This might all be some sort of ghastly misunderstanding. Walter's visits to the clinic might be entirely innocent. And Donna could have gotten things mixed up. She hadn't appeared to be the swiftest boat in the water.

If Walter had any connection with Paterson, he deserved whatever punishment he got, but she would give him the benefit of every doubt until she was sure, until she knew the truth.

She felt a prickling at the back of her neck as she got out of the car. Paterson, somewhere close? She heard the sound of an approaching car and held her breath, but it went on by, splashing a street-side puddle of rainwater.

She considered looking in on Paterson, to see where he was at the moment, but she was afraid to do so, afraid of drawing him to her. The last thing she wanted was for him to find her here, even on the spirit level. She wanted no interruptions in what she had planned.

She went in through the kitchen, leaving the garage door open so that if he should come home, Walter would know that she was here. Better to confront him than to have him call the police to report a burglary in progress. If everything she suspected was somehow a horrible mistake, she certainly did not want the police involved in it. Not even Chang. Not until she knew.

She could understand why the house remained unsold, realty sign notwithstanding. It was a pig sty, dishes piled everywhere, half eaten food moldering on the table, wrappers and cans littering the floor. A sour, rotting smell permeated the air. She thought of the meticulous, neat man with whom she had lived for years. He had vanished, apparently, consumed by another self that must always have lurked within him.

She tossed her jacket on a chair, hardly glancing at the disarray, and went directly to Walter's office. Even living alone, he would probably not have abandoned his safe hiding place. That sort of habit did not die easily.

The carpet on the floor of the closet was loose. She pulled it back, to reveal a trapdoor. The space below was crude, unfinished, just dust covered boards and wooden beams. Nestled in the gap between the beams was a small cardboard box.

She lifted it out, dreading what she might find, and opened the flaps on top. A gun lay inside. She hadn't known Walter even owned a gun. It was impossible for her to imagine him using it.

Next to the gun was a small plastic bag half filled with white powder. Cocaine, she wondered? Speed? She was woefully ignorant about such things, but Chang would know. And, anyway, that wasn't what she was looking for. Just for the moment she couldn't have cared less about any drug problem of Walter's. If there were anything that evidenced a link between him and Paterson, this was where it would be hidden. Right this instant, that was all she cared about.

Beneath the plastic bag were a couple of DVDs, unlabeled, and a manila envelope. The envelope was filled with pictures. She slid them out and looked at the one on top.

Her stomach gave a warning turn. She gasped aloud. Though she had never before seen anything like this, she knew exactly what she was looking at. Chang had called it "kiddie porn," but that label was altogether misleading. It sounded too cute, too innocent, for the filth she held in her hands.

Even "porn" didn't seem right. Time and usage had made that word less wretched than it once was. She had even heard the expression "porn-chic," an implication of something exciting, something sexually advanced, sophisticated.

How, she wondered dazedly, could anyone find this sexually exciting? Yet it was self-evident that *someone* must. This clearly was the business that drove Paterson and Colley: producing just such horrors as these pictures and, she was sure without even looking at them, the videos as well. This was why they needed children, needed to steal them, because how else to recruit these poor, tortured innocents? She leafed through the photographs, having to force herself to look at them when her eyes wanted to slide away. Little girls, and little boys as well. No gender discrimination in this hell, she thought grimly.

She groaned aloud and let the pictures fall from her hands. They fluttered to the floor like leaves from a dying tree.

It was horrible enough to contemplate what Paterson and Colley had done, were still doing, would continue to do until she found a way to stop them. It was worse, infinitely worse, to know that their evil business could not exist were there not people willing to pay money for pictures such as these.

People like Walter. She could not pretend about that. These pictures hadn't simply fallen into his hands. Even if they had come to him through some freak set of circumstances, a normal person, a sane person, would immediately turn them over to the police, would be as sickened and shamed by them as she was. That Walter had kept them, kept them hidden away here in this little cache, told her everything.

She had lived with a stranger for years, shared his home, his bed, borne a child to him, and here, for the first time, she was seeing who he really was. A part of her hated not only him, but herself as well for being such a fool, for unwittingly providing him with a cover of innocence that had allowed him to practice his vice undetected, even unsuspected.

With that thought came another, the most terrifying of all. She snatched up the pictures, riffling through them hastily. She could not bear to think that Becky might be in any of these photos, and at the same time couldn't bear not to know.

That little girl, with blonde hair, her face hidden, could that be her? She stared, horrified, at the image, but she could not say. She went through the pictures again, but there was no one of whom she could be certain. In all but the rarest few, the faces were hidden. They were only bodies, these tiny victims, just flesh to be violated.

She hurled the photos away from her. With a loud sob, she buried her face in her hands. It seemed to her as if she could hear the cries of all those tortured children, their voices clamoring for help, for comfort, for justice.

"Catherine?" Walter said from outside the room. He appeared in the door and saw her kneeling by the closet, his eyes taking in the exposed cubbyhole, the cardboard box, the photos strewn on the floor. "Oh, hell," he said.

"Yes, Walter, hell." She got slowly to her feet, hardly noticing that her legs had gone stiff from kneeling on the hard floor. "That is exactly what I am looking at, at a window into hell."

He stood motionless, hands hanging helplessly at his sides, and began to cry, quietly, tears rolling down his cheeks. "I wanted to tell you." His voice was little more than a whisper, but so sharpened were her senses that she heard him as clearly as if he were shouting. "For so long, I wanted to, but I couldn't. How could I?"

"How, indeed? How could one explain anything like this?" She leaned down to snatch up a handful of the photographs, "To any sane person? What? Why? How?"

"It was drugs. Cocaine." He paused for her to say something.

"Go on," she said in an icy voice. "I want you to make me understand what could have brought you to this. How could cocaine, how could any drug, result in these pictures?"

"You remember, three years ago," he said, speaking in an earnest voice as if he truly wanted to make it clear to her, "when I started up the restaurant, I was working such long hours, night and day it seemed, and one of the cooks offered me some cocaine. Have you ever...?"

She shook her head and said nothing.

"Well, it's hard to describe exactly, it picks you up, like a super tonic, everything goes faster. And at first it helped, I couldn't believe how well, it gave me the energy I needed, it seemed like I could go on forever.

"It was just a little each time to start, a couple of lines, once, maybe twice an evening. After a while, though, I needed more to do the job, and more still. And finally the cook said it would be cheaper and simpler if I got it myself, and he hitched me up with a supplier. I started getting it by the ounce, it was cheaper, like he'd said, and I had all I needed all the time. The dealer was there for me whenever I needed him."

"Paterson," she said, her voice even, emotionless.

He blinked, surprised that she knew the name. "Yes, Paterson. Trash Can, they call him. How do you…?" But her look stopped his question. He hesitated but when she said nothing, he went on. "Well, that worked for a while, I'd buy it from him, and sometimes we'd do it together, at his place, and listen to music and talk. He seemed like such a great guy, he made me feel, I don't know, smart, important, special. Our marriage wasn't, you know, things had long since died out for us."

"Don't, Walter," she said coldly. "Don't suggest for a moment that I am to blame, that our marriage led to this. Yes, I know that I was not a model wife. It was a rotten marriage, I will grant you that, but millions of people survive rotten marriages without turning into monsters."

He gulped and shook his head. "No, no, it wasn't our marriage, it wasn't you. I know that. Paterson is to blame, he's the one who…." His voice broke. He swallowed hard. "Well, one night he told me someone owed him for a bunch of drugs and didn't have the money, so they paid him off with a collection of pornography, and that some of it was pretty weird. He played on my curiosity until I insisted I see it for myself. I was high. You think funny when you're on the stuff.

"Anyway, there was a lot of the usual sort of thing. It was okay, some of it was pretty good, but I couldn't see what he meant about weird. Then he showed me this one movie…it's there, in the hole. It…it disgusted me, Catherine, honestly, it did. But, God forgive me, it excited me too. I couldn't help it. I got turned on watching it. I know it's sick, but we can't help how we are made, can we? I didn't want to respond to it, but I did, despite myself."

He paused reflectively. "What I can't understand, what I have asked myself so many times after, was how did he know? How could he have guessed that movie would turn me on like it did?"

"I should have thought the answer to that would have been obvious, Walter. Water, even filthy water, rises to its own level, doesn't it? Tell me one thing," she came a step toward him and brandished the stack of photographs, "Tell me Becky isn't in these pictures."

He began to sob then, softly at first and then louder, his tears streaming unchecked, his nose running. "I couldn't help it," he said between choking sobs, "They blackmailed me. There were pictures of me with this little girl. I was in some of them. I swear to God I didn't even remember them being taken, I don't know when or how it happened, but it was me, you could recognize me right off. I must have been totally wasted. Anyway, they showed me these pictures, they threatened me with them, if I didn't...they made me...that day...."

She suddenly realized where this was leading. Her heart seemed to stop. In her worst nightmare she could not have imagined this. "You set her up, didn't you?" she demanded, her voice little more than a hoarse whisper, the words coming only with great difficulty. "You let them take her that day?"

His sobs became a bleat of pain. "They promised me they wouldn't hurt her. They swore it. They were just going to take pictures, was all. They even let me be there, so I could be sure, so I could see for myself they didn't hurt her. I would never have agreed otherwise, I swear it. I said I would have to be there. I insisted."

The light. It was there in the room, growing rapidly brighter, beginning to swirl around her. She found it increasingly difficult to keep him in focus. She knew what it meant, knew she was being called somewhere, but she couldn't go, not now. She had to know the rest, all of it, no matter what it cost her. She pushed the light away from her with her mind.

"Wouldn't hurt her? Are you mad? How could you think this?" she waved the photos at him, "this wouldn't hurt her? And they killed her, didn't they? Were you there when they did that, too? Did you not think that hurt her? Me? You?"

"No." He shouted it at her. "I swear, I wasn't there when...I left. I couldn't stand to watch, it was.... I wanted it to stop, but they wouldn't, they laughed at me, told me if I wasn't man enough, to get out. And I did."

"And you left her there?"

"Only, she had seen me, Catherine. She knew I was there. She called me 'Daddy'."

It broke in her then. A moan came out of her like the sound of death. She flung the pictures in his face and ran at him, slapping him with all her strength, pounding his chest with her fists, her own tears pouring down now.

"God damn you, God damn you straight to hell, Walter."

"Yes, yes," he sobbed, and sank to his knees before the fury of her attack. "Hit me, kick me, *kill me*, in the name of Heaven, I want to die."

As quickly as it had come over her, her rage retreated, replaced by a fury too cold for rage, a sense of hatred and odium such as she had never experienced before. She stepped back from him, panting for breath, like she had just finished a ten-K run. "You shall, Walter, you shall, I promise you that."

He sat on his knees, head bent, sobbing helplessly. She turned from him, couldn't bear the sight of him, the sound of his sobs. She left the room, went to where she had tossed her jacket and fished her cell phone out of the pocket.

"Where are you?" Chang answered the call at once.

"I'm at Walter's, at the house. I need to see you, I…."

This time the light would not be denied. It consumed her, blinding her, and inside her head a voice shouted, "He's here!"

The warning was too late. A voice behind her, a real voice, said, "Put down the phone."

CHAPTER TWENTY-FOUR

"Paterson." She spoke the name aloud. He was there, and Colley just behind him. She hadn't heard them come in. A wave of terror sweep over her, settled like ice in her veins. As horrible as the astral confrontations had been, she had known then, at least, that there were on different planes. Confronting him once again in the flesh was infinitely worse. Her legs felt suddenly weak, and she grabbed the back of a chair to support herself.

"Catherine?" Chang's anxious voice sounded faintly from the cell phone. "Paterson? He's there?"

"Yes," Catherine said.

Paterson gestured with the gun in his hand. "Hang it up. Put it down."

Catherine hesitated, not so much wanting to defy him as simply too frozen to move.

"You bitch." He strode to her and snatched the phone from her hand, flinging it to the floor, and struck her hard across the face with the back of his hand. She reeled and crashed into the wall. "I'm going to make you pay for everything you've done to me."

"Leave her alone," Walter said from the doorway of his office. He had the gun from the cubbyhole in his hand. "Do whatever you want with me, but leave her alone."

"You dumb fuck," Paterson said. "Colley! Get that gun off him."

Colley took a step in Walter's direction and Walter fired. With a yelp of pain, Colley staggered and fell onto the sofa, knocking over the lamp beside it. But before Walter could turn back to Paterson, Paterson had shot him. Walter gave a moan and dropped his gun, clutching at the red stain that quickly spread across his chest.

"Catherine," he gasped. He tottered a step in her direction before his legs gave out and he fell face down, his hands splayed toward her.

Catherine screamed. "You've killed him," she shouted, and threw herself at Paterson, hitting his face and chest with all her strength. Her attack surprised him. The gun fell from his hand and Catherine dropped to her knees and snatched it up, but Paterson was too quick for her. He kicked it out of her hand and yanked her violently to her feet, pinning her against his chest despite her struggles.

"A wildcat, ain't you? Over him? He ain't worth it. Anyway, he had it coming." Paterson sneered down at Walter. "Stupid bastard. Quit struggling or I'll bust you again. Get up, Colley, you're not dead. And hand me that gun."

"He got my leg, Trash Can," Colley whined, but he got up as he was ordered, trying to stanch the flow of blood from a wound on his thigh, and retrieved Paterson's gun.

Catherine had stopped struggling but she was still breathing heavily. Oddly, she felt less frightened now. Anger had taken over for the fear. Paterson's gaze switched back to her and he gave her a grin dripping with malice.

"Go ahead, kill me," she said.

"Oh, no, bitch, that'd be too easy. I've got better plans for you. I've always wanted to film a snuff movie, and I just found me my leading lady. By the time I'm through with you, you'll be begging to die."

Her cell phone rang. He put a booted foot on it and ground it to pieces. "Colley, get them pictures, the movies, all of it. And be quick."

Holding a hand to his wounded leg, Colley limped into the other room, blood dripping through his fingers onto the carpet. Paterson snatched up Catherine's jacket from the chair and flung it at her. "Put that on, I don't want you catching a cold. You're an *asset* now," making an obscenity out of the word.

She struggled into her jacket. Her eyes dropped to Walter's gun where it had fallen on the floor. If she could reach that…but before she could try Paterson had produced a set of handcuffs from his belt and cuffed her hands together in front of her. Colley came back, stuffing photos and DVD's into a plastic grocery bag. "Coke, too," he said triumphantly, "A half ounce, maybe."

"Fine. Let's go." Paterson dragged her to the front door.

Outside, stumbling down the steps, she wondered if she could get away from him and make a run for it, but he held her arm in a fierce grip. She looked desperately toward the street, but the stone wall and the citrus trees that had always provided such welcome privacy in the past screened her as well from any likelihood of neighbors seeing them.

It had begun to rain again while she was inside, a steady drizzle that already was collecting in puddles. Walter's Buick sat beside the Jaguar in the garage, and behind that sat a battered gray van.

He threw open the rear door of the van and shoved her violently inside and slammed the door shut. "Get in back with her," he ordered Colley.

"My leg's hurting, Trash," Colley whined, climbing in alongside Catherine and using his hands to pull his wounded leg inside. Paterson swung himself into the driver's seat and fired up the engine. They reversed into the street, and Catherine braced herself to jump from the van, but Paterson, looking over his shoulder to back up, shook his head warningly.

"Don't even think about it," he said, "I'd run you down before you got ten feet."

He handed the gun back to Colley. "If she tries to jump, shoot her in the knee. That'll slow her down. And keep her awake. She's too dangerous when she's asleep."

Catherine shrank as far away from Colley as she could get and leaned her head against the window. Colley glowered at her, alert for any attempt to open the door, but by now they were going too fast for her to jump. He leaned across her and pushed the lock down anyway, just in case.

She closed her eyes, tried to shut out the pain in her jaw where Paterson had struck her. Despair engulfed her. She thought of Walter, poor foolish Walter. He had been no match for Paterson's evil. It had consumed him. He was dead now, and she could even pity him, though she could not forgive. To the end, he had blamed everyone and everything else for his failing. He had died believing that none of it was his fault. God would judge him now.

She had no hope that her fate would be any better. She knew at least what a snuff movie was: a film of someone being murdered, the death recorded for whatever sort of ghoul found that exciting. No doubt it would be a slow, horrible death.

The death itself didn't frighten her, even the ghastly prelude that she was sure she would suffer first. She had died before, and not just when Paterson had shot her. She had died a kind of death when she faced what had happened to Becky. She came back from both of those experiences. She would not come back from this one, but surely it could be no worse than what she suffered then.

THE ASTRAL: TILL THE DAY I DIE, BY V. J. BANIS

The real tragedy was not her fate. Far worse was that these two would live, free to continue their horror, to continue to prey on the innocent, the helpless.

No, she thought suddenly, fiercely. No, that mustn't happen. She *had* died before, and she had been sent back, been given a special gift, all for a purpose: to stop them.

But how?

* * * * * * *

The first thing they saw was Walter's body on the floor, the gun nearby, the blood staining the carpet.

"Oh, God," Jack cried, and then, "Catherine! Catherine!" He ran through the house, from room to room, calling her name and looking for her. "She's not here. They've taken her."

Conners had paused to take in the filth and disorder in the kitchen. "Wow, I wonder if Martha Stewart has an emergency number?" he said. He followed the trail of blood droplets into what appeared to be a home office, half expecting to find another body, but there was no one there. He spotted a photograph half under the desk and stooped to pick it up, grimacing in disgust.

"Check it out," he said, handing the photo to Chang as she entered the room.

"The husband? Into kiddies?"

"It explains a lot," he said. "Like the difference in their M.O. when his daughter was snatched."

"He set it up," she said in a burst of understanding. "Damn. I'm sorry the bastard is dead."

"Where...?" Jack said from the doorway, but she gave him a "wait-a-sec" gesture.

"Get the black and whites on their way," she told Conners, "But tell them it's F.B.I. business, touch nothing. I'll get one of our agents here pronto but I need you to secure the scene till he gets here."

"Where will you be?" Conners asked.

"We're headed for Big Bear," she told him, already on the run, signaling for Jack to follow her.

A siren wailed in the distance as they clambered into the Bronco. She threw the car into gear and made a turn in the wet grass, leaving deep ruts behind, their headlights tearing at the trees. They were gone a full two minutes before the black and white careened into the driveway, lights flashing, siren blaring.

210

* * * * * * *

The van rocked as Paterson swung onto a freeway at high speed, skidding slightly on the rain slick ramp, and gunned his way into the stream of traffic. The Santa Monica Freeway, heading east. To Big Bear, Catherine wondered? She had thought Paterson was in Mexico, had seen dirt roads and shacks—but, she realized belatedly, that could describe Big Bear, too.

By now, Chang had surely reached the house. How could she alert her? She closed her eyes and suddenly she was in the back seat of the Bronco, Chang at the wheel and Jack in the passenger's seat. She leaned forward and tried to tap Jack on the shoulder, but of course her hand went through him. Nor could she make any sound. How in the name of Heaven was she to communicate?

She looked long and hard at the back of his neck. This had worked in the quietness of his office and her apartment, but then it had been little more than a game. Could she make him aware of her presence here, now?

"What if they've already skipped out of Big Bear" Jack asked.

Chang swerved out of the way of another approaching black and white. "They don't know we've busted O'Dell so they still think his place is safe. I'll give you odds that's where they're taking Catherine," Chang said with more confidence than she felt. She had gambled on Paterson's ignorance once before, with disastrous results.

"And if it's not?"

"You got any better suggestions?"

"No. But, if we're wrong...."

He turned toward her and his glance fell on the back seat—and he saw, to his astonishment, Catherine sitting there. She nodded her head frantically.

"Big Bear?" he asked, and she nodded her head up and down again. In the next instant, she was gone.

"Yes, Big Bear," Chang said, puzzled. "Isn't that what we've been talking about?"

"Yes. Yes, Big Bear," he said in an excited voice.

"Are you okay?" Seeing him stare, she glanced over her shoulder into the empty back seat. "What changed your mind all of a sudden?"

"Big Bear," he said again with a grin. "I'll explain in a minute. You were right, that's where they're headed. And don't spare the horses."

* * * * * * *

Colley was shaking her.

"Damn it, I told you not to let her go to sleep, Colley," Paterson said from the front seat, slapping the steering wheel with one hand. "For Christ's sake, do whatever you got to do to keep her awake."

"Anything?" Colley asked with a lewd smirk.

"Keep that in your pants, we'll need it later. Just keep her awake."

Still smirking, Colley reached under Catherine's jacket and pawed her breasts. She sucked in her breath as he tore her blouse open, pawed her bra out of the way, and pinched one nipple viciously.

"That'll keep you awake, I bet." He glanced down meaningfully at his lap, where a growing bulge was becoming evident. "Him, too," he added with a chuckle.

She tried to shrink away from him and realized that her resistance was only fueling his excitement. Instead, she sank back against the seat, letting her entire body grow limp.

"Keep your eyes open," Colley ordered.

She obeyed, looking straight ahead, watching the freeway signs rushing toward them in the rain-streaked windshield and sailing past. Yes, she had been right, they were on the I-10 now, heading east, toward San Bernardino, and beyond that, the mountains and Big Bear.

Had Jack seen her? Did he understand? She'd had no more than a few seconds before Paterson had realized what she was doing. Somehow, he was attuned to her astral projections. That was going to make things even more difficult.

Paterson maneuvered the van into the fast lane. It would be forty-five minutes or more before they left the freeway, maybe an hour in this driving rain, in the dark. For the first time since Paterson had flung her into the van, however, she felt hope stirring within her. She thought wryly that Paterson had made a mistake in bringing her along alive. He might have been wiser, indeed, to have killed her back there with Walter, as she had defied him to do.

She smiled inwardly and closed her mind to the coarse hand mauling her breast. After a moment, Colley grew tired of her indifference, and the hand was gone.

"Icy, ain't you?" he snarled at her, and tugged at his lap to make himself more comfortable. "I need to pee," he announced to Paterson.

"Piss in your pants." Paterson rammed the heel of his hand down on the horn to warn an errant pick up truck out of his way and veered around it, tires momentarily losing their grip on the wet pavement. He swore under his breath and brought the van under control.

The rain came down harder, wipers struggling to keep the windshield clear. He turned them up to the fastest setting, and cursed again. Ahead of them, brake lights flashed as the traffic began to slow in the downpour.

Fifty-five minutes later, they veered off the freeway at Redlands and in a few minutes more they were on Route 38, the two-lane road that twisted and climbed its way into the mountains. As they drove higher, the rain on the windshield turned to sleet and soon after that to snow.

The road would take them directly into Big Bear, but Catherine was sure that the town itself was not their destination. These men would not want neighbors close by. They needed a place off to itself.

Which meant that somewhere between here and Big Bear they would leave this highway. The Big Bear area was streaked with roads and lanes, some of them little more than trails, that led into the forests to isolated cabins where one could live unnoticed for weeks, months even.

Did Chang already know where they were headed? She must have, mustn't she, to have started out on her own for Big Bear? She glanced surreptitiously at her watch. How far behind her could they be? Twenty minutes, maybe, surely no more than half an hour.

The higher they climbed, the harder the snow fell, a dancing curtain of white in the twin tunnels created by their headlights. Paterson was forced to slow down, cursing non-stop as he did so. The road had been recently cleared, but already the new snow had begun to stick. The rear end of the van skidded sideways.

He jerked the wheel and pulled abruptly into a turn off at the side of the road and the van slid to a stop. "We're gonna need the chains," he said. "Give me the gun. I'll watch her. You put them on."

"My leg, Trash Can. You forgetting I was shot?"

"It didn't slow down your pecker any back there a ways. If you can get a boner you can handle tire chains. Go on, they're there in the back. And make it quick, we don't want any company pulling in behind us here."

Grumbling, Colley climbed out, letting a gust of frigid air sweep through the van, and limped toward the rear. Chains rattled as he dragged them out and dropped them to the ground.

Paterson knelt on the front seat and kept his eyes glued to Catherine, the gun propped on the seat back. She looked steadily away from him, at the snow blowing fiercely past the windows. For a moment she hoped that someone would pull into the turn off, but as soon as she thought that, she changed her mind. Paterson would almost certainly kill any unfortunate passerby who stopped. She wanted no more blood on her hands.

Colley went by the window, still grumbling, and knelt out of sight. After a moment, he yelled, "Pull up about two feet."

Paterson turned away from Catherine to fire up the engine again. For a moment she was unwatched. She eyed the forest outside the van and briefly considered trying to make a run for it. If she could only get into those trees he would have a hard time taking a shot at her.

Which, she quickly concluded, would leave her alone and helpless, and handcuffed, in the woods, at night, in the middle of a near blizzard, and God only knew how far the nearest cabin might be. Even if Paterson and Colley didn't come after her and catch her, she would likely freeze to death before she found anyone who could help her.

She closed her eyes and tried to send herself swiftly to Jack and Chang. She had a brief glimpse through the windshield of Chang's Bronco, saw the freeway sign for Redlands. They were gaining ground. She opened her eyes back in the van, and suppressed a smile.

Paterson yanked his head around, his eyes narrowed. "What are you doing?" he demanded. He closed his own eyes for a second. "Somebody's following us, ain't they? You've tipped 'em off, haven't you? I ought to...." He lifted the gun as if to strike her with it, and she cringed, but the blow did not come. "Let 'em try to find us," he said with a smug expression. "You can't talk to them, can you? You can't steer the car for them. All I care, you can go sit on his lap, that won't tell them diddly."

She looked directly into his eyes. Surely even this man must have some spark of humanity in him. If only she could find a way to appeal to that. Wasn't that what they said a hostage should do, bond with your captors?

"How did you...how did you get into all this?" she asked.

"This?" He looked genuinely surprised by the question. "What do you mean?"

"The children. The sex, violence, all of it?"

He laughed. "Everything I know I learned from my daddy. Daddy got me off to an early start."

She could not conceal her horror. "You can't possibly mean that he, that your own father molested you?"

He sneered. "Hell, he was just making sure he got the cream off the top. Same as he did with my sister, wanted to be the first. What, you think that was something horrible, like? It wasn't. I got her after him, or between times, anyway. Hell, same time other boys were wishing they knew how to get themselves some I had it steady, and I didn't even have to go out of the house to get it. Pretty good way to grow up, you ask me."

Despite her disgust for the man she could not altogether escape a feeling of pity as well. Her dark angel, Gabronski had called him. A demon, even, who destroyed families, violated children. Yet he was once a child himself, and innocent. Innocence corrupted, the corrupted becoming the corrupter.

"Your sister...is she...?"

His grin faded. "She's dead," he said, voice flat. "Stupid bitch killed herself. Killed the old man, too. She'd have taken me with them if I had come home that day like she told me. What do you need to know all this shit for anyway?" he snapped, suddenly angry. "Colley, get your ass in gear, we ain't got all night."

"They're on," Colley said. He stood up and came around to the van's door, brushing snow off himself.

"Get the blanket out of the back," Paterson told him. He looked at Catherine again. "Something warned me not to come home that day, though. I always did have me a guardian angel, looking out for me. That's something you ought to know: she's never failed me yet."

Colley got the blanket from the back, letting another gust of frigid air into the van and climbed in again beside Catherine, tossing the blanket on the seat between them. Paterson passed the gun to him and drove back onto the road, the chains clacking rhythmically and loudly.

The chains gave the van's tires more grip on the snow covered pavement but they slowed them too. They were crawling now on their increasingly steep way up the mountain. Paterson drove in the middle of the road. Catherine glanced out the window at the sheer drop just beyond the edge of the road, and hoped they didn't meet any oncoming traffic on one of the curves.

"What's that up ahead?" Colley suddenly asked, alarmed. There were people and cars in the road ahead, taillights and hazard lights blinking. Red and blue Highway Patrol lights flashed a warning. A uniformed officer stepped into the center of the road and held up a hand as they neared.

"It's a road block, Trash."

CHAPTER TWENTY-FIVE

"Highway patrol," Paterson said, peering through the fogged-over windshield. "Chain stop. Get her down on the floor and put that blanket over her."

The van slowed. Highway Patrol vehicles blocked the road ahead. Half a dozen cars were pulled into a turnoff and men were putting chains on them.

"You heard the man," Colley said, and shoved her down between the seats. He threw the blanket over her. It smelled and she had to resist the urge to sneeze.

"Cock her if you have to," Paterson's muffled voice said.

They were barely moving now. A highway Patrolman strolled in the van's direction. Paterson rolled down his window.

"Evening, sir," he greeted the uniformed man with a smile, his hands gripping the wheel tensely. The officer glanced down at the tires with their chains and nodded his approval. Half the fools driving this road had to be told they needed chains.

"Where you headed?" he asked.

"Big Bear. Road's still open, isn't it?"

"It's open but it's snowing over pretty quick. Drive carefully, now," and he waved the van on through the checkpoint. The window went up. The van crept forward, picking up speed.

"Did I know him?" the patrolman wondered, looking after it. Something teased at his memory, but another vehicle was already rolling to a stop. He forgot the van, walked up to another rolled down window. It was a cold job. He rubbed his gloved hands together. Cold and busy. He wished his shift was over.

* * * * * * *

Catherine thought briefly about screaming, but under the cover of the blanket Colley pressed the gun against her head. She remained silent. She had no doubt that they would kill her, and the highway patrolman too. The van picked up speed again, and the cold air was cut off as Paterson rolled the window back up.

"You can get up now," Colley said, poking her with the gun, and yanking the blanket off her.

She crawled back onto the seat and sneezed. In the brief moment under the blanket, she got another glimpse of Jack and Chang. They were through Redlands already, gaining on them, the four-wheel drive Bronco able to make better time in the weather than Paterson's van could.

In the mirror, Paterson shot her an evil look. Did he know? He seemed almost to read her mind. She looked away, blowing a piece of lint off her lip, and tried to look hopeless.

* * * * * * *

It seemed an eternity later when the van swayed and tilted as it turned off the main road. Catherine peered intently through the windows, looking for signposts. There, a highway marker: mile thirty-one. On the opposite side of the road, a log fence with one timber fallen from its place, half buried in the snow.

Their pace slowed even more. This road was obviously unpaved under its deep blanket of snow. They were barely crawling now, the van pitching and slewing over ruts and bumps, the body groaning. Paterson wrestled with the steering wheel and flipped the headlights to bright, but they barely penetrated the curtain of white.

"Think we'll make it?" Colley asked, bracing himself against the back of the front seat as they jarred their way over some particularly large obstacle.

"Shut up, you fool," Paterson snapped, "I got my hands full here. You just keep your eyes on her."

Colley glanced dutifully in her direction, but clearly he was more concerned with their progress, and almost instantly he leaned forward again to peer anxiously through the windshield. Catherine stared too, though there was little to see beyond the endless whiteness swirling in their headlights.

They hit something, a rock, Catherine thought, and bounced even harder. The van came down with a crash, and stopped, wheels spinning helplessly in an effort to get traction.

"Now see what you did," Paterson shouted. He banged his hands on the steering wheel and gunned the motor ferociously, to no avail. The van remained stubbornly where it was, hung up on a rock.

"We'll have to walk," he said. He switched off the engine and flung his door violently open. Catherine shuddered in the onslaught of icy air.

"It's gotta be two miles from here," Colley said. "We'll freeze to death before we get there."

"Well, we sure as hell will freeze to death sitting here, won't we? We got to get to that cabin."

"If we can even find it," Colley grumbled under his breath.

"Shut up your griping. The cabin's not but twenty feet off the road, we can't miss it. Anyway, it's a dead end road. If we miss it first pass, we just backtrack. Get her out of there."

"Damn it to hell," Colley said, but he climbed out and, coming around to Catherine's side of the van, yanked her door open and tugged her out. She sank shin deep in the snow.

They started off, Paterson in the lead, bending into the wind that seemed to cut right through them. Colley gripped Catherine's arm tightly and followed him, limping and trying to step in Paterson's tracks. Catherine was grateful at least that Paterson had let her bring her jacket, but it was woefully inadequate for this kind of cold and her shoes were soaked within a few steps.

Paterson plunged ahead but it was quickly clear that neither the wounded Colley nor Catherine could match his pace, and he was forced to stop often, glowering impatiently at them and waiting for them to catch up.

It was impossible to judge the terrain under the snow and they all three stumbled frequently, catching themselves on the trees and shrubs hovering close on either side. Once Catherine tripped and, with her hands cuffed together, was unable to get a grip to steady herself. She fell to her knees in the snow.

Colley jerked her roughly to her feet. "You think I'm carrying you, think again," he snarled.

"You've got to take these off." She held up the cuffs.

"Go ahead," Paterson said impatiently, tossing him the keys. "She ain't got nowhere to go. You hear me, Miss High and Mighty? Best thing for you is to stay with us, you try getting away you'll end up freezing your tight ass off out there."

She didn't bother to answer. A fresh wave of despair swept over her. He was right: she was at their mercy.

Colley took the cuffs off and she rubbed her wrists where they had chafed. *No*, she told herself ferociously, *I won't think that way*. The important thing for the moment was that she was still alive. So long as she was alive, she had a chance.

"Let's go, move it," Paterson snapped. "You two're slower than molasses." He started off again in the lead. Colley gave Catherine's arm a yank, but she needed no urging. They had a destination and that meant shelter, at least, and surviving just that much longer.

She must concentrate on that, on staying alive. That was everything at the moment, just surviving. Paterson might suspect that someone was after them, but he couldn't be sure. And Jack and Chang were gaining on them, that was another thing she knew that Paterson did not. It was an advantage, if only a slim one.

She brought one foot down in front of the other, and then again, and again, and tried not to think of her toes freezing into pieces of ice.

* * * * * * *

She felt as if she could go no further. Beside her, Colley was reeling and stumbling and even Paterson, who seemed to possess a supernatural energy, was beginning to flag. In the dark, in the snow, she could just make out his back ahead of them, bent over against the wind.

He suddenly stopped in his tracks, looking around like a wild animal sniffing for a scent. Were they lost, she wondered, despite his macho-man confidence?

After a moment, he pointed his chin to their left. "It's over here," he said, though she could see nothing but the relentless sheets of snow.

"I don't see nothing," Colley said, but he followed in the deep prints Paterson left as he went now with a quicker pace.

"You're a moron," Paterson said, but even his insults sounded more good-natured.

He was right. Suddenly, as if by magic, a cabin loomed through the whiteness. Colley gave a little yip of excitement and even Catherine felt her spirits rise. Whatever might happen there, at least it would be a respite from the snow and the cold.

Paterson struggled at the door with numbed fingers. Catherine dropped helplessly to her knees on a hard wooden floor, too weak for the moment even to get to her feet.

Colley shoved the door shut behind them, a dusting of snow having already followed them in. Even without any heat, the cabin was blessedly warm after what they had just endured.

"Get her on the couch," Paterson said, and strode across to a soot-blackened fireplace where logs were already stacked waiting to be lit. He crumpled up a wad of newspaper, found a match on the mantle and lit it, and shoved it under the wood. In a minute tinder began to crackle and flame.

Shoved onto the couch like a bag of potatoes, Catherine had a moment to look around. It was not much of a cabin, just one large room with a couch and a bed and a pair of chairs, a make-do kitchen across one end. Just at the moment, it looked like a palace.

Having tossed her onto the couch, Colley rushed to the kitchen, snatched a can of something from one of the shelves and, hastily opening it, began to spoon the contents furiously into his mouth.

The fire started, Paterson followed his example. He opened a can and paused to give Catherine a measuring look. He thought about killing her, but somehow that idea didn't excite him the way it had before. He wasn't really a killer, except when he had to be.

The thought came to him of a sudden that the two of them had been brought together for some other reason, sucked to one another like nails to a magnet. No, couldn't be, he shoved that thought aside. What the hell could they have to do with one another except murdering? She'd have murdered him, that was for damned sure, if he'd given her the chance.

Still, he had been thinking on the ride up the mountain, that he hadn't realized before what a beauty she was, even with the fatigue and all. He could see easy enough how she could bewitch a man, how she had made such a fool of that weak-sister husband of hers. That dumb sap had not been enough of a man for her, ever. This was a woman that needed a real man, a man who....

He shook himself like a dog climbing out of water. Where in the hell had that kind of thinking come from? Jesus, she was witching him, too.

* * * * * * *

The news at the chain stop-point was dispiriting. The patrolman in charge thought he recognized the pictures of Paterson and Colley. "Two men in a van," he said. "About half an hour ago, maybe forty minutes."

He was sure, however, that they had been alone. "No woman," he repeated when Chang asked him a second time.

Had they already killed Catherine, disposed of her body somewhere between here and Los Angeles? Or simply concealed her in the van?

"Nothing we can do at this point but go on," she said. "And pray a lot."

Her phone rang. It was Conners. "Where are you," she asked.

"Right behind you," he said, "Your man Renner's on the scene, didn't need me. I should be gaining on you."

"That truck four wheel?"

"Yes. And mine's bigger than yours. Anyway, it's snowing where you're going. You'll need someone to keep you warm."

"You're a crazy son of a bitch," she said, but she grinned in spite of herself. She would be glad for the reinforcements. It would improve their odds.

* * * * * * *

Catherine watched Paterson's face with its odd changing landscape of expressions. This was her first opportunity to really study him in the flesh. She thought of something she had once read, about the glamour of evil. Paterson was far from handsome: ugly, actually, and his body was scrawny like an alley cat's. Yet he had too that alley cat's nervous vitality, an energy that even now, exhausted as he surely must also be, radiated from him like the heat from a furnace.

She could see how women might be attracted to him, to his menace even. Why someone like Colley, hardly a softie himself, would bend to his will.

She looked away from his face to the can of soup he was holding in his hand. For all her fatigue and numbing despair, she suddenly found herself ravenously hungry. She refused to beg, and half expected him to let her starve. To her surprise, he crossed the room in three easy strides and shoved the can and a spoon into her hands.

"Here," he said, in an angry voice. He went to the shelf and got himself another can and began to eat noisily, his back to her.

She ate gratefully, hardly noticing what it was she shoveled into her mouth: some kind of soup. The most delicious soup she had ever tasted.

She finished it, wiping her mouth with the back of her hand, and pondered whether there was any point in asking for more. Probably not, she decided, and set the empty can on the table next to the couch. She supposed she ought to thank him for what she'd had, try again to bond with him. For the moment, though, she was simply too bone-weary to think of any more stratagems. She leaned back against the couch, closing her eyes.

"Oh, no you don't." Paterson was there in an instant. He grabbed her shoulders and shook her hard. "You stay awake, damn you. Colley, you see to it."

Colley sighed wearily. "Man, I'm dead on my feet. Let me sleep a bit, just half an hour, okay, and then I'll look after her."

"She gets to sending her mind out, you'll be more than dead on your feet, you'll be dead on your ass. Mind her, I tell you. I got to get some sleep so I can think clear. I got to think for the both of us, don't I? That's more important than you resting your sorry butt."

"Well at least I got to pee," Colley said in a petulant voice. He limped into the bathroom and closed the door with a bang. They heard him urinating loudly.

Paterson stood just in front of her. She glanced up and found him studying her again with an expression she couldn't read.

"You know," he said, "About your little girl. It wasn't supposed to...well, we never did that before, offed any of them kids. It was kind of like, an accident. It was your old man, if you want to know the truth of it. The whole business was him from the get-go. He wouldn't stop yapping about it: why didn't we, couldn't we, wouldn't it be great? He was the one messed it up, too, couldn't stay where he was supposed to be. I should have killed him, the stupid bastard. Hadn't been for him, she'd have been okay, I swear it. We always took care of those kids. All of them. Lots of dope...well, hell, kids like that shit once they get a sample, and it gets them over the hump, so to speak. Kept them well fed, too, saw they was set up good after. People think it's something horrible what we did, all that shit they talk, but it ain't like that. I could let you talk to half a dozen kids, they'd tell you they got it real good now, they're like on top of the world, all kinds of money, plenty of dope, lots of sex."

He paused, waiting for her to say something. She could only stare at him, could scarcely grasp what he was trying to say.

"I just wanted you to know: it'd have been like that for her, too, hadn't been for your old man, that dumb shit." He paused again, swallowed, ran a tongue over his lips.

Catherine stared. Did he really believe what he was telling her? Could anyone's thinking be that twisted?

Yes, of course, she thought: people, even horrible people, want to convince themselves that what they did was right. The reality was, people were scarcely any better at knowing themselves than they were at knowing one another. The mirror lied to one and all, and few could see the reality in the depths of the glass.

She swallowed. Her mouth was Saharan. When she finally did speak, the words surprised her, seemed to come unbidden, from someone other than herself: "I want to forgive you, Mister Paterson."

They surprised him too. He blinked, speechless for a moment, staring at her like he hadn't heard her right.

Where had they come from, those words? She had not even imagined herself saying such a thing. They had simply spilled out of her.

Yet she meant them. Or at the least, she *meant* to mean them. She might be close to death. It was even possible, it had occurred to her before, that she had been dead all along, and everything that had happened since she had been shot was only a dream.

In either case, she was suddenly sure of one thing: she didn't want to go back into that light carrying all the hate and bitterness and anger with her. She wanted to forgive him if only for her own sake. And, perhaps, she hoped, for his as well. If she hadn't quite done that yet, if the words she had spoken were not quite yet the truth, surely that lie would do less damage to her soul than continuing to bear the bitter burden she had borne so long.

"Someone called you my dark angel," she said.

He actually grinned. "Yeah? What does that make you? My, what, my bright angel?"

The question caught her off guard. She hadn't thought of that. What was she to him? Not his angel, surely—but something, something she herself did not understand.

His grin faded. For a crazy moment he actually thought he saw, like, a halo of light around her head. What if she was, some kind of angel? What if that was what had been drawing him to her, not to kill her but to, well, to what? *An angel?*

To her surprise, he dropped to his knees in front of her, the wooden floor creaking. "Listen," he said, eyes fastened on hers, "I wish we hadn't gotten off on the wrong foot the way we did, you and me. I'm not such a bad guy once you get to know me. And... well, shit, I guess you've heard this a lot, but you are a fine-looking piece. I could've made you happy. Still could." He grinned. "That's what I do best. Make women happy. I'm real good at it."

He ran a hand slowly along the inside of her thigh, fingers gently kneading her flesh. Smiled into her eyes. In the bathroom, the toilet flushed noisily.

Without even thinking, she spat in his face. His eyes flamed, nostrils flared. The malevolence of his smile told more clearly than any words could the depth of his anger. He wiped the spittle from his face and stood. Colley came out of the bathroom and gave them a curious look.

Ignoring him, Paterson went to the fire, now casting a welcome warmth into the room, and poked violently at it. Satisfied that it was okay, he threw the poker into the bin and gave Catherine a warning glance. "Don't try anything," he said, and to Colley, "Wake me up in thirty minutes. Then you can have your turn."

He curled up on the bed, back to them, and within minutes was snoring. Colley pulled a tattered armchair around so it was near the fire, facing Catherine. He settled himself into it, cast a resentful glance at Paterson and glowered at her.

"Ought to have killed her back then," he mumbled, but not loud enough to disturb Paterson's sleep.

He tried to keep his eyes fixed on Catherine, but the warmth of the fire and the draining fatigue began to take their toll. His eyelids flickered. He started and gave his head a shake, and glared at her afresh.

Catherine pretended not to see his exhaustion, tried to ignore him altogether, and fought to stay awake herself. Sleep tried to creep over her, but she dared not surrender to it. This might be her only chance, and she could not be certain what would happen if she dropped off.

Something stirred in the corner, some forest creature, no doubt, a mouse or a squirrel, annoyed at having his comfortable winter lodgings intruded upon. Outside, the wind howled, and the snow blew against the window in ceaseless gusts, rattling the panes.

The contest of wills tilted in her favor. Colley eyes were barely half open now, and they drifted shut more frequently and stayed that way longer.

A log snapped loudly in the fireplace. He jerked upright, looked quick and hard at her and around the room, and settled back into his chair. His eyes drooped again. The wind clawed at the window. Shadows danced on the wall.

His eyes closed and stayed closed. His breathing grew deeper, more regular, and he too began to snore.

Now, she thought. She closed her eyes and sent herself into the ether.

* * * * * * *

"Yipes," Chang cried as Catherine suddenly appeared in the seat between her and Jack. The Bronco slid briefly before she got it once more under control. She took one hand off the wheel and felt in Catherine's direction. "Oh, Lord." Her hand went right through the apparition, "She's like a ghost. I forget."

"She's not physical at all," Jack said. "She's here to guide us."

"How, if she can't talk and she can't take hold of anything?"

"She can nod." He looked down at their directions. "Highway marker mile thirty-one?"

Catherine nodded vigorously…and disappeared.

"Jesus, that is weird," Chang said.

"Anyway, we know for sure they're taking her to O'Dell's cabin," he said. "And the directions are right. We just have to watch for mileage marker thirty-one."

* * * * * * *

Paterson was shaking her violently. "Damn you to hell, what are you doing? You're leading them here, aren't you?"

"…Sleeping," she mumbled, trying to act as incoherent as possible. It wasn't all that difficult. The fatigue almost had put her to sleep.

"Bitch." He slapped her hard, bringing the sting of tears to her eyes. With a muttered oath, he threw her back against the sofa and dashed to the window, yanking the curtain aside to peer out as if someone might already be pulling up outside. Over his shoulder, she could see only a white blur of snow in the faint light from the window and, beyond that, darkness.

He dropped the curtain and paced back and forth for several minutes, considering. Catherine reached out tentatively, trying to read into his thoughts, but that only served to draw his attention back to her. He stopped in his pacing and snapped his head around to glower at her, and seemed finally to reach a decision. He opened a closet and took out a shotgun, propped it against the wall. Then he grabbed her coat off the chair and flung it at her.

"Put it on."

On the chair nearby, Colley groaned and opened his eyes. "Man, I could sleep for a week," he said drowsily.

"You weren't supposed to be sleeping at all. You dumb jerk, I warned you what would happen."

"I couldn't help it, Trash. That bullet wound is hurting bad. I just closed my eyes for a minute, anyway, I swear to God." He looked at Catherine struggling into her coat. "What's happening?"

"I'm taking her out of here." Paterson shrugged into his parka. "Hurry it up," he told Catherine.

Colley sat up, wincing. "Where we going?"

"Not we. You can't move fast enough like that. You wait here in case they show up. If they do, use that." He nodded his head toward the shotgun leaning against the wall.

Colley got unsteadily to his feet. "Hey, Trash, no way, you can't leave me behind, we're in this together."

"If I get away and they don't show up here, I'll come back for you. If not, well, we're both screwed, is how I see it."

"'Cept I'm the one's most screwed, waiting here for them to come and pick me like an apple off a tree. I'm going with you, that's how it's gonna be. Don't worry about me, I can keep up." He limped toward where his coat dangled from a wall hook.

Paterson shot him in his other leg. Colley went down with a yelp and a crash, taking a chair with him. The fresh wound spewed blood. He swore and clutched at it. "Jesus, Trash," he groaned, "What'd you go and do that for? I'm gonna bleed to death here, you bastard."

Paterson shrugged his unconcern. "Bleeding, frying, you're just as dead one way or the other. Come on." He yanked Catherine to her feet. At the door, he looked back at Colley squirming and sobbing on the floor.

"Get yourself together. Wrap something around that. It's just a flesh wound, for Christ's sake. And drag your pansy butt over to the window so you can watch for them. If I hear shots, I'll know they showed up."

"If you hear shots it'll be me trying to nail your ass." Colley started to crawl in the direction of the shotgun.

Paterson laughed. "That's the way, show a little backbone for a change."

He pulled Catherine out into the snow and shoved the door closed behind him with his foot.

CHAPTER TWENTY-SIX

They had stepped into a world of white, of wind swirled snow. He hesitated, looking in every direction, and began to walk as swiftly as the storm allowed up the hillside to their left.

The wind fought against them, trying to push them back, as though it resented their intrusion. Catherine struggled to keep up, her knees threatening to buckle under her. When she stumbled he jerked her roughly back to her feet. In the dark, in the snow, it was impossible to see where they were going. He seemed to be obeying some inner radar. Of course, she thought, he's psychic too. She wished she could enter into his mind, but that was too dangerous, especially in his present violent mood.

"We'll never make it through this," she told him breathlessly. His only answer was to tug again at her arm and propel her forward. Her feet and hands were numb, her nose a block of ice.

The hillside grew steeper and thicker with trees, but at least the trees provided some break in the wind, so that it was easier to see where to put their feet down. They skirted rocks and thin outcroppings of brush, climbing steadily and laboriously now. Something tore at her shin, stinging, and she looked down to see droplets of red against the blanket of white.

A trail, she thought hopefully, and immediately realized the futility of that. The blood would be obliterated in minutes by the falling snow. She would have to find some opportunity to travel.

She stopped dead in her tracks and fell back against the rough bark of a Ponderosa pine. "I've got to catch my breath," she said.

He gave her an angry look and was about to say something, then checked himself. He let her lean there for a minute while his eyes searched the forest around them. Dawn was near, but the pale light barely penetrated the storm.

Catherine closed her eyes and tried to project herself into the car with Jack. She saw him, peering anxiously over the back of the front seat. He saw her, and relief washed over his face. She pointed at the

228

sheet of directions he still held in his hand and shook her head frantically back and forth.

"No, you don't." Paterson took her arm again and resumed their climb. Frustrated, Catherine stumbled alongside him. Had there been time? Had Jack seen her fleeting signal?

Her feet were numb, but she was afraid if she fell, or tried to stop again, he would shoot her and be done with it. Her job now was to stay alive and to delay them as much as possible in whatever way she could. Jack and Chang would find them, she was certain of that. They must.

"Come on," he ordered when she slowed her pace slightly.

"I can't go any faster," she said breathlessly. "Please, just leave me here."

"Fat chance, you'd be waving them in my direction before I had gone twenty feet. Hot damn, here we are."

They had crested a small knoll. Below them about thirty feet away a wisp of smoke rose from the chimney of a cabin. A blue pick up truck with enormous tires sat in a freshly cleared driveway.

They scrambled down the hillside, half running, half sliding. It was a relief to feel the solid surface of the driveway beneath her feet. He slunk to the side of the truck and peered through the window, disappointed the keys were not in it.

"I'll have to get them, then," he said aloud. He looked toward the cabin and then, appraisingly, at her. He couldn't take her in with him. There was too much risk of her alerting them to his arrival or, in a struggle, finding some way to get away.

Choosing the lesser of two evils, he grabbed the handcuffs from the pocket of his parka and, clamping one around her wrist, fastened the other to the truck's outside mirror.

He grabbed her by the throat and lifted her nearly off her feet, choking her.

"None of your fancy crap," he hissed at her. "So help me, if you pull anything...." He waved the gun under her nose. "We're getting out of here, the two of us. And if we don't, I promise you, they won't take either one of us alive."

He was gone, running at a crouch. She gasped for breath, raising her free hand to her bruised throat, and watched him slide up to a lighted window and peer cautiously inside.

If only she had some idea who was inside, or how many. A single woman, unarmed? Or a pack of hunters, guns at the ready. Whoever they were, they were certainly oblivious to the evil that was about to burst upon them, as sudden and as deadly as the strike of a viper. Should she scream, try to warn them?

She had no doubt that he meant his threats. It was too much of a risk. Safer to do what she knew how to do.

* * * * * * *

She soared through darkness, reaching through space to find Jack. Where was he? He couldn't be far. She had left them nearing on the main road. She saw the ribbon of the highway winding and undulating beneath her and then she was standing alongside it, no more than five feet from the mileage marker they were watching for. A marker that now would lead them astray.

She strained to see through the snow and darkness. After a moment headlights sliced through the blinding snow and a turn signal began to blink. She caught a glimpse of red: the Bronco. An hour ago that would have been the right road for them to take, but now it would lead them only to a wounded Colley. She wasn't concerned about him. If no one showed up to find him, he almost certainly would bleed to death as he himself had predicted.

But if Jack and Chang went that way, they would never find her in time. She and Paterson would be gone before they picked up the trail again.

She stepped into the road and waved her arms desperately.

* * * * * * *

The window gave onto a kitchen. At the stove, a man in jeans and a green flannel shirt stirred something in a pot, his back to Paterson. Oldish, so near as Paterson could tell, thin, but with an athletic look. A pair of cross country skis, still wet from a recent outing, leaned against one wall. A skier, then, no pushover.

Paterson's eyes scoured the room. A book open on the kitchen table, coffee cup. One plate. One cup. Hank Williams mourned from a countertop radio. Probably the man at the stove was alone. He would have to chance it.

He looked back toward the truck. He couldn't see her. For sure she was up to her stunts, but unless he stayed with her full time, there was no way he could prevent that. Probably he should just have killed her. Why hadn't he, just gone ahead and killed her back in L.A.? Snuff movie—he didn't need no snuff movie. For sure he should have wrung her neck when she spit in his face. *Angel my ass. Angel bitch, was more like it.*

Well, it was too late to cry about that. For now, the most important thing was a getaway vehicle. He'd deal with her once that problem was solved. Anyway, he might need her if things got hairy.

The man in the green shirt got his plate from the table, carried it to the stove, and began ladling something onto it. It reminded Paterson that he was hungry. Hank Williams had given way to a woman singing, "What child is this?"

Christ, it was practically Christmas. Tomorrow was Christmas Eve, wasn't it, or the next day? For the briefest of moments, he thought about the situation he was in and how he came to be in it.

It was only a little while ago that everything was going his way. Business was good; there were plenty of people willing to pay top dollar for the specialty porn he provided. Colley was stupid, but he had been a useful sidekick, willing and, in his own crude way, good at suckering unsuspecting parents.

They'd had plenty of money and plenty of sex as a side dish. In a few months they'd have moved on to another city, say Seattle, he had always liked Seattle. And it was never smart to stay in any one place too long.

It was her fault: that bitch back by the pick up. She was the one had messed it all up for him. It was people like her who made the world such a shitty place. For a moment, he almost changed his mind and went back to choke the worthless life out of her.

His better sense kicked in. He pulled his gun from his belt and crept to the back door. Through its uncurtained window he saw the green shirt still at the stove, salting something on his plate.

Patterson hit the door hard, crashing it open, and yelled "Don't move."

To his surprise, the damn fool threw the plate of food at him. It missed by a mile but it broke his concentration, gave the old fart a minute to wheel and run toward the kitchen counter. Reflexively, Paterson pulled the trigger of his gun, and heard a dull click instead of a blast. Christ! He was out of bullets. Talk about luck.

He snatched up a chair and flung it. It hit the old man squarely in the back of his head and he stumbled and fell against the counter but he didn't go down. He reached instead toward a wooden block sitting there with knives sticking from it.

He had one in his hand by the time Paterson was upon him. For a minute or two they wrestled. Just as Paterson had feared, he was no weakling, wiry but muscled. Desperate, Paterson struck him hard on the temple with the empty gun, stunning him. In an instant, he had grabbed the knife and, crouching back on his heels, stabbed viciously downward with it. The old man gave a moan of agony and fell on his back, blood gushing from the wound in his belly.

"Stupid bastard," Paterson told him. "If you'd done as I said I might have left you alive."

For good measure he stabbed him again and twisted the knife to be sure there wasn't any chance he would survive. The eyes staring up at him grew dim and a bubble of blood appeared between his lips.

Paterson got up and gave him an angry kick. Some days nothing wanted to go right. No wonder he got so pissed at everything. He wiped the knife off on a kitchen towel, thrust it into his belt, and shoved the gun there too. Even an empty gun could come in handy. He looked around quickly and saw keys on the counter near the open kitchen door. Yes, house keys, obviously, and there were the recognizable truck keys as well.

He snatched them up and was out the door in a second.

* * * * * * *

"Damn you!" Paterson was slapping her awake again. He yanked her violently to her feet and drew back his hand to strike her again. She cringed away from him, but instead of hitting her, he snorted in exasperation and fumbled for the key to remove the handcuffs.

He threw open the door of the truck. "Get in," he ordered, brandishing the butcher knife under her nose, "And no funny business."

There was a sudden crashing and thumping to their left. Paterson's head snapped around as a dark gray muzzle appeared out of the trees. Burros. As he watched, the rest of them trailed out of the bushes behind their leader. One or two of them cast wide-eyed glances sideways.

"Dumb fucks," Paterson said, laughing at his own skittishness. "Shoo, git."

He let go of her wrist just for a second. In that same instant, there was a flash of light, like lightning only brighter still. It glared off the curtain of snow, blinding both of them.

"What the hell...?" He blinked, and thought for a moment he saw another woman standing there in that fierce radiance. Startled, he took a step back. *Where did she come from?*

The sudden bolt of light startled the pack of burros into flight. They stampeded in his direction, passing him so closely that one or two of them jostled against him, throwing him off balance. He fell heavily against the truck.

Run. The voice echoed inside her head. Catherine hesitated no more than a split second before she whirled away from Paterson and dashed down the driveway in the wake of the burros, in the direction of the road.

* * * * * * *

"We'll never find her in this mess," Chang said. In the dark, in the snow, she could barely make out the pine trees that lined the road.

Jack looked frantically out his window. She had to be this way. That had certainly been her in the road a mile or two back, signaling them not to take the planned turnoff.

Chang glanced in the rear view mirror, thought she saw a pair of headlights in the distance. Conners was gaining on them, was only a couple of miles behind the last she'd talked to him. She'd be glad for the reinforcements, but what good would that do if they couldn't find Catherine?

"There!" Jack shouted suddenly, pointing.

Chang saw her then too, trailing a pack of stampeding burros down a driveway they had just passed—and Paterson running after her, and gaining.

She hit the brakes, hard, felt the Bronco slide.

* * * * * * *

"Get back here, you cunt," he shouted behind her, but she only drove herself harder. She heard his footsteps pounding after her. Twenty yards away, she saw a flash of red on the roadway. The Bronco. Jack and Chang. She was saved.

It passed the driveway. She gave a hoarse shout, and was rewarded with the flare of brake lights. The Bronco slid in the snow and began to back up rapidly.

Her elation turned to agony. Her feet were too numb. She was too weary. She stumbled, almost falling, and Paterson grabbed her arm, jerking her around so violently she thought her arm had been pulled from its socket. She fell against him, out of breath, too weak to struggle any further. Behind her, a car door slammed and Jack shouted, "Catherine!"

* * * * * * *

Chang was out of the Bronco while it was still rolling, dropping into a crouch. Behind her, she heard a pickup truck sliding to a stop. Conners. Man, that boy was something! She held the Glock in both hands, couldn't shoot because Paterson was holding Catherine in front of him.

"Don't," she said when Jack would have dashed past her. "He's got a knife. He'll kill her."

* * * * * * *

Paterson grabbed her throat and forced her head back, forced her to look directly into his face, twisted with fury. "I told you," he hissed, "I told you, they wouldn't never take neither of us alive."

They were face to face, his eyes boring into hers, eyes filled with hatred...and with something larger than that, something she could not define.

Her dark angel, Gabronski, had called him. Yes, she could see it now: they had been tied together all along, since that moment when he had shot her. Still, even here, even now, something like a magical bond linked them.

She had never contemplated what an intimate act murder might be: to feel with a shock of pain and invasion his knife tear into her belly. She put her hand down and felt the warm blood thawing its numbness. To have this man of all men thrusting into her....

And, in a burst of light as fierce as any she had yet experienced, she understood finally, clearly, why she had been sent back, what it was that only she could do. Not to trap him, not to kill him, not even to imprison him. It was this moment, and she, and she alone, who could set him free. And herself as well, by doing so.

The snow became a vortex into which she was falling, falling, down, down, down...she must say it before she vanished: "I forgive you," she whispered.

This time, it was true.

* * * * * * *

She sagged in his arms, eyes closing, lips parting on a final breath.

Christ, he had killed her. His head swam. What if she really had been...? She'd said something as she died—what? *I forgive you.* That was it, that was what she'd said. Something surged through him, like an electric current.

In a distance, as if miles away, he heard car doors slamming, someone shouting. He looked up, and there was a frizzy haired woman with a gun, some kind of cop, and two guys, the boyfriend and another one he didn't recognize.

He'd killed her. *Jesus, Paterson, you are crazy.* He let her fall, dropped the knife with her, reached to his waistband for the gun, and held it out in front of him, aiming it at the redhead.

* * * * * *

Suddenly, Catherine was out of the way, sinking to the ground in a river of red, and Paterson was in the clear. "Catherine," Jack yelled and ran toward her.

Paterson ignored the man charging toward him. From somewhere a gun appeared in his hand. He lifted it and aimed it straight at Chang.

Behind her, Chang heard Conners hit the ground on the run. *I hope I get another chance to jump your bones, you cute little bastard*, she thought. She steadied the Glock, sighted carefully—best shot in her class at the bureau—and fired. A crimson stain blossomed like a rose in the middle of Paterson's forehead and he dropped to one knee. The gun slipped from his fingers and he collapsed in a heap in the bloody snow, one arm falling across Catherine as if to comfort her.

EPILOGUE

She was there, in the light again, just as before. She sensed familiar spirits waiting for her somewhere ahead, felt herself weightless, free of pain and care, flying into the light.

And again, someone separated herself from the whiteness and moved toward her. Catherine squinted, and felt her heart turn over.

"Mommy," a voice that seemed to be within her cried.

"Becky?" she asked, thrilled beyond all meaning. "Becky, it's really you?"

She remembered then what Gabronski had said about her guardian spirit: without sex, without age. And knew who had been guiding her all along.

They embraced. Even without a physical self she could sense the arms encircling her, knew that she held her daughter to her breast once again, knew that her tears flowed.

"My darling, I'll never let you go again," Catherine vowed. "We will be together forever."

After a moment, Becky seemed to retreat from her slightly. "No, you must go back."

"No, no, I can't, I won't," Catherine cried and reached out, trying to grab her daughter back to her, but Becky was receding. "Don't leave me, Becky, don't go."

"You must go back," her voice growing fainter. "You must take care of my baby sister. But I will be with you always, my love will never leave you, or yours leave me."

"Becky," Catherine sobbed again. The silvery glow was swirling, eddying about her. A drop of light, turned liquid, fell upon her cheek. She opened her eyes, and found herself lying in the snow, in Jack's arms.

Beyond him, from a far, far distance, someone shouted, "They're on their way."

"Catherine, hold on," Jack sobbed, kissing her brow, "Don't leave me again, darling, I couldn't bear it."

236

Her lips parted, and she found the breath to whisper, faintly, "I'm here." She closed her eyes, and felt another of his tears fall upon her cheek.

ABOUT THE AUTHOR

V. J. BANIS is the critically acclaimed author ("the master's touch in storytelling…"—*Publishers Weekly*) of more than 150 published books and numerous short stories in a career spanning nearly a half century. A native of Ohio and a longtime Californian, he lives and writes now in West Virginia's beautiful Blue Ridge.

You can visit him at http://www.vjbanis.com

www.ingramcontent.com/pod-product-compliance
Lightning Source LLC
Chambersburg PA
CBHW032040240626
47154CB00003B/1014